FAMILY LIES

by June E. Hudy

Order this book online at www.trafford.com
or email orders@trafford.com

Most Trafford titles are also available at major online book retailers.

Note for Librarians: A cataloguing record for this book is available from Library
and Archives Canada at www.collectionscanada.ca/amicus/index-e.html

Printed in Victoria, BC, Canada.

ISBN: 978-1-4269-1360-0 (sc)

*Our mission is to efficiently provide the world's finest, most comprehensive book publishing
service, enabling every author to experience success. To find out how to publish your book, your
way, and have it available worldwide, visit us online at www.trafford.com*

Trafford rev. 8/12/2009

 www.trafford.com

North America & international
toll-free: 1 888 232 4444 (USA & Canada)
phone: 250 383 6864 ♦ fax: 812 355 4082

Acknowledgements

First, I would like to thank my husband for his patience with my writing mind and helping me to self-publish so many of my projects. Thanks to my family for their support and encouragement with my writing endeavors; a special thanks to Teresa for her insight and a listening ear when I have become frustrated and ready to quit. Thanks Teresa for keeping me going.

Chapter 1

"I CAN'T BELIEVE YOU are so stubborn about this," Amy's mother, Gladys Stern slammed her cookie sheet into the sink and wiped her hands on the towel laying there. "You know I haven't been well and I need your help around here; but it figures. You always were selfish, thinking of yourself first. What is your boss going to say? I worked hard to get you that job, you ungrateful brat!"

Amy shrugged and turned away. She was used to her mother's tantrums, but this time her mother wasn't going to win. She had been looking for a change in her life for some time and when she spotted the ad in the paper, it seemed the answer to her problems.

The ad read: HELP WANTED: Southern Alberta sheep ranch looking for permanent help. Must be willing to learn and take directions. Applicant should be able to lift at least fifty pounds, enjoy the outdoors and like animals. Apply in writing with references and phone number to Box 1745, Milk River, Alberta.

Amy had received a reply several days before, but had been reluctant to break the news to her mother because she knew there would be a scene, just like this one. Ever since Amy had returned to Medicine Hat from Calgary after her marriage failed, her mother had been trying to control her life. When she first moved back, she had moved in with her, but Amy couldn't stand the constant nagging and accusations about her failed marriage. After she got a job, she rented a tiny apartment where she could enjoy her own company.

Her boss at the Dairy Queen was very nice and she had worked herself up to assistant manager, but there was no where else to go. She was tired of the dead-end job and ready for a change. She hoped life on the ranch in southern Alberta would help her put some direction in her life.

She had decided to hang on to her apartment for the next month just in case things didn't work out. She wasn't sure she could lift fifty pounds but she was willing to give it a try. The big plus was not having her mother breathing down her neck and phoning all the time with errands and chores for her. And no more scenes like the one they just had.

"Mom, you will just have to hire someone to help you or get Edith to come over. She has offered lots of times but you always turn her down," Amy said as she put on her coat and picked up her gloves.

"I don't want strangers touching my things and I sure don't want nosey Edith over here. Well, go on with you. Don't waste your time worrying about leaving your sick mother to go gallivanting on a lark; to a sheep ranch, of all things! You won't last a week. You never were good at sticking to anything. You'll be back."

"Maybe," Amy answered as she walked over and kissed her mother's cheek, "Take care of yourself."

Her mother turned away and didn't answer. Amy wasn't surprised. She had expected the silent treatment. As she left the house, she heard her mother slamming the dishes into the sink and wondered how many were broken this time. That would be her fault too, she mused as she carefully shut the gate and got into her car.

Chapter 2

WITH HER LITTLE Sunbird loaded with as much as she could fit in, Amy backed out of her parking spot, drove down the street to the main thoroughfare and headed west out of Medicine Hat on Highway 3. It was early morning and a beautiful day. The sun was up, casting shadows on the small snow drifts that had accumulated in the ditch and along the highway. It was early April and most of the snow was gone, but a skiff had fallen the day before. With the wind blowing, it had ended up in the ditches. The highway was clear, so Amy set her cruise at 100 K. and relaxed a bit. It was nice to get away from the hustle and bustle of the city. She had a map beside her and the phone number of the ranch. She was to call when she reached Milk River.

Watching the traffic, Amy thought about her mother and her problems with her. It wasn't all her mother's fault, she thought. She had been a problem teenager, running wild and getting pregnant when she was only fifteen. Her father had died when she was just a toddler so her mother had to deal with things on her own. Gladys had worked in a department store downtown but the wages were not great at that time. So when Amy got into trouble, it was a financial hardship for Gladys as well as upsetting.

Amy was sent to a home for unwed mother's in Calgary. When the baby was born in August, Amy wasn't allowed to see it or hold it. They said it was better that way when a baby is put up for adoption. Many times Amy's heart ached to be able to see and hold her child. She didn't even know if it was a boy or girl. As time went on, it started to seem like just a bad dream. It had been eighteen years since she gave birth.

After she had the baby, Amy returned home to Medicine Hat and her mother. Life had been unbearable. Her mother imposed strict curfews, wouldn't let her join any clubs or go out with friends. Amy managed to stay the two years and complete her grade twelve. When she turned eighteen, she applied for government funding to go to beauty college in Calgary. Finishing her course, she took a job at a hair salon in the city. While there, she made friends with another beautician by the name of Susie Bacon. They had great fun together and Amy was happy for the first time in her young life.

Twice a year, she went home to Medicine Hat to see her mother. The visits got increasingly difficult. Her mother resented the fact she was living in Calgary and had not returned to her home town. She bore a grudge against Amy and everyone. At first, she seemed to think Amy was leading a life of sin; then after she married Raymond, she was not a good wife. Amy gave up trying to please her.

It was through her friend Susie that Amy met Raymond. Susie had called her one night and asked if she would be willing to go on a double date with her and her boyfriend Arnold. Her brother Raymond was in town and she didn't want to go out and leave him at home. Amy had heard a lot about Susie's brother. He was an airline pilot with Air Canada and Susie was very proud of him. Amy accepted, being as he was Susie's brother.

Amy and Raymond hit it off right away. He was funny and considerate, not to mention very good-looking. After only two dates, Amy knew she was smitten. She liked to hear him talk of all the places he had visited and the sights he had seen.

"You will have to fly with me sometime!" he would always say.

They dated for six months. Every time Raymond flew to Calgary, they were together. They burned up the phone lines when he wasn't there. Susie was thrilled her best friend and her brother were in love. When Raymond asked Amy to marry him, she said yes immediately. She couldn't think of life without Raymond.

When Amy phoned her mother to tell her the good news, she said,

"Are you knocked up? Is that the big hurry?"

"Can't you be happy for me just once? For your information, Raymond and I are waiting until we are married," Amy had responded.

Her mother's attitude was the main reason they decided to get married in Calgary. Amy's mother was sent an invitation but she refused to come, saying she was too sick to travel.

The first years of their marriage were one long honeymoon. Raymond would be gone for a few days and when he returned, they would spend long hours, catching up on everything. On one layover, they finally took a road trip to Medicine Hat to see Amy's mother. Amy had been shocked by Gladys' behavior. She couldn't do enough for Raymond, making sure he was comfortable, catering to his every whim. That was not the mother Amy knew.

When Raymond stepped outside to have a smoke, Gladys said to Amy, "How did you manage to snare him? He's way too good for you. Does he know about your sordid past?"

How do you respond to a vicious remark like that? Amy had just walked away and went to the bathroom.

A few years into their marriage, things started to change. Raymond started taking more flights overseas and when he was home, he seemed pre-occupied. When Amy asked him what was wrong, he said nothing. He was just tired. Even his sister Susie was worried about him. She thought he was working too hard.

Amy had kept her job at the hair salon as they were saving for a down payment on a house. It was then five years into their marriage and they had no children. Amy saw specialist after specialist and when she mentioned having a child when she was young, they all concurred that could be the problem. It had been a difficult birth. The specialists wanted Raymond to get tested, but he refused. There was nothing wrong with him, he said.

Then, out of the blue, seven years into their marriage, Raymond came home from an overseas flight and announced he wanted a divorce. Amy was in shock. After so many years of marriage, and he now wanted out? Finally the story came out. He had been seeing a flight attendant for the last four years and they had one child together and she was expecting their second. Amy couldn't believe all that had been going on and she knew nothing about it. 'How stupid can I be,' she had thought. The signs were there; she just had to open her eyes. No wonder he knew there was nothing wrong with him! He had two children to prove it. That was the reason he had quit talking about them getting a house. When they filed for divorce, Amy found out he had purchased a house for his "other family". There was very little to divide up. He had put the house in his lover's name so Amy couldn't touch it.

Amy went into a deep depression. Her best friend blamed her for her brother's infidelity. She couldn't work, so lost her job. Finally, she went home to Medicine Hat.

The first thing her mother said to her was, "I don't blame Raymond. You never were good enough for him; and he wanted kids and because of your past, you couldn't have any. A man needs prodigy."

⇉ ⇇

"Well, here I am," Amy thought, "A change is needed all around. That looks like Milk River up ahead. I sure hope I pass muster with the sheep ranchers!"

Chapter 3

As Amy drove into Milk River, she spotted a restaurant and decided to have some lunch before she called the ranch. It was still early in the day and she wanted some time to unwind. Everything seems easier on a full stomach, she thought as she parked and got out of her car. She noticed a few flakes of snow coming down. I hope we're not in for a change in the weather, Amy mused as she strode into the restaurant. The place was busy with the early lunch crowd. Amy took a seat at the counter and picked up a menu. When the waitress found her way over, she ordered chicken fingers and salad with a cup of tea.

As in all small towns, everyone seemed to know everyone else, so it was no surprise when the man sitting next to her asked, "Are you from around here?"

Amy glanced over and answered, "No, I'm from Medicine Hat."

"So you're just traveling through?"

"You might say that," Amy wasn't about to give any more information to a complete stranger.

"I'm sorry to hear that," the man replied.

Surprised by his response, Amy shot a quick glance in his direction. He was smiling as he held out his hand, "I'm perfectly harmless. Ivan Johnson, at your service."

Hesitating for a moment, Amy finally reached out and shook his hand, "I'm Amy. Nice to meet you."

Ivan had the look of a rancher to Amy. He was tall and rugged and had on wrangler jeans and a western shirt. On the floor at his feet was a cowboy hat and Amy noticed he was also wearing walking western boots. He was far from good-looking but had an outdoor kind of appeal about him. He was friendly anyway.

Amy's lunch arrived and Ivan picked up his hat and stood up.

"Hope to see you again some time," he said as he turned to the check-out.

Amy concentrated on eating her lunch. If she was going to work in this area, there was a good chance she might see him again. She was amused by his friendliness. If all the people around here were as open as Ivan, she just might enjoy living in this area.

She finished her lunch and taking her check, she headed to the till.

"Oh, your lunch is paid for, " the waitress said as Amy opened her purse.

"What? By whom?" Amy demanded.

"Ivan paid on his way out. I think he likes you," the waitress smirked.

"I can't let him do that. I pay my own way. The next time he comes in, you give his money back."

"Suit yourself. Do I get to keep the tip?"

"I don't care." Amy paid, then headed to the payphones. What nerve! To assume I would accept him paying, Amy grumbled to herself as she dialed the ranch.

It was answered on the first ring, "Laura Collins here."

"Mrs. Collins? This is Amy Bacon. I am here in Milk River. Can you give me directions?"

"Well, hello Amy. I'm sure glad to hear you have arrived. I'll do better than directions. One of our neighbors had to run to town for supplies. I'll call him on his cell phone and you can follow him out. Where are you?"

"I'm at the restaurant on the highway. I drive a blue Sunbird."

"Okay. Hang tough. He'll be there shortly."

Well, that's good, Amy thought. This way I have no chance of getting lost. It was snowing a bit and Amy was worried the back roads may not be too good. She went out to her car and waited.

Before long, a Ford 4X4, green in color and very dirty, pulled up beside her. Who should get out but Ivan!

"I said I hoped to see you again some time, but I didn't think it would be this soon. So you're Laura's new hired hand?"

"Yes, I guess I am. But........ one thing I want to straighten out right now. I'm not accustomed to letting strange men pay for my meals. Is that understood?"

"Perfectly. Just trying to be friendly, is all. But I don't think I'm that strange," Ivan laughed, " That your car?"

"Yes it is; what about it?"

"A bit small for these parts. Hope you don't get hung up on some rut," Ivan commented as he looked the car over.

"Don't worry about my car. Can you just guide me out to the ranch?"

"Sure enough, little lady. Don't get your knickers in a knot. Do you think you can keep up?"

"Try me." Amy turned and got into her car. Ivan smiled as he sauntered back to his 4X4 and climbed in. This summer just started looking better all the time. He helped out with the heavy work on the ranch, besides looking after his own. Yes, things could be interesting on the Collin's Ranch with a tenderfoot in residence. He started his truck and eased out on to the highway and headed south.

Chapter 4

AMY KEPT RIGHT behind Ivan as he headed out on the highway. She was a bit miffed at him. Making fun of her car like that; and the nerve of the guy, thinking she would accept him paying for her meal! Maybe he was just being friendly, but that she could do without.. She had enough of men to last her a long time, maybe forever. She understood that Mrs. Collins handled her sheep ranch on her own with her eighteen year old son. No man around to give orders and complicate things.

Ivan was signaling a right turn, then he left the highway and took a gravel road heading west. It had stopped snowing so Amy was grateful for that. The dust was flying so Amy had to ease back so she could see the road. She hadn't thought to ask Ivan how far it was out to the ranch. All she could see off in the distance were hills and rolling pasture land. Here and there, she spotted some cattle and an odd building site, but nothing that looked like a ranch.

After what Amy assumed was about twenty miles, Ivan signaled a left turn. Amy glanced in that direction and saw a winding road heading into the hills. She slowed as Ivan pulled off to the side of the road. She stopped and Ivan came over to her car as she rolled her window down.

"Why are you stopping here?" she asked Ivan.

"Well, I don't think you can get lost now. Just stay on that road and you will drive right into the ranch. My ranch is up the road a piece, but our property is back to back. Good luck, little lady. Be seeing you around."

Amy watched as Ivan got back into his truck and drove off to the west. She put her car in gear and turned south up the road he had indicated. She suddenly felt very alone and in the middle of nowhere. She wondered how far it was to the ranch? Why hadn't she asked Ivan when he was here? She glanced at her fuel gauge. The tank read over half, so she should be okay.

The road wound into the hills and she went over a couple of Texas gates. Now she was seeing more cattle and some horses in the pastures on either side.

She had driven for a time when she topped a hill and stopped the car. She just stared. Stretched out before her was a wonderful view. Below her was the ranch, with the ranch house set back against the side of a hill surrounded by trees. To the right of the house was a two car garage. Behind was a creek that came out of the draw between the hills and flowed down toward the barns. There were corrals everywhere and in the corrals, more sheep than Amy could ever imagine. Next to the garage was a trailer which Amy assumed would be her new home.

Butterflies were fluttering around in Amy's stomach. Had she bitten off more than she could chew? What did she know about sheep? Or ranching, or country life for that matter? She must be crazy! Oh well; never say never, she thought. Face it up and give it a try. She sure didn't want her mother to be right.

She started the car and drove down the hill and through the ranch gate which sported a sign that said. COLLINS RANCH, Abe and Laura Collins. Registered Columbian Sheep. Stock for Sale.

Amy crossed over the Texas gate and drove up the driveway to the ranch house. She parked beside a pickup that was there. Two border collies set up a ruckus as she got out of the car. Barking wildly, they attracted the attention of a woman down in one of the corrals.

"Down here," she called up to Amy, "Don't mind the dogs; they're friendly."

Amy shut her car door and walked down the path to the corral, flanked on each side by a dog. As she neared the fence, the dogs headed back up to the house. A face appeared over the corral.

"Hi! You must be Amy. I'm Laura. Glad to see you got out here safely. Ivan gave you directions? I won't offer my hand, as you can see, I'm a little busy here. This is the fourth ewe to lamb this hour. I'll be glad when Shane gets home from school to take over for a bit so I can put my feet up. We really need the help around here. Have you ever been around a sheep ranch before?"

"No, I haven't. As I said in my letter, I was raised in the city and haven't spend much time in the country. I'm at a crossroads in my life and wanted a change of pace, and scenery. I'm a good worker and I'm strong and willing to learn."

"Well, that's the only recommendation I need. Oh, oh; looks like she's finally getting busy. See that water bag at her rear? That's the sac surrounding the lambs. Once that shows, things are starting to proceed. She will really push now and with any luck, we'll have two new additions on the ground shortly."

"How many sheep do you have here on the ranch?" Amy asked as she watched the ewe circling and pawing the ground. She finally laid down and putting her nose in the air, started pushing again.

"Oh, give or take, around five hundred ewes, I guess. Shane keeps a good record of all the ewes and their breeding records. I don't know what I'd do without him. Since his Dad died, he's been the only man on the place, so he had to grow up early. Oh there comes a lamb!"

Amy was fascinated. As the ewe pushed, the little lamb slid out on to the straw. Immediately the ewe got up and started licking the lamb.

"Now is the time we have to be careful. If the ewe is having another lamb, she may desert the first, or ignore the second when it is born," Laura said.

Right on cue, the ewe quit licking the lamb and started pawing the ground again. Soon she laid down and pushed out another lamb. She didn't get up immediately but kept talking. The first lamb was answering so she finally got to her feet. Seeing the second lamb behind her, she started to clean it, while talking to it. Not to be ignored, the first lamb answered and soon she had them both talking and was licking both.

"Well, I think that old girl has everything under control. We'll just leave her for a spell. It's best if you don't handle the lambs until she bonds with them. Later we'll put iodine on the navels and see if the plugs are out of both teats."

"I hate to sound stupid," Amy said, "but I don't understand. Why do you put iodine on the navel and what is a plug?"

"The iodine is a disinfectant. We put it on the navel to speed healing and prevent navel ill, which will kill a lamb quickly. The plug is a waxy substance in the end of the ewe's teat. It is there to prevent the udder from developing problems. In some cases, the plug is so tough, the little lamb can't dislodge it to get the milk. In the wild, those lambs would starve."

Laura opened the gate on the small pen and came out.

"Let's head up to the house and I will fill you in on what a sheep ranch is all about. Then we'll get you settled. Shane should be home soon and will spend some time out here."

Chapter 5

Laura washed up in the entry to the ranch house and removing her boots and coveralls, put on a pair of slippers.

"Come in, come in," she beckoned to Amy, "never mind your shoes; they're clean."

"What a lovely home you have here," Amy stated as she gazed around at the open kitchen/dining/living area. It was all open beam, definite ranch style. Amy was so used to small living quarters that the ranch house seemed huge.

"Thanks," Laura answered, "Sometimes it's a bit much for me to look after. I'm sixty years old and feel every day of it at times. I find lambing time very exhausting. Since Abe passed on, I have been struggling to manage this spread by myself. Shane does what he can, but he has to attend school He will graduate in June. He will work here for a year, then go on a mission with our Church. We're Mormons. You are familiar with our church?"

"Yes, I am," Amy replied, "My last boss belonged to your church."

"So you can see why I need some help. Shane will be away for two years. He says he wants to ranch when he comes home, but time will tell. We will cross that bridge when it comes. In the meantime, we have to get you settled. Do you have any work clothes with you?"

"Well, I do have jeans, but no barn boots or coveralls."

"I'll take you to your trailer and get you settled in, and tomorrow, while Shane is here to look after things, I'll take you shopping. Oh, here's Shane now."

The outside door slammed and a tall, blond young man entered the kitchen.

"Hi, Mom, who's car................. oh, Hi!"

"Shane, I want you to meet Amy. She's our new hand around here. I'm just going to take her over to the trailer. After you get changed, could you check at the pens? Number 83 and 104 look close."

"Right O. Glad to met you, Amy. Hope you last longer than the last one."

Amy looked over at Laura, who shrugged, "We had a guy here last fall to help out, but he only lasted two weeks. I don't think he liked working for a woman, or he didn't like sheep. I don't know. On payday, he said 'Thank you, but no thank you, I'm out of here.'"

"That's too bad. Well, I sure hope I can do what you require. I'm willing to learn."

"I'm sure you'll do fine. Now, let's get you settled in. How do you feel about cats?"

"I like cats. Why?"

"Because you have a resident cat in the trailer. She thinks that's her house. We can remove her if you don't want her, but she's a good mouser, so no worries about varmints in the trailer."

'I would sooner have the cat than mice," Amy answered. I sure don't like mice."

"Well, let's go meet Happy Cat."

Amy gathered one of her suit cases from her car and followed Laura down the path, past the garage and to the trailer.

"Shane will help you carry the rest of your things after supper," Laura commented, "You will have suppers with us, but look after your own breakfast and lunch. We eat at 6:00 PM sharp unless there's a crisis in the sheep yard. And that usually only happens during lambing. Most of the time, it's pretty quiet around here. Abe always wanted his meals on time, so I guess we just got in the habit."

Laura opened the door to the trailer and a large grey and white cat appeared around the corner.

"Well, hello Happy Cat," Laura bent down and stroked the cat's head, "Come and meet your new room mate."

Amy knelt down and Happy Cat smelled her fingers, then proceeded to rub against her hand.

Laura laughed, "I think she likes you. You two will get along just fine. She has her own "cat door" so can go in and out on her own, so no litter-box to contend with. All you have to do is be sure she has water in her dish and cat food. I have the cupboard stocked with lots of food. Just let me know when you run out."

Amy had Happy Cat on her knee and was busy stroking her soft fur. The cat was purring loudly and trying to kiss her.

"Hey, you two; quit with the love-making so I can show the rest of the trailer."

Amy stood up and set Happy Cat on the chair; "Sorry Mrs. Collins. I guess I got a little carried away. I never had a pet, even growing up. My Mom figured them an expense we didn't need. I had no idea they can be so loving."

"There is something about the outside of a cat which is good for the inside of a soul", is an old saying; something like that; and my name is Laura. All my friends call me that. Follow me for a quick run through, then I must go and get supper started."

After Laura left, Amy sat down at the table and gazed around at her new abode. There was a kitchen/dining combination, living room, bathroom and two bedrooms. Laura had explained that several years before, they had run nearly 1000 ewes and had a couple hired to help out. They had a little boy while there. They had stayed with them for ten years, then the boy had become allergic to the sheep, so reluctantly they had left. Since that time, they had trouble keeping good help so had downsized their flock. Then Abe had his first heart attack. He survived that one, only to have a massive coronary a year later. He never returned home from the hospital and passed away a week later. Because of good neighbors, Laura had managed to hang on. All she had were the sheep and the ranch. Now she was holding on for Shane. She hoped when he returned from his mission, he would take over.

Amy was touched by such a sad story. She was going to do her very best to learn the business and help out. Unpacking her suitcase and checking out the closets, she put everything away. Glancing out the bedroom window, she could see Shane moving some bales around with a tractor. 'I wonder if I'll get to drive one of those,' she thought, 'Only time will tell.'

Chapter 6

PRECISELY AT 6 PM Amy presented herself at the ranch house. The smells coming from the kitchen were out of the world. Shane let her in and took her coat.

"I sure hope you're hungry. Mom's been cooking up a storm, a 'Welcome to the Ranch' supper."

"I'm famished. Something sure smells wonderful."

"That's my Mom's famous fried chicken. You haven't tasted fried chicken until you try Mom's. No one does it as good as Mom."

"Quit with all the flattery; it won't get you an extra piece." Laura came into the entry, wiping her hands, "Come in, come in. Supper is on the table."

Shane and Laura bowed their heads to ask the blessing on the food. Amy quickly followed suit. She should have known that they would say grace. They were Mormons, after all. Not everyone was so dedicated.

Shane wasn't elaborating; Laura's chicken was exceptionally good. But so was her stuffed potatoes, creamed broccoli and apple crisp.

"Boy, I'm going to have to work hard to burn off the extra calories, or I will put on the pounds," Amy told her hostess, "Your food is entirely too good!"

"Told you," Shane answered, " Mom's the best cook in the district."

Laura paused from picking up the plates and ruffled Shane's close-cropped hair, "You're prejudiced."

Amy jumped up and started to help clear the table, but Laura stopped her.

16

"Go on. Shane will help you carry your stuff in. You have a lot of unpacking to do. Tomorrow morning we'll head to town and get you some boots, coveralls, a heavy coat and some gloves. You will need those things for sure. Then tomorrow afternoon, we'll get you in the swing of things. I have a dishwasher so no big deal here."

Amy moved her car down to the trailer. She was glad of Shane's help unloading. For the time being, she planned to leave some of her boxes packed. She didn't know how things would work out and she was feeling a little overwhelmed at the moment.

"Anything else you need help with?" Shane asked as he stooped to pet Happy Cat.

Amy shook her head, "Everything is fine. I appreciate all your help, Shane."

"Okay. I'd better go do a sheep run. Ewes are right in the midst of lambing and we want to save every lamb we can. See you tomorrow."

Amy watched at Shane loped off toward the barns. The two border collies raced around him yipping and enjoying the moment. Shane stopped and petted each one before opening the gate and passing into the corrals. Again, the two dogs returned to the main house. 'I thought sheep dogs remained with the sheep' Amy mused as she watched. 'I will have to ask about that.'

Piling several of her boxes into the spare bedroom, Amy took the remaining ones to the proper places and started unpacking. It was 10:00 PM by the time she was finished. As she glanced out the window, she could see the lights were on in the barn. Needing a bit of fresh air, she put on her jacket and shoes and stepped outside. The air had a nip to it, so she tucked her hands into her pockets and walked down the path toward the barn. As she neared the corral where she saw Laura earlier, she looked in. The ewe was laying in the corner and her two lambs were snuggled up next to her. Amy could see tags with numbers in the ear of each lamb. Shane must have tagged them, Amy thought. She walked over to the barn and quietly opened the door. She could hear a voice down at the end of the alley so she headed that way.

Shane's head appeared over the partition.

"I thought I felt a draft. Come look."

Amy reached the stall and looked in. There was a ewe in the stall and with her were three lambs.

"Wow! Do they often have that many?" Amy asked.

"Well, it depends. We usually like to just have two, but every so often a ewe will surprise us and drop three and sometimes four. It is difficult for the ewe to nurse more than two as she only has two teats. With a ranch this big, bottle lambs are a bother. Sometimes we're lucky and can give the bottlers away."

"So why is this ewe inside?"

"She had the first lamb, then had trouble birthing the second. It was cool out, so I figured if I had to help her, I'd rather do it where it's warmer. I just picked up the first lamb and she followed me in here. When she laid down to push, I checked and her problem was the two lambs were both trying to come at the same time. I pushed the one back in, pulled the first one out, and the last one came easy. While the ewe was down, I pulled her plugs and now she's up and doing fine. I'll put her back outside in the morning. Right now I have to make a pen check. Want to come?"

"I'm not really dressed for it, but I'd like to."

Shane stepped out of the stall and latched the gate. Walking to the back of the barn, he opened a door and took out an old coat.

"Put this on. It's not fancy, but it's warm."

Amy slid her arms into the jacket. It felt fleecy and warm.

"Thanks; this helps a lot."

They went out the side door into the sheep pen. The ewes were laying all over. Most were chewing their cud, but several were grunting and stretched out.

"Look for any that aren't sleeping, are pawing the ground or look uncomfortable," Shane said.

"They all look uncomfortable. Look at the bellies on them! The poor things!"

"I guess a woman probably feels the same way close to her due date. Do you have any kids?"

The question caught Amy unprepared. She hesitated, then said, "My husband and I never had any children." She didn't want to lie and that statement was the truth.

"What happened to your husband?"

"We're divorced," Amy replied shortly.

"I'm sorry." Shane apologized, " It's really none of my business. I'm glad you're here as we really need the help. I worry a lot about Mom. Losing Dad really took a lot out of her. She misses him a lot. She works way too hard; I think trying to forget. She and Dad were very close. They did everything together. I don't remember them ever going places without each other. Mom wants to keep the ranch intact for me when I'm ready, but at what cost? I would rather she sold off the ewes and took care of herself. If I want to ranch, I'll find some way to build a flock back."

Amy touched Shane on the arm and said, " I will do what I can to help your Mother. Maybe I'll be able to take some of the pressure off her. Oh look, Shane, there's a ewe that looks like she's getting ready. Isn't that a water bag?"

"Good eye, Amy. I'll open the gate on that empty pen there and we'll quietly guide her in there."

Amy was excited. Her first conquest. She had been watching and listening. Shane no sooner shut the gate than the ewe laid down and started pushing. It wasn't long before two feet appeared, then a nose. With a final big push, the lamb slid out. The ewe was on her feet immediately and started talking and licking the lamb. While she was busy with the first lamb, a second slid out. The ewe was ignoring the second lamb and it wasn't moving. Shane was away checking the rest of the flock and Amy could see the lamb had the sack still over it's head and nose, so it couldn't breathe. Amy knew she had to act quickly. She opened the gate and slid into the pen. The ewe wasn't happy and stamped her foot. Talking quietly to the ewe, Amy reached down for the second lamb and cleaned the sack off it's face and nose. It still didn't move. Taking the sleeve of the jacket, Amy rubbed the little fellow's sides briskly. Suddenly, it gave a gasp and started to flop in the straw. The ewe bleated and stomped her foot again, so Amy eased back out the gate. The lamb let a little bleat out and the ewe answered. Soon she was licking the second lamb.

Amy was trembling. She was so happy the ewe took over.

When Shane returned, Amy told him, "I'm afraid I mucked up your jacket," and she proceeded to tell him what she did.

"You did the right thing. The lamb would have suffocated. Boy, you learn fast!"

"Thanks, but now I'm heading up to bed. See you tomorrow."

Once Amy got into the trailer, she let her guard down. She started to shake all over. She had been so scared, but instinct told her the lamb needed help. She had taken basic CPR in her beauty course so understood what was needed. Maybe she would be okay once she got the hang of things. She sat down on the sofa and Happy Cat jumped up on her lap.

"Yes Happy Cat, you are good soothing company. I'm glad you're here."

Being away from her mother's influence can be nothing but good, Amy thought. Then she remembered she hadn't phoned her mother to let her know she had arrived safely. Oh well, would have to do that in the morning. It was way too late to call now. Her mother will be angry, either way. There was time enough to deal with her in the morning.

Chapter 7

A BANGING ON HER door awoke Amy the next morning. Wiping the sleep from her eyes, she glanced at the clock. 7 AM!! She couldn't believe it! She never slept so sound. It must be the fresh air and exercise, not to mention how quiet it was.

"Just a minute," she called out as she struggled into her housecoat. Shane was on the step when she opened the door.

"Good morning, sleepyhead! Mom says to come to the house for breakfast as she knows you didn't have time to stock your cupboards."

"Okay, what time?"

"Well, we usually eat at 6:30, but we've been letting you have a little extra shut-eye. I told Mom about you being out in the pens last night."

"Oh, you should have awakened me. I don't want to mess up any routine. I don't eat much breakfast, usually just a coffee or juice and maybe a slice of toast."

"Well, you won't get coffee in our house, because as you know, we're Mormons. But juice and toast we have. After you've been working here a while, I'm sure you'll start the day with more sustenance. You wear it off very quickly."

Amy laughed and turned back into her kitchen, "We'll see. Tell Laura I'll be over in ten minutes."

"Okay; I'm off to the barns. We had five more ewes lamb in the last hour. I didn't get in until 5:00 AM and Mom's been up since 4:00. See you."

Dressing quickly, Amy ran a comb through her long hair and tied it back in a ponytail. Then she hurried over to the ranch house. The two collies met her on the path and their excited yips made Amy realize she didn't even know their names. As if reading her mind, Laura, who had stepped out on the porch, said, "They are Lad and Lady."

"I meant to ask you yesterday and forgot. Why are they up here by the house and not with the sheep?"

"During lambing, we keep the dogs out of the pens. They get the ewes excited and they may step on their young." Laura beckoned Amy into the kitchen and poured her a large glass of juice. "Sorry I can't accommodate you with a coffee, but we'll go shopping today and you can pick up what you want for your breakfast and lunch. Shane and I always start our day with juice, oatmeal, toast and fruit. Sometimes we even have eggs and ham or bacon. It sticks to our ribs better if we happen to get really busy and miss lunch."

"Well, I'm not officially working yet, so juice and toast will be fine."

"I heard you were out in the pens last night. Shane is really impressed with how you catch on. And you took the initiative to save the lamb. Good for you. I'm happy to tell you the ewe and both lambs are doing fine."

"That's good. I was so scared but I didn't want Shane to see me shaking so I got out of there."

"It will get easier. I've been at it for probably close to thirty years. This used to be my Dad's place. He ran cattle on it. When he passed away, the ranch was left to me. I was an only child. I was a newlywed at the time and my husband was working in the mines in the foothills. He hated it. So we decided to pull up stakes and move to the ranch. I was working as a secretary at the mine so we both quit our jobs. When we got to the ranch, we found the hired man had walked off with the cattle and everything of value. When we finally caught up to him, he had a paper on him, signed by my Dad, giving him permission to take anything he wanted. I'm sure Dad didn't know what he was signing."

"That's terrible! What did you do?"

"We couldn't find anyone who thought Dad was incompetent so we had to let it go. We couldn't afford to buy cattle back, so decided to go into sheep. I got a job in town for the first few years. Things were tough but we made it through."

Amy took another bite of her toast and washed it down with the apple juice. Wiping her mouth, she commented, "I can't imagine how you managed. Don't you need special fencing for sheep?"

"Yes, you do. Abe managed to get a really good dog and between them, they herded the sheep for the first year. By the second year, we had saved enough to start fencing. We just went year by year. We, of course, had good corrals and could run the sheep in at night. Coyotes were bad in the early years and we lost more than a few head to them."

"I never thought about predators."

"The worst ones are neighborhood dogs. They will run the sheep and kill for sport. At least the coyote kills to eat."

"So is Shane the only child you and Abe had?"

"Not really. I lost two babies in the first years we were married. I couldn't seem to carry past four months. Abe and I were saddened by the losses."

"But then you had Shane. I imagine you were overjoyed!"

"Shane is adopted. I was never able to conceive after my two miscarriages."

"Oh, I'm sorry. I shouldn't have pried into your personal life."

"No problem. Shane knows he's adopted. We never kept that from him."

"That's good. Honesty is the best policy."

"So we always say. Well, if you're done, let's hit the road and do some serious shopping. I'll just check with Shane to see if he needs a hand before we leave."

Laura headed out the door. Amy picked up her plate and glass and headed to the sink. She felt bad she had asked so many questions. What a sad story! But they seemed to make it out on top. It was too bad Abe had died so young. He really was needed here. Amy put on her shoes and grabbing her coat, headed to the trailer to get her purse.

"I think I'm going to like it here," she mused aloud as she walked back to the house, " And I know I really am needed."

Chapter 8

THE SUN WAS up and shining brightly when Amy and Laura pulled onto the highway and headed into Milk River. It looked like a beautiful day. The frost on the windshield had disappeared before they left the ranch.

"It's sure nice to see the weather warming up," Laura commented, "It's not fun, making sheep checks when it's freezing out. We have to be so watchful at those times because a lamb can get chilled very easily."

"How many sheep usually lamb at night?" Amy asked.

"As many as lamb in the day," Laura answered, "An old sheep herder once told me if I only turn my rams out in the day, all lambs will be born during the day. Well, on this ranch, that would be impossible to do, so I can't prove or disprove that theory. So we just work day and night during lambing."

"How long does lambing last?" Amy inquired.

"Well, we usually get three weeks of pretty intense lambing, then the stragglers can last another three. If your rams are good and you have enough of them, not too many ewes get missed on their first cycle after the rams go in. The ram has a very keen nose and can detect a ewe in heat even before she knows it!" Laura laughed and shifted down as they entered town. "Let's get your shopping done and head back to the ranch. I don't like to leave Shane for too long in case he has trouble."

Amy hit the dry goods store and with Laura's help, managed to find some good boots, a warm, but light jacket, good gloves, and three pairs of coveralls. Laura said she would need at least that many as she would be wet and dirty. One purchase Amy insisted on was an alarm clock so she wouldn't sleep in again. Laura insisted on paying for everything and told Amy she would take it out of her pay checks.

Then they headed to the feed store where Laura made some purchases. The grocery store was last. It was still morning when they headed back to the ranch.

Shane was waiting for them and he helped to unload their purchases and bring them up to date. He had a very busy morning. Fifteen more ewes had lambed in the three hours they had been gone. They had twenty-nine more lambs on the ground and seven or eight more ewes were looking close.

When they finished unloading, Shane said he could use a hand moving some ewes and lambs to make room for more.

"Okay," Laura said, "I'll be right there."

"Why don't I help Shane?" Amy volunteered, "then you can put your groceries away and get lunch."

Laura hesitated, then smiled, "That's a deal. Have to start you somewhere."

Amy hurried down to her trailer with her purchases. She put her perishables into the fridge, donned her new boots and coveralls, then headed out to the sheep pen. It was warm enough she didn't need her coat or gloves. She was excited. Her first official day in the pens. She hoped she wouldn't embarrass herself.

Shane met her at the barn door. "We'll move the flock of older lambs and ewes to the outside pen. We always like to keep the most recent lambs closest to the barns in case of sickness. As we put the group down the alley to the gate leading to the outer pen, be watching for untagged or sick lambs, etc. Sometimes one gets by us. Look for lambs with droopy ears or bunged up tails. Scours can kill a little lamb quickly."

Amy was listening closely. Shane was so full of information. It was hard to take it all in.

When Shane opened the gate, the ewes hung back and eyed it warily. Quietly, Shane walked through the gate into the pen and motioned for Amy to go to the back of the flock. Suddenly one ewe bolted for the opening and others quickly followed. There was close to seventy ewes in the group and all the lambs. Some of the lambs got left behind so there was quite a racket as ewes tried to find their young. When the last lamb was through the gate, Amy shut it. When the dust settled, Amy could see Shane had a lamb in his arms.

"Could you go to the barn and bring me the first-aid kit? It's where I got the jacket for you last night. This little guy needs a shot."

Amy dashed off to the barn and found the kit. When she returned, she watched Shane give the lamb a needle.

"As you can see, this little guy has the scours. It sometimes happens when they take on too much milk or they pick up an infection from the yard. He's not bad, so should be okay. We'll keep an eye on him."

"How will you catch him again if he's out in this pen? It's pretty big."

"Well, if he's that well, he won't need treated. But I have an ace in the hole. These lambs are pretty sturdy, so I call in the back-up crew. Lad and Lady can pick out a sick lamb as well as I can. They will corner it and help me catch it. Lady had even been known to hold a lamb down until I could get there, and she doesn't leave one mark on the lamb."

"Wow, that's impressive. But what about the ewe? Doesn't she object?"

"Probably, but she is defenseless against the dogs. Well, let's get those other ewes out of the small pens and into the one vacated. Then it's time for lunch."

Another ewe in the waiting pen was lambing so Shane told Amy to go have her lunch. When she got back, he would go. Amy hurried off to her trailer and quickly made a sandwich and had a glass of milk. She grabbed an apple and headed back to the pens. Shane had the ewe already in the small pen and one lamb was up and sucking.

"I think this old stinker is only going to have one. She's got a bit of age on her, so I've marked her as a cull."

Shane showed Amy his clip board. Beside #172, he had put a black X.

"That means to cull. On these sheets are the #'s of every ewe we have. When one lambs, we find her # and mark beside it; how many lambs and any other pertinent info, like if she refuses her lamb or if she has trouble. When we cull in the fall, we take all these facts into consideration. I'm heading up for lunch now. You can check the pen for anymore looking ready and I'll be back shortly."

Amy took the clipboard from Shane and hung it on the nail on the side of the pen. She took one last look into the pen. The ewe was laying down and chewing her cud so she didn't look too worried about anything. The lamb was curled up beside her. She eyed Amy suspiciously and smelled her lamb.

Walking slowly through the holding pen, Amy tried not to upset the ewes. They were so huge, and as they lay there, they were grunting and trying to find a comfortable position. About twenty or so were at the hay feeder, so Amy didn't bother to check them. She figured if they were eating, they couldn't be in labor. There were still about fifty other ewes in the pen to check. Most of them seemed to be sleeping.

"Good," Amy thought, "I'm not quite ready to try this on my own." She again checked the ewe with one lamb, but she was sleeping. "So much for her. Now I can move the clipboard."

It wasn't long before Laura showed up.

"How are you doing? I sent Shane to bed. He'll take the night shift, so I thought you and I could handle today, okay?"

"Fine with me. Just tell me what to do."

"Well, first we're going to head out to that left pen and check for any ewes that are making bag. That means they're getting closer to lambing and should be brought in to the inner pen. We have moved over 100 out already so makes more room. For this job, we will need the dogs. They will round them up and put them into the chute. As they go through, I will check. You work the gate. I will say left or right and you swing the gate that way. Okay?"

"I'll do my best. Is it the gate or the pen that is left or right?"

"The pen. Come on, I'll show you."

Laura whistled for the dogs and they all headed out to the left pasture. Laura showed Amy how to operate the gate and with a series of whistles, the dogs had the ewes heading toward the chute. Laura closed the gate when the last one passed through. What a commotion! There was baaing and dust everywhere. The dogs went to the back of the flock and started pushing the sheep toward the squeeze. As each ewe passed into the chute, Laura checked it's bag and vulva, then said left or right. Left meant not close and the ewe went back to the pasture. Right put her into the next pen that opened into the holding pen. It was a good system and easy to use. Amy was impressed with the set-up they had. It was time-saving for sure.

After they ran all the ewes through, Laura called the dogs into the next pen and opened the gate to the holding pen. It didn't take much encouragement for the ewes to head in.

Laura and Amy were covered with dust and in need of a drink.

"Let's grab something wet before we do another check," Laura said. Amy didn't disagree. Her throat was parched and her eyes full of dust.

They headed to the tack room and the fridge there. With a cold drink of water, they sat on the chairs and enjoyed a little break.

"Well, how's your first day going? Are you starting to relax and take things in your stride, Amy?"

"I hope so. I have so much to learn. I want to be able to help you as much as I can."

"I think you're doing fine. One of us will always be available to help you out, so don't sweat it."

"Shane sure knows what he's doing. You're lucky to have a son that is willing to work like he does. I see so many of the young men in Medicine Hat that just want to hang out with their friends. I can't imagine any of them doing what Shane does."

"He's a good boy, but he worries about me too much. I'm doing okay. I want him to get his education and go on his mission. Tomorrow is Sunday. We take turns going to Church on Sundays during lambing. Tomorrow is my turn, so Shane will be here. Usually we don't work on Sunday, except to feed the stock, but lambing is different. I hope you don't mind working on Sundays for the next little while?"

"Of course not. I don't attend any particular church so I'm willing to stay and work. Why don't you both go? It's only for a short time and I could manage."

"No, that wouldn't be fair to leave you on your second day. We'll have to season you a bit more. Besides, our church is three hours, plus going and coming back, so way too long to leave you. Well, time for another check. Let's get to it."

Chapter 9

THE NEXT FEW days were a blur to Amy. She did manage to find time Sunday morning to call her mother. Gladys was cool to her, just as Amy suspected.

"Couldn't find the time or have the decency to call your mother to let her know you're okay. But that's what I would expect from you. Are you still on the ranch? They haven't fired you yet? Won't be long."

"Nice to talk to you too, Mom. No, Laura and I get along just fine. She has been very kind to me. And her son is easy to work with."

"Her son? How old is he? I suppose you have your eye on him. It doesn't seem to take you long to find another man."

"For your information, Shane is coming eighteen years old. I'm old enough to be his mother. I have to go now. I'm on duty."

"What?!? They don't give you Sundays off? What kind of employer is that?"

"The sheep don't know what day it is. I'll call you in a couple of weeks."

"Don't bother. I wouldn't want to interrupt your work. Your old sick mother will just muddle through."

"Whatever. Take care."

Amy hung up the phone and put on her jacket and gloves. There was a chill in the air; from the phone as well as outside. Her mother never changes. It would be better not to call her too often, Amy thought as she headed to the sheep pens and work.

⇒ ⇐

All the next week, they were extremely busy. Lambing was definitely in full swing. They would no sooner get one ewe settled and another started. At times they has two or three lambing at the same time. Some ewes had problems and they had to help with the birth. Amy even got to deliver a few lambs.

At night, she was so tired, she had a shower and fell into bed. Shane was on school break as it was Easter time, so it helped to share the work. So far, she had managed not to disgrace herself. She knew the routine and did her best. Laura and Shane had little to say as they worked from one pen to another. If Amy had a question, they would answer it. The rest of the time, they seemed to know the other's moves. They worked well together.

Before Amy knew it, it was Sunday again. Shane left for church. Because Laura had been in the pens since 3:00 AM, Amy persuaded her to go and have a rest.

"I'll call you if I have a problem," Amy told her and Laura didn't argue too much.

"I am pretty tired. Think you'll be okay for a bit?"

"Sure thing. Don't worry."

After Laura left, Amy got the clip board and recorded all the new ewes in the lambing pens. Laura had been too busy to do the recording. Amy could see by the ewes checked off, that they were over two-thirds lambed out. Not bad for just over two weeks. With any luck, maybe things would slow down in a week or so. Laura had said around three weeks for the first cycle.

"Let's hope not too many are stragglers," Amy thought as she headed to the tack room and a cup of hot coffee. She had put her coffee maker into the tack room as she spent most of her time at the barns. Laura had left some cinnamon cake there too, so she took a piece and enjoyed a minute or two of relaxation.

As she headed back to the pens, a dirty green 4 X 4 pulled into the yard.

"Oh, no, not Ivan!" Amy moaned as she shut the gate behind her. "Hopefully, he'll go see Laura."

But Ivan jumped out of the truck, petted the wildly excited dogs, then headed for the barn. Amy went on with her ewe check. When Ivan appeared over the fence, she tried to ignore him.

"Hey, tenderfoot! How's the job going? Got run over by any sheep yet?"

Amy paused and took her time answering, "No, these sheep are well mannered. Better than some people I could mention."

"Ouch, that hurt. It's too early in the day for daggers. Where's Shane and Laura?"

"Shane has gone to church and Laura is laying down."

"And they left the greenhorn alone with the ewes? They must trust you pretty good."

"A person has to earn trust. Maybe that's something you should think about."

"Why? Don't you trust me? I told you; I'm harmless. I like to tease, but can be a good and loyal friend."

"I don't need friends. I have my work. That's enough for me."

"Okay, but I think you're going to need help in a few minutes. I can count three ewes about to give birth."

With that statement, Ivan opened the gate and entered the pen. He was right. There were three different ewes, all pawing and circling, getting ready to pop out a lamb.

With Ivan's help, they managed to get each one into a pen. Glancing over the flock, Amy say two more showing signs. One already had a water bag out. Doing a quick check on the rest, she hurried back and opened two more pens. The one ewe went right in but the one with the sac protruding wouldn't leave the spot where she started labor. Because some of the fluid had leaked on the ground there, she thought her lamb should be there. She kept smelling the ground and bleating.

"Just leave her and look after the others. She will lamb right there, then we'll get her in," Ivan said as he checked the other pens, "Looks like lots of action here."

For the next two hours, Amy and Ivan worked side by side. Amy had to admit she appreciated his help. He knew what he was doing and worked quietly and efficiently. When thing settled down, they had eighteen new lambs and were both ready for a break.

"Have you got anything to drink in that fridge in there?" Ivan gestured toward the barn.

"I think there's some orange juice and water. I also have coffee on the go."

"You drink that poison? Not good for you and bad on the nerves. I'll take the water though. Let's take a break."

Amy led the way as they headed off to the tack room. She knew she looked a sight. She hadn't bothered to even comb her hair as she hustled out to the barns in the early morning. She removed her gloves and washed her hands at the sink before getting Ivan some water. He moved to the nearest chair and sat down.

"Boy, I don't know how Laura does it. I'm twenty years younger than her and it plays me out just for a few hours. Sheep are so touchy. It is so easy to lose lambs. That's why I have cattle. They all calve right out on the pasture. Only an odd time I have to rope one and help it. I keep them all in the pasture below my house during calving and I can watch them from my porch, using field glasses. If one is having a problem, I saddle Scamp and go make a visit."

"How many head of cattle do you have?"

"Oh, must be about three hundred head, not counting the calves. I've had pretty good luck this year. I only lost one cow and three calves. I finished up a couple of weeks ago. I like to get done before Laura starts lambing. That way, I can help her if she needs it."

"You must be pretty good friends."

"Laura is just like a mother to me. I was just a little duffer when she and Abe took over the ranch. Shortly after that my mother died, so Laura sort of took me under her wing. My Dad was so lost, he was no father to me. I actually stayed here with Abe and Laura for a few years. Then one day, out of the blue, Dad came to get me. Said it was time I came home. I was about seven or eight at the time."

"I imagine Laura really missed you when you left."

"I suppose, but being a kid, I was only thinking of myself. Things were easy with Abe and Laura. They spoiled me. Years later, I found out they tried to adopt me, but Dad wouldn't budge."

"Well, your Dad had just lost your mother. He wasn't going to want to lose you too. I'm surprised the Collins' tried to take you from your Dad."

"I guess they thought I was being neglected. You see, Dad was courting a new woman and was gone a lot, leaving me alone. I was pretty young at the time. Then one day, he brought her home and announced she was my new mother. That's the day I ran away and came back here."

"He didn't give you any warning?

"Nope. Just dumped her on me. Well, that one lasted all of one year. Then there were a series of women in and out of our home. When I was eighteen, Dad finally found May. They were a perfect match. She had money and Dad was looking for money. Of course, she wouldn't live on the ranch so Dad moved out and left me the ranch."

"Where do they live?"

"Dad died two years ago. He had cancer. May, as far as I know, still lives in Calgary. She never contacts me."

Amy set her coffee cup down. "Well, my break is over. Thanks for your help, Ivan; and the conversation. All this helps me to know everyone better. See you another time."

"What?!? Are you firing me already? It's Sunday and I have nothing better to do than help a pretty greenhorn with her duties. We'll let Laura rest. I'll help you until Shane gets home. Laura will have to work tonight as Shane has school in the morning."

"Laura could sure use the rest,' Amy reluctantly agreed, "I will take you up on the help. It's a lot easier with two."

"Did Laura tell you I help out here quite a bit? I do a lot of the heavy work for them, and we hay together. So you'll be seeing lots of me, so I hope we can be friends."

Amy smiled, "Well, I guess I could use another friend. I already count Laura and Shane in that group so I guess I could add you."

"Great! Now, let's go do some sheep-ing."

Chapter 10

T HE NEXT WEEK or two just flew by and soon the lambing was nearing completion, with just a few stragglers left. Amy had learned to drive the tractor and move bales around, how to feed the ewes, deliver lambs, deal with problems and make friends with Lad and Lady.

With the end of lambing, Laura was starting to perk up and she was preparing her garden for planting. She got Ivan to come over with his garden tractor and work it. She was also out in her flower bed whenever she had time. The weather had turned very warm. It was the end of April and the hills were bursting forth with crocuses' and green grass was appearing everywhere.

"We'll turn the ewes out next week," Shane said one morning. "We'll keep in those ones that haven't lambed yet. How many do we have?'

"On last count, I think there was twenty-three," Amy answered as she measured some feed into a pail.

"Good; they should be finished in the next week or so. We don't usually get too excited when we get down to so few. The weather is warm so we let them work things out. We won't be doing all night checks anymore. We'll take turns doing one check in the middle of the night."

"Sounds good to me. I am feeling a bit worn down."

"Amy, you are looking great. You've put on a lot of muscle since you arrived and you have a tan."

"Fat, you mean. Your Mom cooks way too good."

"No, I bet you gained muscle. That's what wrestling sheep does for you. Do you mind if I ask how old you are?"

"No, I don't mind. I'll be thirty-four this year."

"Wow! I sure didn't think you were that age! I wouldn't put you a day over........say........twenty-five."

"Well thanks, Shane. That is a nice compliment. Some days I feel fifty, so it's nice to know I don't look it."

"I bet if you were all dressed up, you would be really pretty."

"Oh, I'm not pretty now?" Amy teased.

Shane blushed. "I'm sorry; I didn't mean it like that. What I meant is because you are pretty, if you were all dressed up, you would knock the men's socks off."

"I'll second that, Shane."

Amy jumped and looked up to see Ivan sauntering toward them.

"Hi, Ivan," Shane tried to look busy, "What you doing over here?"

"I was just driving by heading into town so I wondered if anyone wanted to go or needed anything?"

"Check with Mom," Shane answered.

"I could use some supplies," Amy spoke up, "I'll give my list to Laura if she's going with you."

Amy handed the pail of feed to Shane and headed out the gate.

"Wait up," Ivan said, hurrying after her, "I'll walk up with you."

Laura came out of the house as they approached. Ivan repeated his invitation, but Laura declined.

"Why don't you go, Amy? You can get your own stuff and pick up a couple of things for me. I'll get some concentrate for the ewes if you're going to the feed store, Ivan. Just put it on my bill."

"Come on Amy. It will do you good to get away for a few hours. You've been living and breathing sheep for weeks now."

"Okay. I just have to change and wash up. Can you wait ten minutes?"

"I can wait forever for a pretty girl," Ivan answered as he sat down on the porch swing. "I'll be right here."

Amy dashed off to her trailer. She slipped off her coverall, and headed to the bathroom. Having a quick shower, she found some clean jeans and a blue T-shirt. She toweled her hair dry and left it loose. No need to put it up out of the way and it would dry better that way. She hoped it wouldn't get too frizzy. Because of her natural curl, it was inclined to do that.

Amy grabbed her purse and headed back to the main ranch house. Laura and Ivan were sitting on the porch.

"All ready," Amy announced as she reached the bottom step.

"What beautiful hair you have," Laura commented, "It's exactly the same shade of brown as Abe's was. He also had a natural curl. You could almost pass for his daughter."

"Thank you," Amy replied, "I have problems controlling it sometimes. Maybe I should get it cut."

"Don't you dare," Ivan finally spoke up, "You would regret it."

Amy laughed, "Probably. I'm ready; let's boogie."

"Okay, little lady."

As they strode toward Ivan's truck, Amy commented, "Don't you ever wash your truck?"

Ivan glanced over at her and smirked, "Why? Don't you want to ride in my dirty truck? It's not too bad inside. The last passenger was my cattle dog and before that, a calf. But I brushed it out."

Amy punched him on the arm. "You are always a barrel of laughs, aren't you? I was asking a legitimate question.. Don't you ever wash your truck?"

"Not often. This way, no one can see all the rust on it."

"Is that true? Is that why you don't wash it?"

Ivan laughed and patted her shoulder. "You ask the weirdest questions, little lady."

"My name is Amy. I prefer you use it."

"Okay, okay…. Amy." Ivan held the door open for her, "May I have the honor of your company, Amy?"

Laughing, Amy climbed into the 4 X 4. It was clean and tidy inside. What a spoofer, Amy thought. It sure didn't smell like a calf or dog had been in there.

Laura waved from the porch as they left the yard. Amy suddenly felt very carefree. It was good to get away from the pressures if only for a few hours.

Amy had called her mother the night before and it had been the same old story She was a cruel, mean daughter to leave her mother alone like this. How had she managed to stay on the ranch this long? Was she giving favors to the ranch son? Amy had hung up as soon as she could. Her mother always depressed her. Wouldn't she have something to talk about if she knew Amy was going to town with the bachelor neighbor. Then a thought struck her. Was Ivan a bachelor or did he have a wife back on the ranch?

Turning toward Ivan, she said, "So, did your wife give you a big list too?"

Startled, Ivan responded, "What makes you think I'm married?"

"Well, you never have said one way or the other, so I was wondering?"

"If I told you I was single, would it make a difference between us?"

"Why should it?"

"Well, maybe you would feel safer if you thought I was married."

"I feel safe with you. For Pete's sake, I just wanted a straight answer!"

"Okay, okay. I was engaged to be married when I was twenty-three, but she decided I didn't make enough money on the ranch and I wouldn't move off so she left for greener pastures. Since then, I haven't found anyone who measures up. I guess I'm pretty fussy. How about you? How come you're single?"

"Who says I am?" Amy teased right back, then added. "I was married for seven years, and one day he came home and asked for a divorce. That's when I found out that for four of those seven years, he had a honey on the side and had a child by her and another on the way. He even bought her a house, while we were living in an one bedroom apartment."

"Did you have kids?"

"No. I guess it was my fault. He proved he could. My mother says that's why he left. A man needs prodigy."

"Bull! I hope you don't believe that? He was fooling around on you before the kids came along. Those kind of men need shot."

"My Mom thought he was wonderful. So did I for a long time. He was funny, witty, and so good-looking. I guess he turned my head. Well, I learned my lesson. No man will turn my head ever again."

"That's too bad. Just because you had a 'lemon in the garden of love', doesn't mean all men are snakes. Take me for example; I'm witty, funny, oh-so good looking ... and loyal besides."

That made Amy laugh. If anything, Ivan sure wasn't good-looking, but he did have a great sense of humor and Amy was finding she enjoyed being around him. He wasn't bad for being a man. She couldn't believe she had opened up and talked to him about her marriage.

"So you're tooting your own horn, are you?" Amy responded.

"Is it working?" Ivan grinned as he shifted down to enter Milk River. "It's now 11:45. Why don't we have lunch first, then do our shopping?"

"Only if I pay for my own," Amy said.

"Okay. You sure can burst a man's bubble, when he wants to prove he's a real gentleman .... And loyal, too."

"I hope you're joking," Amy glanced over at Ivan, "This has nothing to do with you being a gentleman or loyal. I just like to pay my own way and not beholden to anyone. Can we stop at the bank first so I can cash my cheque?"

"Sure thing."

After a hearty lunch at the local restaurant, they got the shopping done and headed back out. They chatted constantly on the way home and before they knew it, the ranch loomed below them.

"Before we get to the yard, I wanted to ask you a question. Now that lambing is coming to an end, I wondered if you could consent to go to a movie with me some night?" Ivan asked.

"Like on a date?"

"Well, we could call it just two friends enjoying a movie together. What do you say?"

Amy thought about it, then answered, "Ask me again when lambing is over. Then I'll see."

"Fair enough. Here we are, home safe and sound. I'll help you unload."

Chapter 11

THE DAYS PASSED quickly during the balance of lambing. There were many little jobs that needed tending to that had been neglected during the push of lambing. Along with those chores, Amy helped Laura plant her garden and work around the house yard. Laura was starting to look more rested and seemed happy to have Amy around.

On her day off, which was usually Sunday, Amy took to the hills, following the animal trails. Lad and Lady usually traveled with her on the outings. Shane and Laura would be off to church. The first few Sundays, they asked her to come but she declined and now they no longer asked her.

This particular Sunday, Amy was enjoying her quiet time in the hills. It was early May and she discovered a profusion of wild prairie flowers in full bloom; crocuses, three sisters, and violets were a few she could identify.

"Who says the prairie isn't beautiful?" Amy mused as she knelt down and smelled the flowering perfume. She found a rock and sat for a spell, gazing around at all the distant hills. Lad and Lady lay down beside her, their tongues lolling out, waiting for her.

Amy felt a great peace descend over her. There was something about the smell of flowers, the picturesque scenery and the company of her canine companions that made her soul awaken and a feeling of 'this is right' come over her being.

"Who says I need to go to church?" Amy spoke aloud, "You can't get any closer to God than right here!"

After her rest, Amy decided to walk a bit further. It was a beautiful warm day and she wasn't ready to head home yet. She noticed a structure on top of a hill off to the west and being the curious type, she decided to investigate it. Lad and Lady were ready for the adventure and they bounded off ahead.

As she trudged along, Amy thought about all the changes that had taken place in her life. She went from a beautician to a waitress to a shepherdess in a very short time, and she discovered she liked sheep a lot better than some of the customers she had to deal with as a hairdresser or waitress. She also found she didn't miss the city at all and definitely all the noise and traffic. Sometimes, she missed the shopping, but really, what did she need out here? She hadn't put a dress on in over a month. Some day she would have to do that and surprise everyone.

That made her thoughts turn to Ivan. She wasn't too sure how she felt about him. She had accepted the movie date and had a great time. Since then they had been on one other date; out for dinner one night, which she let Ivan pay for without argument. Ivan was very busy with spring work so he hadn't been to the ranch for a few days. Amy found she missed having him around. She missed his crazy humor and his teasing. It was nice to have good friends, and she was glad Laura and Shane had someone they could rely on in Ivan.

Soon Amy realized she had reached the foot of the hill. As she gazed up, she could see the structure looked like an old cabin, though it was in a bad state of repair. Lad and Lady had loped on ahead and as they disappeared around the cabin, they started yipping, then suddenly stopped.

"That's strange," Amy thought aloud, "I wonder what they spotted?"

She reached the cabin and took a glance inside the doorway. The cabin was a mess. It looked like a tornado had gone through. She walked around to the back side and then, startled, she jumped back. She nearly walked into the back end of a horse!

When she gathered herself together, she saw movement to the right and there were Lad and Lady, sitting calmly beside Ivan, who was sitting on a rock, grinning.

"Are you trying to scare a person half to death?" Amy groused, as she took a couple of steps toward him. "I'm lucky I didn't get kicked in the head!"

"Old Scamp wouldn't hurt a fly. He's sleeping. He's like me, got a bit of age on him so harmless."

"Sometimes a bit of age can cause other problems, like not knowing what side of the fence you're on," Amy responded, "I sure didn't expect anyone else on Collins' land."

" I hate to tell you this, but these hills you are so fond of walking belong to the Johnson spread. As you'll notice, when you left the lower pasture, you crossed through a fence before you started up the hill. We consider it neutral territory between the two ranches. I only pasture these hills on dry years when I don't have enough grazing on the flats."

"Well, I'm sorry I'm trespassing. I won't do it again. No one told me."

"You are not trespassing. I love seeing you walking these hills."

"Why, have you seen me before?"

"Nearly every Sunday. I find a certain peace up here in the hills. It's like I'm close to nature or something. I used to bring Rover with me but he's getting pretty old and prefers to sleep. A bit like me."

"You're not old. Older perhaps." Amy found a rock and sat down. She thought she would be annoyed by finding Ivan in her special place, but she was touched by his saying he found peace in the hills. She felt the same way.

"Did you bring a lunch?" Ivan inquired as he stood up and stretched.

"No, I didn't. I usually eat at home after my walk."

"Well, I did and I packed enough for two," Ivan responded as he headed to the horse and picked up the saddle bags from behind the saddle.

"I don't want to take your lunch. I can eat when I get back to the trailer."

"You're not taking my lunch. I packed enough for you. I planned to meet up with you."

"How did you know I would come up this far?"

"I didn't. I was watching you. If you had turned and gone the other way, Scamp and I would have caught up to you."

"You were spying on me all the time!"

"Not all the time; just when it suits my plans."

"And what plan is that?"

"To have lunch with you. We'll call it a date."

Amy had to laugh. What a round about way to get a date.

"Why aren't you working today, or is the spring work all done?"

"I never work on Sunday, except to do chores. I guess that's my church upbringing."

"What church is that?" Amy asked.

Ivan looked surprised, "Laura didn't tell you? I'm a Mormon too."

"Then why aren't you in church? All the Mormons I know attend church regularly."

"That's a personal question and one I don't plan to answer right now. Let's have lunch."

Ivan took a blanket from his saddle bag and spread it on the ground. Then he took out two bag lunches and two bottles of water. Beckoning Amy to come over, he sat down cross-legged on the blanket and opened his bag. Amy obliged and opening her bag, found a ham sandwich, some carrot sticks, an apple and two cookies. Amy bit into the carrot stick while studying Ivan through her lowered lashes. The information she had just received put him in an entirely different light. He was a man with secrets and Amy was determined to find out that secret. She knew he had been engaged at one time. Was that the reason he didn't attend church? She knew what she would do. She would ask Laura. If anyone would know, it would be her. It didn't really surprise Amy that Ivan was a Mormon. He was practically raised by the Collins' so they would be a big influence on him.

"How's your lunch?" Ivan broke the silence as he dug into his bag and pulled out a second sandwich, "Did I pack you enough?"

"More than enough," Amy answered, "I can't possibly eat all this."

"Yes, you can. You need to keep your strength up. Just because lambing is over is no reason to slack off. Haying will start before you know it and then there will be lots of bales to stack. Laura likes to have a stack of square bales for lambing as they are easier to handle in the lamb pens. The rest we will round bale."

"Where does the ranch get their grain for the ewes?"

"Well, I seed their cultivated acres for them and we usually plant a mixed grain. If they run short, I have extra on hand most years."

"So you rent their cultivated land?"

"We have an agreement, I guess you could say."

"I think that is nice that neighbors can help each other out. People sure aren't like that in the city."

"I know. That's why I prefer the land."

"I can understand why. I am beginning to love it out here. I hope I never have to go back to the city."

"Well, I'm sure that can be arranged," Ivan commented as he started to clean up the lunch.

"What do you mean?" Amy took a quick glance at Ivan.

"What I mean is Laura and Shane really like you and I'm sure if you want to stay permanent, it could be arranged. Come on, want to come see my ranch? We can ride double on Scamp."

"What?!? I've never ridden a horse. I'd probably fall off and break my neck."

"No way. You can hang on to me. We'll just walk."

"I don't know."

"Come on. What's the harm? You haven't even seen a working cattle ranch yet. I'll give you a ride home in my truck later."

"What about Lad and Lady?"

"No problem." Ivan turned to the dogs, " Lad, Lady, go home!"

The dogs hesitated for a moment and looked over at Amy. Then they took off. Amy watched as they headed over the hills back toward the Collins' ranch.

"Well, I never! That's really neat. They sure are well trained."

"All sheep dogs are. Let's get going. There looks to be a cloud building up."

Amy managed to scramble up behind Ivan on the ever patient Scamp. She was a bit reluctant to put her arms around him, but he persisted.

"Hold on tight. The terrain is a bit rough, but you'll be okay. I don't bite. Just put your arms around my waist."

Amy did as she was told. Soon she was enjoying herself and watching all the sights.

"Oh, look! Isn't that an eagle?" she asked Ivan as she pointed to a large bird soaring overhead.

"Yep. It sure is. They have been known to take a lamb or two, but mostly they hunt rabbits and other small varmints."

"It sure is pretty, soaring through the air like that. What freedom!"

"Do you want to be free, Amy?" Ivan asked.

"Well, that depends on what you mean by free. I am free to make my own choices in life, but the freedom that eagle has is the unfettered type; no restrictions."

"I know what you mean. We're a lot alike, you and I."

"I don't know about that," Amy replied.

They were approaching the Johnson Cattle Ranch. Looking around Ivan's shoulder, Amy could see rows and rows of stacked feed next to several large corrals. Behind that she could see a large hip-roofed barn, red in color with white trim. Scamp's walk had sped up as he headed straight for the barn. At the door he stopped and Ivan helped Amy slide to the ground. He then dismounted and opened the barn door. As he took Scamp into the barn, Amy gazed around the yard. She hadn't seen the house when they rode up to the barn, but now as she walked around the corner, she could see the two story structure. It was surrounded by a hedge and white picket fence and was painted white with red trim. It wasn't a large house, but definitely big enough for a bachelor. She wondered what kind of a housekeeper Ivan was.

When Amy stepped into the barn, Ivan was rubbing the horse down.

"Getting lonely yet? I'm just about done. What would you like to see first?"

"By the looks of the clouds, we only have one choice," Amy said, "I think it will be raining shortly."

"We could use the rain, so that's good."

Ivan set down the brushes and gave Scamp a pat on the rump. Scamp flicked his tail and went on eating his oats.

"I'll leave him in here until later," Ivan said as he closed the stall door and came toward Amy. "Let's go. Looks like we'll have to make a run for it."

Sure enough, the rain was starting to fall. As they took off running toward the house, Rover, Ivan's old stock dog spotted them and started to bark. Amy could feel her shirt starting to stick to her back and she couldn't see where she was going. She ran into the back of Ivan as he stopped to open the gate into the house yard.

"Whoa, Nellie!" he laughed as he put out his hand to steady her, "We're almost there."

They dashed into the porch and shut the door against the wind and rain. Panting and laughing, they collapsed on the bench there.

"Wow, did that ever come up fast. We're lucky we made it home before it hit, " Ivan commented as he wiped his face on his sleeve. "Come in. We have to get you out of that wet shirt before you catch cold."

"I'm okay," Amy chattered as she rubbed her hands together to warm them.

"You're not okay. I have a housecoat you can borrow. You head to the bathroom. It's right there, on the right and I'll get you the robe. Put your wet things in the dryer."

Amy was grateful to be able to get out of her wet clothes. Her shirt was soaked and her jeans were not that dry either. She decided to remove them both and dry them. She dried her body the best she could and opening the door a crack, found the robe on the chair there and she put it on. It was way too big, but at least it was dry and cozy. It smelled faintly of Brut, men's cologne.

She ventured out to the kitchen to find Ivan had put on the kettle and was making them hot chocolate.

"That sure will hit the spot," Amy said as she took a chair by the table. She glanced out the window and could see it was still raining.

"I called Laura and left a message on her machine to let her know you are with me. She knows you go walking in the hills on Sunday and she might worry when the dogs are back and you're not, especially since it is raining."

"Thank you. That was very thoughtful of you. I should have thought of it."

"You were occupied. Hope this chocolate is strong enough. Let me know."

As Amy sipped her chocolate, she glanced around the kitchen. Everything was neat and tidy. Looking through to the living room, she spotted a typical ranch room with hardwood floor, western style furniture, and a Russell painting on the wall. Everything was neat. Ivan was just full of surprises. Amy wondered just how many women had seen this place. So thinking out loud, Amy asked, "So how many women have you managed to bring home to your little nest?"

Ivan grinned over at her and answered, "All that I can. Usually I pick them up in the hills and hog-tie them on the back of my horse and bring them, kicking and screaming down the hills to my love-nest. You were the easiest."

Amy felt properly chastised, "I'm sorry. It was a dumb question, which deserved a dumb answer. I guess, what I really wanted to know is do you date a lot?"

Ivan took a sip of his chocolate and responded, "Actually, you are the first woman I have been out with in a long time and the first woman, other than Laura, who has been in my house. I don't make a habit of picking up women, unless they're young and pretty and walk into the back of my horse!"

Amy laughed, "It was quite a way to meet, wasn't it?"

"I loved it. I hope we do it often."

Finishing her chocolate, Amy stood up, "I really should be heading home now. I have some laundry to do and housework. My trailer is a mess compared to your house. You put me to shame."

"What's the hurry? You haven't seen the rest of the house yet."

"Okay, a quick look-see, then I have to go," Amy was curious about the rest of the house, but she didn't want to appear too interested.

The main floor had the kitchen, living room, bathroom and office. In the office, Amy saw several plaques of awards Ivan had won with his cattle.

"What kind of cattle do you raise?" Amy enquired.

"I have purebred Black Angus. They do well and they are easy calving. They are a bit hard on the fences but a good electric fence cures that."

"How many awards have you won?"

"Too many to count. Most have come from the prodigy of one bull I had several years ago. He was a champ himself. I imported him from overseas. He cost me plenty but paid for himself over and over again by the sale of his daughters and sons for breeding stock."

The upstairs housed two bedrooms and the main bathroom. It also had a small sitting area at the end of the hall where there was a window that looked out toward the barns. Amy could imagine sitting there looking out the window, knitting or reading a book on a rainy day like today. It was very appealing. Ivan's bedroom was done up in greens and browns. The floors were all hardwood and had rugs in front of the beds. The second bedroom was smaller and done up in blues.

"This used to be my bedroom when I was a tyke," Ivan said, "but when Dad moved out, I moved into the larger room."

"You have a very nice home, Ivan, " Amy answered, "I can't imagine anyone not liking it."

"So you think it's not bad?"

"It's better than any place I have lived. I've only lived in apartments and at home with Mom. Our home wasn't nearly as nice."

"You had a tough time, didn't you?"

"Some of it was my fault. I wasn't the best teen in the world. I got away as soon as I could. I went to beautician school in Calgary and then got a job there."

"Is that where you met your ex-husband? He is an ex, isn't he?"

"Yes, and yes. I was best friends with his sister. Of course when we divorced, Susie blamed me."

"Funny how that works. The injured one always gets the blame."

"Yes, my mother even blamed me. Isn't that a kick?"

"What kind of a mother would do that?"

"My kind of mother. I've learned to try to ignore her. She really can depress me. You wouldn't understand unless you knew her. She can fool even the sharpest. She had my ex fooled."

"I'm pretty hard to fool. I'm a good judge of character. You should invite your mother for a visit. Maybe the ranch would do her some good."

"Not on your life. This is my little corner of the world. I don't want her to ruin it for me."

Ivan laughed and touched Amy's arm, "It's your life and I'm glad you like our little corner of the world, as you so eloquently put it. Nothing can ruin that unless you let it."

Amy turned and gazed up at Ivan. Yes, he was part of that little corner. She put up her hand and touched his cheek. The next thing Amy knew, Ivan's lips brushed hers with a feathery touch. She stepped back quickly and nearly fell. Ivan reached out to steady her.

"Sorry for that. It just seemed a good idea at the time."

Amy touched her lips and turned away, "Don't be sorry. I touched you first. Just a kiss between friends, right? That's all it was."

"If you say so - that's right. A kiss between good friends."

"I have to go now." Amy was a little upset. She valued Ivan's friendship and she didn't want things to change between them.

"Sure thing. I'll get the truck from the garage and meet you out front."

Amy headed to the bathroom and got her clothes out of the dryer and put them back on. As she stepped out on the deck, the sun was starting to peak through the clouds. Ivan drove up to the gate and jumped out of the truck.

"Look at the rainbow! I think that's a good omen, don't you?"

Amy looked when he was pointing. Sure enough, there was a magnificent rainbow, not just a single, but a double. Was it really a good omen? A good omen for what? That she and Ivan would always be good friends, or something more? She was getting the feeling that maybe that was in Ivan's mind. The planned meeting and bringing her here. Well, she would have to put a stop to his plans. She wasn't ready to make any future commitments.

Ivan was silent on the drive back to the Collins' ranch. Amy commented on how fresh everything looked and he only grunted. As he dropped her off at her trailer, he wished her a nice evening and left her standing by her door. He didn't even stop at the main house.

"So he's probably sulking," Amy mused as she headed into her trailer. "I'm not going to let it spoil the rest of my day."

Chapter 12

"I CAN'T BELIEVE I was so stupid," Ivan spoke aloud as he drove away, "A good way to scare her off before I get to first base. What an idiot!"

Ivan shifted gears and headed out on the grid road. He didn't know what came over him. Amy was way too skittish to do a bold thing like that. She had his head muddled up for sure. Since the first time he laid eyes on her, he knew she was someone special. Look how she had fit right in on the ranch, doing her share and then some. Laura and Shane had nothing but praise for the way she had turned out. Ivan sure didn't want to do anything to cause her to leave when Laura really needed her. He would have to back off - stay away from her for a while, until she forgets his error. It wouldn't be easy, but he would try. He had the seeding to finish and then they would be starting to cut hay in June. Maybe after seeding, he would take a quick trip to see his buddy Ace and his family in Montana. He could get Shane to check on things for a week or so. Yes, that's what he would do.

Amy kept busy for the next few days, getting all the lawns mowed and cleaning out the sheep pens and corrals. She had mastered the garden tractor as well as the yard tractor so didn't mind. The work kept her busy and her thoughts away from Ivan's kiss.

It was just a 'spur of the moment' thing, Amy was convinced. She was sure he was sorry about the whole thing and wished he could take it back.

She hadn't seen hide or hair of him since then. Wasn't that a sure sign he was sorry it ever happened? Shane had been over at Ivan's and said they had finished the seeding and harrowing. He mentioned Ivan was talking about going to Montana. Well, that cinched it! He was trying to avoid her. Running away like a coward! Well, let him. Who needs him?! Amy shifted the yard tractor into a lower gear and lowered the bucket for another scoop of refuse. It was almost 5:30 so she'd better hurry. Laura didn't want anyone late for supper.

It was 6:00 sharp when Amy slid into her chair at the table. Shane sauntered in from the bathroom.

"Hey, Amy, what are you doing - burning the midnight oil, so to speak? Your time ends at 5:00 now that things aren't so hectic."

"I know, but I wanted to finish that one corral today, but there is a lot more buildup than I thought. I'll get it done in the morning."

"No hurry. We don't need the corrals until weaning time, which is October. If you don't get them all finished, I can help you after I'm out of school. Right now, I'm weighed down with studies. I'm hoping for a scholarship. If I get one, I might go to college this winter. The courses will be done before April so I would be back for lambing, but that all depends on you."

"Why? What would I have to do with it?"

"It depends on if you plan to stay. I can't leave Mom here by herself."

"Well, I like it here. It's the first time in my life that I feel relaxed and really happy. I want to stay if you and your Mom are happy with me."

"Yes!!! I knew I could count on you. You're the best thing that's happened to us. Isn't that right, Mom?" Shane asked Laura as she came into the dining room with a bowl of stew.

"I couldn't agree more. Now, if we can only get her to eat more, everything will be perfect."

Amy laughed, " If I eat any more, I'll soon be as fat as those pregnant ewes were!"

"I must say you have picked up a bit of muscle since you arrived. It looks good on you," Laura said as she sat down, "Shane, will you offer the blessing?"

As Amy bowed her head, she thought about Ivan and what she learned. She would have to question Laura about him. Maybe tonight would be a good time. Later, when Laura was in the garden.

Amy helped Laura with clean-up, then headed back to her trailer. She had some personal items to attend to. Then she would watch for Laura.

"The garden is really coming along," Amy commented as she opened the gate into the garden to join Laura.

"You should be resting, not out here," Laura scolded her, as Amy dropped to her knees and started weeding the tiny cucumber plants.

"I am resting," Amy responded, "I find working in the garden very relaxing."

"So do I. I can't imagine not having one. And I love my flower garden. Cut flowers seem to cheer up the most dismal house. I always like to have some inside everyday when they are available."

"My mother never had the patience for gardening. As long as I can remember, she let the neighbors plant our garden patch. She said she was too sick. Maybe if she had worked in a garden, she wouldn't be sick."

"You and your mother didn't always get along, did you?"

"You can say that again," Amy continued to pull the weeds and pile them to be taken off the garden.

Laura sat back for a moment and then, out of the blue, she asked Amy. "What happened between you and Ivan?"

Amy felt the color rising in her cheeks. She turned away and answered, "What do you mean?"

"Oh, don't be coy. I know something is up. I didn't live sixty years without learning something. You avoid his name like the plague and Ivan hasn't been here for a few days, so what's up?"

Amy sighed and sat back too. She looked at Laura and said, "I don't know what's happened. I think maybe Ivan got the wrong impression, or I did; I don't know."

"Why do you say that?"

"Well, we, by accident.......... Well, I mean we, sort of had a kiss when I was at his house. I was a bit startled and reacted. Ivan apologized, but now I don't know if he meant it or if he is sorry. I like Ivan but only as a friend. I have too much baggage dragging behind me. I had the impression he was looking for more, but now I'm not sure. I'm so mixed up. He's probably sorry about the whole thing and wants to put it behind him."

"So how did you come to that conclusion?"

"You can see, as you said, he never comes around here anymore."

"Do you want to know what I think?"

"I'm sure you're going to tell me."

"You're right. Ivan isn't coming around here because he's embarrassed and thinks he may have stepped over the line you have drawn in the sand. Anyone with eyes in their head can see that he is nuts about you. Maybe even he doesn't know it yet, but it's obvious to me."

Amy stared at Laura with her mouth open. What had she missed? She had no idea Ivan felt that strongly. No, Laura was wrong. She had misjudged the situation.

"Ivan loves to tease and we are good friends. That's all."

"That's where it starts. Abe and I were good friends before we started dating. He wasn't a Mormon, but joined my church before we got married so we could be sealed in the temple in Cardston. It was the happiest day of my life, the day we were married for time and all eternity."

"What does that mean; for time and all eternity?"

"It means not only are we husband and wife here on earth, but our church believes we can be together always, even in Heaven."

Amy thought about that. She pondered it a bit, then said, "What if you and your husband were unhappy together? What then? You sure wouldn't want to spend eternity together!"

Laura laughed, "That's why it is so important to marry the right one!"

Suddenly Amy remembered the reason she wanted to talk to Laura.

"Laura, why did Ivan quit going to church?"

"He told you he was a Mormon?"

"Yes, but when I asked him why he didn't go to church, he told me he wasn't ready to talk about it."

"Well, none of us are sure why he quit, but it happened after Cindy broke their engagement. The first few times he went to church, the people were all sympathetic, but soon he started hearing stories that took Cindy's side. I guess she had told several people that Ivan had promised to sell the ranch, then reneged on it. That wasn't true at all, as I'm sure you know, Ivan would never sell the ranch. She had her followers so Ivan became the 'bad guy'. It wasn't long after that, he quit completely."

"That is sad. Why would people who profess to be Christians treat someone like that?"

"Not everyone that attends church is perfect. We, as Mormons should know better, but Cindy came from a very prominent family so was hard to ignore. I breathed a sigh of relief when that family moved to Regina, but Ivan didn't come back to church. It breaks my heart as he was very strong. He was engaged to Cindy right after he returned from his mission."

"I didn't know he went on a mission. Where did he go?"

"He went to Scotland. I think that is the reason he was set on raising Black Angus cattle."

Amy stood up and brushed off her jeans. "Thanks for talking to me. You've given me more insight into things."

"Just don't count Ivan out of your life. If you care for him at all, think about what I've said. Ivan needs a good woman in his life. I happen to think you are that woman. No, don't argue with me. I think you know it too, but you're running scared. Ivan isn't your ex-husband. He would never be unfaithful. When he falls, he falls hard, and I know you are the one."

Amy turned and left the garden. She had a lot to think about. She headed back to her trailer and Happy Cat where she could do some deep thinking without interruptions.

Chapter 13

S HANE WAS OUT of school finally, having graduated with honors. Laura
was very proud of her son. As a graduation present, she gave Shane
his own truck, a nice metallic blue GMC ¾ ton 4X4. It wasn't new but
only had 129,000 kilometers on it. Shane was really excited about it. Laura
had enlisted Ivan's help in picking it out. Amy was thrilled for Shane. He
had worked so hard over the years so it was nice to see him rewarded. He
had been accepted for college in Lethbridge, so would be needing a vehicle
to come home on the week-ends.

Ivan had returned home from Montana by the end of May and though he
had been over to the farm as he was busy cutting hay, he never mentioned
the kiss and did seem to want to forget all about it. Amy was only too glad to
oblige. Ivan didn't joke with her as much and she hoped it was just because
he was busy. She didn't want their friendship spoiled by some silly misunderstanding. Laura kept busy in her yard, tending her flowers and weeding
the vegetable garden.

Because Shane and Ivan were busy with haying, Amy would take the dogs
and check the sheep most every day. Every ten days, the sheep were moved
to a new pasture. Now that the collies were used to Amy, she could manage
the move on her own with Lad and Lady. On one of the moves, she saw the
talent of Lady at work. She moved among the sheep and singled out a ewe
and kept turning it back. It was then that Amy noticed the ewe was limping.
She recorded the number and later that day, Shane helped her catch the ewe

and doctor it for foot-rot. They isolated her with her lambs, so they could continue to treat her and hope it didn't spread to any more of the flock.

The days had turned hot and the hay was maturing fast. All the ranch was busy, with getting the hay baled and stacked. Amy's job was to pick up the square bales with the truck and trailer and stack them in the hay shelter. Shane showed her how to put a load on the truck and trailer so it was stable and then how to build a stack so it was secure. It was hot, itchy work and Amy was exhausted and ready for bed each night. When she crawled out in the morning, all her muscles screamed for mercy. It would take a nice warm shower for things to loosen up and she could get mobile. She now knew what they meant by being able to lift fifty pounds. Some of the bales were closer to eighty pounds. Amy was grateful she had a couple of months on the ranch to work into this job.

Lad and Lady usually came with her to the field and as she picked up each bale, they would check under for mice. They were good company and she enjoyed watching them frolicking in the field.

By the middle of July, all the square bales were hauled in and Amy got a break from the hay. Ivan and Shane were nearly finished with the main hay crop. Shane was cutting, using the haybine. Ivan was baling and he would haul the bales in with his large bale unit. He took 1/3 of the bales for his share. Laura said in dry years, Ivan always made sure they had sufficient hay to last them through. A few years ago, they had to buy hay, as it was so dry. All the pastures and hay land had burned up. Then the profit on the ranch went to next to nothing. But the last years had been good.

Now that the work was getting caught up, Laura decided to go to visit her sister and family in Calgary. Amy and Shane assured her they could manage. She left on July 25th, planning to be back by the 1st of August as her garden vegetables would be needing attention.

"I'm glad Mom decided to get away from the ranch for a few days," Shane commented to Amy. "She never takes enough time off, and I'll be leaving in September for classes, so this is a good time."

"Your Mom loves it here, but I have noticed she gets tired quickly. Maybe it is her age. I guess we'll all find out when we get to that stage of our life."

"Mom hasn't been the same since Dad passed on. They say people can die of a broken heart. I think the only thing that keeps her going is the ranch.

She and Dad worked so hard at it. I hope to find a wife that is as special to me as they were to each other."

"I don't think that will be a problem. You're a very attractive, hard-working, kind young man. The girls would be blind not to fall for you."

"Hey, hey! I said wife, not wives!"

Amy laughed and patted Shane on the arm, "Not up to handling several, eh? Well, I envy whoever you pick. You're a special young man."

"Say, don't give me a swelled head. Vanity is a sin, you know."

Shane reached down and patted Lad on the head, "Hey boy, let's go check out the lower pasture fences. We want to put the ewes back in there by Friday."

Lad and Lady responded to Shane's voice and went bounding off down the path to the barn.

"Work calls." Shane said as he waved to Amy and sauntered after the dogs.

Amy finished pruning the tomatoes and taking off her gloves, she wiped her brow. It was only 8:30 AM and already it was hot. Her little trailer got extremely warm during the day, but cooled off at nights so she could sleep. She didn't mind the heat, but she knew if it didn't rain soon, the pastures would start to dry up.

She heard Shane start the quad and head out to the lower pasture. She was glad he was around for the next month to take some of the pressure off. When Laura got back, Amy planned to ask for a couple of days off so she could go to Medicine Hat. She didn't look forward to the trip but knew she had better go. Gladys didn't sound good the last time she talked to her. Usually she had some snide remark to say, but this time she just sounded uninterested. It wasn't like her mother. She was sure Laura would let her have a day or two. She could go on a Sunday, but would prefer more time.

Chapter 14

LAURA WAS GONE two days when Shane announced one morning that he was heading into town for some supplies and asked Amy if she wanted to come. Amy did have a few things to pick up so agreed.

She quickly changed into a pair of walking shorts and a light T-shirt. She put her sandals on and brushed her hair. She decided to leave it loose for a change.

"Wow," Shane remarked as she climbed into his truck, "You look young enough to be my girlfriend. All the guys will be jealous."

"Is that why you asked me to come - to make your friends envious?"

Shane blushed and returned, "No - no way! I wanted you to come. Can't a guy give you a compliment without the third degree?"

"I guess not. I'm sorry. I was just trying to be funny. Maybe I'm not so good at the humor thing. Anyway, I sure could not pass for your age. I look every bit at least............ twenty-five!"

Shane laughed, "Well, you got me there. Have to eat my own words."

The ride into Milk River was enjoyable. They chatted about the ranch, about Laura, about school and then eventually, the talk got around to Ivan.

"What's up with you and Ivan? You two used to talk and laugh together a lot. I thought you two were going to become an item. Then wham! Nothing - not even talking."

"Why don't you ask Ivan?"

"I did. He told me to mind my own business."

"Well, maybe that's good advice."

"Ivan is like a bear with a sore head. I don't like to see him unhappy. And he definitely isn't happy."

"What makes you say that?"

"Because he usually spends a lot of time here. When it's not busy, Mom always has him over for supper on Sundays, but he's been avoiding coming. When we were haying together, he was pretty quiet, just not the old Ivan."

"What makes you think it has anything to do with me?"

"I see him looking at you. A guy would have to be blind not to see how he feels about you. You could do worse, you know. Ivan is a good, reliable man. A bit crusty around the edges, but loyal."

"Your Mom told me the same thing. But I think you both have missed the picture. Ivan isn't interested in me. If he was, he wouldn't be staying away, especially after…….."

"After what?'

"Never mind. Forget I said that. He has his reasons for not being around, I'm sure. It's nothing to do with me."

"I do believe the lady protests too much!"

Amy turned away so Shane couldn't read her thoughts. Most of what Shane said was the truth. She was sure Ivan was staying away because of that one mistake. Well, she was going to fix that. She didn't want Laura and Shane deprived of Ivan's friendship because of a silly misunderstanding. She would make a point of seeing Ivan soon.

They pulled into Milk River just as it started to rain. They had not seen the clouds building as they had been so busy talking. They hurried through their shopping, wanting to get home as they had left windows open on the house and trailer. As they were leaving Milk River, they noticed Ivan's dirty green 4X4 parked at the restaurant, but neither commented. Enough had been said.

Chapter 15

A MY DIDN'T GET a chance to see Ivan or talk with him for the next few days as the storm brought bad roads and some of the fence was washed out in the lower pasture by the swollen creek rushing over it's banks. It was a much needed rain, but even so, Shane and Amy were glad all the haying was done.

They moved the sheep to the upper left pasture next to the hills. It took them the better part of two days to get the fence rebuilt. First they had to tear out the broken boards and posts and cut and move the wire out of the way. It wasn't easy working with the sodden ground. In places, the water was up to the tops of their rubber boots. The ground was too wet to bring the tractor down to tighten the wire so they decided to leave it for a day or two. It was starting to look like rain again.

As they headed back to the yard, Shane commented to Amy, "It's funny Ivan hasn't been over to see how we're doing. He usually checks any time we have a storm. He knows Mom is away too. I think maybe I'll run over there and see how he's doing."

"Okay. I'll start supper. Try to bring Ivan back with you."

"I'll try. See you later."

Shane dropped Amy at the ranch house and took off down the road. Amy had been helping Shane with suppers since Laura left. She had phoned the night before and said she had decided to stay a few more days if everything was okay at the ranch. Amy was glad Laura was getting a break, but it would mean Amy would have to postpone her trip to Medicine Hat.

Amy removed her rubber boots and gloves in the entry and headed to the bathroom to wash up. She had taken some salmon steaks out of the freezer for herself and Shane, but decided she had better take out another in case Ivan decided to come. She popped it into the microwave to thaw as she got out the rice cooker and measured the water into it. While the water heated, she dug out some salad makings and put the garden peas into a microwave bowl for cooking. Dessert would be the apple pie she had taken out of the freezer the night before. Laura had left lots of baking for them, which Amy was grateful for. She really didn't like baking that much, probably because she would be tempted to eat it. Shane really enjoyed his desserts but never gained an ounce of fat.

"Oh, to be young again," Amy mused as she put the pie in the oven to warm.

She heard Shane's truck return, but as she glanced out, she could see he was alone.

"He's too much of a coward to face me, is that it?" Amy asked Shane as he sauntered in.

Shane looked surprised, "I don't think so. He's coming in his own truck. Why did you say that.......that bit about facing you? What happened between you two?"

"Nothing. Can you set the table? We're almost ready."

"As soon as I wash up." Shane headed into the bathroom. Something was going on. He was sure of it. When he asked Ivan to come for supper, Ivan asked him if Amy agreed. When he told Ivan it was Amy's idea, Ivan's face lit up like a Christmas tree. Oh, yeah, he had it bad. And that comment from Amy, about Ivan facing her; what was that all about? Well, maybe they could resolve things tonight. I sure hope so, Shane thought as he dried his hands and entered the kitchen.

Ivan arrived shortly after Shane had the table set. As he walked into the house, he commented, "Smells good in here. I'm famished."

Amy came into the dining area carrying a bowl of rice, "Everything is ready so set yourself down."

"Thanks for inviting me, Amy. I was getting tired of my own cooking."

"You know you are always welcome here anytime," Amy answered as she set the bowl on the table.

Shane asked the blessing and they all dug in. The conversation was animated as they talked about the storm, Laura's visit to Calgary, and ranch and Shane's classes at school. All very safe topics.

When they had finished up with the apple pie, Shane excused himself to check some things out on the Internet.

"I'll help Amy clean up," Ivan said to Shane as he rose and picked up his and Shane's plates.

"You don't have to do that. I can handle it," Amy responded as she also stood up and gathered up some of the empty dishes.

"I always help with clean-up when Laura is here. I started doing that when I was a little duffer. I guess I just can't break the habit. So you're stuck with me."

Amy laughed, "Well, in that case, hop to it. I don't want to be in the kitchen all evening."

"Okay, okay," Ivan grinned as he headed to the kitchen.

Before long, everything was cleaned up and put away. Amy found that Ivan knew more about Laura's kitchen than she did. He was fussy about things in the right place. Laura trained him good, Amy thought.

As Amy hung up the tea towel, she turned to Ivan and said, "Would you like to walk to the upper pasture with me? I want to check out the ewes for any signs of foot rot."

Ivan raised his eyebrows, then grinned, "I'd be honored to walk with you. Can I borrow a pair of rubbers, as I just wore my runners?"

"I'm sure Shane won't mind if you borrow his. Your feet look about the same size."

"I think he wears a size 11 and I'm a 10, but it should work."

As they headed out the door, Shane watched from the office and smiled to himself, "Well, here's hoping they patch things up. It would be great if they would get together. Mom will be so excited when I tell her they are speaking again. I'll phone her later."

Amy and Ivan headed out to the upper pasture with Lad and Lady cavorting by their side. They crossed the creek on the little foot bridge and Ivan pretended to push Amy in. She retaliated by stealing his cap and sprinting away up the hill. By the time Ivan caught up to her, she was at the top sitting on a rock, wearing his cap.

"Oh, so now you're playing games, eh?" Ivan gasped as he collapsed on the rock, "What are you trying to do, kill this old codger? I'm not a young squirt like you."

"Ha! You're only seven years older than me. You just haven't been working as hard as me. You're soft!"

"There's all kinds of work, you know. I do a lot of mental work. Not brawn, just brains."

"Are you saying I don't have any brains?"

Ivan drew a mock sober face and said, " Since when does wrestling sheep around take more brains than brawn?"

"Oh, you! I should know better than argue with you. You always win. Anyway, we'd better hoof it. The sheep appear to be over the next hill."

"Just a minute, Amy. I want to say something to you first."

"Okay, say away."

"I'm grateful you invited me for supper as I wanted to talk to you, but just couldn't break the ice, so to speak. What happened at my place; it never should have. You didn't know me that well, and you trusted me and then I caught you off guard. I'm really sorry."

"Are you sorry it happened or sorry you caught me off guard?"

"I'm sorry it happened when it did."

Amy turned to look at Ivan and studied his face. He was staring down at his hands and waiting for her reply.

"Ivan, I want to know how you feel about me?"

Startled, Ivan quickly looked at Amy, then glanced away, "What do you mean?"

"Laura and Shane have the idea that you are in love with me or some such crazy thing. I told them they are wrong. Am I right?"

"Yes."

"Yes, I'm right?"

"No; yes, I'm in love with you. I have been since I met you in that restaurant in Milk River. Even when you cut me down about paying for your lunch. Then the way you fit in here and worked so hard; I knew you were the one."

"Ivan, you know I was married and my husband had me completely fooled, so you have to understand that I'm not ready to completely trust any man right now. I like you a lot, Ivan, but only as a friend. Let's just keep it at that, okay?"

"Are you saying there will never be any hope for me? I'm not getting any younger, you know," Ivan smiled sadly.

Amy reached over and took Ivan's hand, "No, I'm not saying I will always feel this way. Things can change. Right now my priority is Laura and this ranch. She needs me here to help her when Shane is away."

Ivan squeezed her hand and stood up, "Fair enough. As long as we can communicate and have fun together. Will you agree to going out on dates with me, like we started to? I promise to behave."

"Maybe I won't," Amy retorted as she punched Ivan on the arm, "Race you up the other hill?"

"No way. This old fogey is going to walk up the hill."

"Okay, I'll walk too. I'm not as tough as I want everyone to believe. I can feel the strain of that last hill."

Chapter 16

LAURA RETURNED TO the ranch the first week in August. She looked rested and was happy to see everything in order. Shane and Amy had kept the garden and flowers weeded. But now the peas and beans were ready for freezing. Amy helped Laura with the garden when she was done with her other chores.

"I'm sure happy to see you and Ivan back to normal," she commented to Amy while they were busy in the kitchen, "I missed seeing him around here."

Amy responded as she sealed another bag of beans, "We talked things out. He knows how I feel now, so it's okay. And you were right about him."

"Told you. I don't miss much, especially when it's someone I care about."

"I don't want to hurt Ivan, but I'm just not ready for a serious relationship. I think he understands. So we are back to being friends."

"Sometimes it takes a good friend to get us over the hurts in our life. That's what Abe did for me. I've never told anyone this before, but I was engaged to be married before Abe. We had set a wedding date, bought my dress and everything was all arranged; then one day I found my groom-to-be kissing my bridesmaid in the cloakroom at the church. Needless to say, that ended the engagement and my friendship with that bridesmaid. It wasn't too long after that, Abe came into my life. He was a friend and a confidant and then it turned to love."

"I really don't know how I feel about Ivan but I don't want to rush into anything. And he respects that."

"Ivan is one in a million. Mark my words, you will be Mrs. Ivan Johnson someday." With that, Laura grabbed her garden pail and headed back out to the garden.

Amy continued bagging beans and pondered Laura's words. Her story was similar to Amy's and look how happy Laura and Abe had been. Well, Amy thought, I'll just let nature take it's course. Right now, I'm happy and contented. I hope that never changes.

Later in the week, Laura approached Amy and said, "We have to plan Shane's 18th birthday party. I want to invite several of his friends from school and the church. What do you say we have a barbecue and music and dancing on the lawn?"

"Sounds wonderful. What day is his birthday?"

"August 13th. I'm sure Ivan will help us set up some tables and put up a few decorations."

When Laura said August 13th, Amy felt a jolt go through her. She had also given birth to a child on August 13th! How many years ago was that? Amy was sure it was eighteen years. She quickly did the math in her head. Yes, it was eighteen years!

"Are you okay, Amy? You look like you're coming down with something."

"I'm okay. Just realizing how fast the years go by. It's been sixteen years since I was eighteen."

"When's your birthday?"

"I was born on December 24th."

"We'll have to remember that. Mine is in September. I'll be sixty-one on the 20th. If Abe was still here, he would be sixty-three on September 21st. We always celebrated together."

"When is Ivan's birthday?"

"On October 14th. He will be forty-one. Not getting any younger."

"That's what he told me when we had our talk. He's got lots of years ahead of him."

"That's what Abe and I thought too. No one knows. Only God knows."

Chapter 17

Now that Laura was back and the garden was caught up, Amy asked for a couple of days to head to Medicine Hat. She wasn't looking forward to it, but knew she had better make the trip before the summer was over. That way she could be back in time to help with Shane's party. She had given up her apartment after her first month at the ranch so she planned to bring back some of her things that were in storage. She figured a day or two with her mother would be all she could handle.

She left on a Sunday morning, just as Shane and Laura were leaving for church. As she came out of the hills and headed down to the main road, she spotted Ivan's truck parked at the entrance to the road. He got out and came over to her car.

"Thought I'd better come and see you off. Do you think that little bug will make it there and back?"

"What? More comments about my car? At least it's clean, not like your truck."

"Touche! Well, have a safe trip and hurry back to us. We'll miss you around here."

Amy opened her door and stepped out, "I'll miss you too, you big galoot."

She reached up and pulled Ivan's head down and kissed him smack right on the lips. Ivan's eyes widened with surprise. He didn't have time to react before Amy was in her car and speeding away. He stood and stared after her car disappearing down the road in a cloud of dust. Touching his fingers to his lips, he tried to stop the wild beating of his heart. Amy had kissed him! And right on the lips! Yahoo!! Ivan threw his cap in the air and did a wild dance. Amy did care. He knew it! Wow!! Maybe this was going to turn out to be a spectacular fall after all!

Amy didn't know what possessed her to do such a fool thing. Maybe she did care more than she let on. She sure did surprise Ivan, that's for sure! He didn't even have time to react. Amy laughed to herself. She bet she would have a lot of explaining to do when she got back and Ivan caught up to her. Oh well, time would tell.

Amy stopped in Milk River and filled up with gas. She checked her oil and water levels. Then she headed out.

She arrived in Medicine Hat shortly after noon. Not wanting to drop in on her mother before she ate, she headed to her old stomping grounds at the Dairy Queen. Her ex-boss was overjoyed to see her.

"Are you back for good? We could use you around here. You look great. What have you been doing to yourself?

Amy laughed and shook his hand, "No, I'm only back to see Mom. I love it down at the ranch. I don't know about looking good, as I get a lot of sun and I've gained weight with all the work and good food."

She ordered a burger and chatted with some of the staff she knew. There were several new faces as it was summer time and a lot of regulars were on holidays.

Knowing she was putting off seeing her mother, Amy ordered an ice cream sundae. Oh boy, here's pounds going on, she thought, as she dug into it. Oh well, who cares?

It was nearly 2 PM when Amy arrived at her old home. She sat in the car and perused the house. Nothing had changed. The front steps still needed painted and the gate latch was still broken. What did I expect?" Amy thought as she got out of the car.

As she rang the doorbell, she could hear voices coming from inside. After a brief interval, her mother opened the door.

"Well, look what the cat dragged in! Came crawling back home, did you? Well, there's no room for a daughter who doesn't care a fig about her mother."

"And hello to you too, Mother. May I come in?"

"Why? To give me a hard time, or because you care?"

"Oh Mother, you know I care or I wouldn't be here," Amy replied as she brushed past her mother and into the living room, only to stop short. There, on the sofa sat an elderly gentleman, holding a teacup and saucer.

Gladys came up behind Amy and stated, "Ed, this is Amy, that wayward daughter I told you about. Amy, this is Ed, my new boarder."

Amy stared at her mother. What happened to 'not having strangers touching my things?' This was indeed a surprise.

"Hello Ed. Nice to meet you."

Ed rose and bowed over Amy's hand before taking it, "How nice to meet the daughter of such a gracious lady."

Gracious lady? Her mother? Boy, was this guy fooled! "So how long have you been living here, Ed?"

"Ed moved in the 1st of July," Gladys butted in, "He has your room now as I told him you never come home. If you plan to stay the night you will have to sleep on the sofa."

"That will be fine. How have you been doing, Mom?"

"Well, better since Ed moved in. He does all the heavy work for me."

"I'm glad you have some help around here. Where are you from, Ed?"

"I've lived here in the Hat all my life. I was a carpenter by trade. Anyway, I'm going down to the Mall. I'll see you later."

When the door closed behind him, Gladys said, "Now don't you start with me. I've heard it all from my so-called friends at church and the neighbors."

"But Mom, just what do you know about this guy?"

"Well, when you left me high and dry, without a thought to how I would manage, I had to find someone to help me out. Ed was looking for a place to stay as he hasn't much money. So we made a deal. He helps me out and I give him room and board."

"Where did you find him?"

"He came to Bingo's at the church on Tuesdays."

"It doesn't look good, him staying here, but I guess you know what you're doing."

"Yes, probably more than you do. When are you going to come to your senses and move back where you belong?"

"Mom, I think I've found where I belong. I love the sheep ranch. Laura and Shane are wonderful to work for. They are very patent and teach me everything I need to know. The country is beautiful and I enjoy long walks with Lad and Lady."

"Lad and Lady? What crazy names!"

"Not if you're a dog. They are border collies. They help with the sheep. And in my trailer, I have a roommate; Happy Cat."

"A cat? What a filthy animal to have in the house. You'll get all kinds of diseases from them."

Amy laughed, "That's not true. Cats are clean animals. Happy Cat goes outside to the bathroom. She is the friendliest thing."

"Well, better you than me. I suppose you're going to want supper. I only have enough meat out for two."

"Why don't I take you out for supper? I can afford it."

"Just me and not Ed? That wouldn't be right."

"We can take Ed too, if you like."

"Okay. What should I wear? You know I never go casual like so many today. Where are you taking us?"

"Well, I thought maybe McDonalds."

"What? Well, that cinches it! I'm staying home!"

"Mom, I was just joking. We'll go to The Hat restaurant."

"What has that ranch done to you? I don't care for your jokes."

Amy was wondering that herself. She must have lost her mind, joking with her mother. Cool it, kid, she admonished herself. Just get through this day and you can head home tomorrow. Home? Yes..... That was what the ranch was - home!

Chapter 18

I T WAS RAINING by the time Amy arrived back at the ranch. She parked her car by the trailer and made a wild dash for the door. She would have to wait to unload her car. Happy Cat greeted her at the door, purring loudly and rubbing against her leg.

"I missed you too, you crazy cat. Let me get my shoes off."

"Did you miss me a little, too?"

Amy nearly tripped over her shoes as she jumped back and looked about for who spoke. Ivan was standing on the step, getting wetter by the minute. "Going to ask me in?" he inquired.

"Oh sorry. Sure, come in. No sense getting any wetter. What are you doing here? I didn't see your truck."

"It's down by the pens. I was delivering some feed for the ranch when I saw you drive in. It just started raining here. I thought I would welcome you home."

"Thanks. Where's Shane and Laura?"

"I think they headed to Lethbridge. Laura had a doctor appointment and Shane was going to look into a place to stay for college."

"Laura's not sick, is she?"

"I don't think so. Just a yearly check-up, she said. Do you need me to carry anything in from the car?"

"It can wait. No sense getting any wetter. Sit down. I'll see if I have anything in the fridge to drink."

"Thanks. I sure could wet my whistle."

Amy hurried over to the fridge and took out the carton of apple juice. She got a couple of glasses from the cupboard and set them on the table.

"Can you excuse me for a couple of minutes?" Amy asked as she headed to the bathroom. She closed the door and leaned up against the vanity. This was the first time Ivan had been in her trailer and it was a bit over whelming. Especially after the rash thing she did when she left. She really hoped he wouldn't mention it. She washed her hands and checked her hair, then sauntered back out and sat opposite Ivan at the table.

"So how did you find your mother?" Ivan asked as he took a sip of his juice.

"You would not believe the shock I got," Amy answered, "Mom has moved a male boarder into my old room."

"A male boarder?"

"Yes. I would say he is probably in his seventies. I tried to tell her it was improper for him to be there alone with her, but she told me 'not to start'. She does seem happier and has company and help. I can just imagine what her friends are saying behind her back."

"Maybe nothing. Sometimes things are not what they seem."

"Well, it seems to me he is taking advantage of a lonely elderly lady. I wonder just how much he does for her?"

"That's really her business, right? She is old enough to know what she wants, even if it is just company and someone to complain to."

"Yeah, about her wayward daughter."

"If that's what it takes, let it be."

"Sounds good to me. So how are you doing? Has Laura commandeered you to help with Shane's party?"

"Sure did. I'll be glad to help. I sure hope it doesn't rain that day, especially since she wants it outside."

"Ivan, you were twenty-two when Abe and Laura adopted Shane. Do you know any of the details?"

"Well, I do know Abe and Laura had given up on getting a child of their own. They were turned down for adoption because they didn't have a stable enough income and they were getting older. The authorities didn't even take into consideration all the recommendations from friends and Laura's big heart. Then, out of the blue, Abe got a phone call from some woman who said she had a child for them. It didn't take them long to jump on that news."

"Where did they get the baby from?"

"I'm pretty sure they went to Calgary. Laura said something about a young girl and a home for unwed mothers. It seems the girl was only sixteen and still in school so the mother forced her to give up the baby. It seems so sad when a young girl gets into trouble, then has to give up a part of themselves. I can't imagine ever giving up a child, IF I ever had any."

Amy listened intently to everything Ivan said. Could it be? Could Shane actually be her son? Her heart was beating so fast in her chest, she thought she would faint. Ivan looked over at her with concern.

"Amy, are you okay?" He rose and came around to her side of the table and touched her arm, "Is something wrong? Why all the questions about Shane?"

Amy swallowed the lump in her throat and tried to smile at Ivan, "No reason; just curious. I am a little tired from the trip. Do you mind? I think I'll lay down for a bit."

"Okay, if you're sure. Tell Laura I'll see her tomorrow."

Ivan left and Amy laid on the sofa. Happy Cat cuddled up next to her and continued purring.

Amy didn't know what to think. Could it possibly be? She tried to mentally run over Shane's features. He didn't look anything like her. She couldn't really remember what his father looked like. It was eighteen years ago and time has a habit of dulling the memory. A memory she wanted to forget. What woman had phoned Abe? Was it someone from the home? Wasn't there usually a long waiting list to adopt? How would Abe be able to get in first? Unless he had some pull. Maybe he paid extra to get a baby! That didn't sit well with Amy. Would Abe have stooped that low to get Laura what her heart desired - a baby? Amy figured that could be possible if what Shane said about his parents was true.

"Why am I feeling this way?" Amy mused, "I should be really glad that Shane had such a wonderful home. If he is my son, so much the better. I knew I was drawn to him; now I think I know why. I have to find out, but where do I go? Back to the home for unwed mothers? Talking about mother's, what did mine have to do with all this?"

Amy gently stroked Happy Cat as all these thoughts raced around in her head. She heard Shane and Laura come home but because she didn't feel like facing them, she decided to stay at the trailer and make a quick omelet for supper - if she could eat. She really wasn't very hungry.

"I'll get through Shane's birthday party, then I'm going to find some answers," Amy spoke aloud as she set Happy Cat on the floor and went to wash her hands.

Chapter 19

THE DAY OF Shane's birthday party was sunny and clear. Amy and Laura had been up since 6:00 AM getting things organized. Ivan showed up rather early too and went to work. He and Shane set up several long tables Laura had borrowed from town. Then they constructed benches from low saw horses and planks. Amy and Laura then covered the planks with material and stapled it to the underside.

"We don't want anyone to snag their favorite pair of shorts or jeans," Laura said, "when I was young, I went to a party at one of my friends. I had my best dress on and I snagged it on a nail from one of the chairs. I was devastated, so I know how it feels."

Shane laughed and replied, "We sure won't see any dresses at this party. They all know it's casual, a barbeque. Just the way I like it."

"That's good," Laura responded, "I'm glad you don't turn eighteen every year. You'd wear me out."

"Well, sit down and rest for a bit. Ivan and Amy have everything under control."

"I just might do that. Amy, have we got enough ice or should someone run to town for more?"

"We have lots; don't worry." Amy stapled the last cloth on, then stood up. She brushed the dust off her jeans and glanced over at Ivan. He was watching her with a little smile on his face. She turned away as she felt the color rise in her cheeks. Why does his looking at me bother me, she admonished herself? Just ignore him! She grabbed the stapler and the rest of the material and headed into the house.

Laura was standing at the kitchen sink and she was holding her head and drinking a glass of water.

"Got a headache?" Amy asked as she came up beside her. Laura smiled and responded, "A bit. I'll be fine. I'm just going to lay down for a bit. Everything ready?"

"Sure is. You go have a good rest. I'll take care of anything that needs done."

Laura gave Amy a little hug and said, "I'm so glad you're here, Amy. I don't know what I'd do without you. Just to have another woman around is a treat for me."

"I'm glad I'm here, too. I love this place and you guys are all like family to me."

"Even Ivan?" Laura quizzed as she smiled at Amy.

"Yes, even Ivan," Amy admitted as she turned away to put the material in the laundry room.

At 4:00 PM, the young people started arriving. Ivan had gone home to change and he was now back, directing traffic. Amy had also changed into white walking shorts with a matching top. She wore her white sandals and left her hair loose. As she looked in the mirror, she liked the woman who looked back. She realized she had regained her confidence. Her sad marriage was behind her; she was only going to go forward.

When Amy left the trailer, Shane was welcoming everyone to the ranch. He was in his glory, making everyone feel at home. Amy hurried into the kitchen and grabbed the appetizers from the fridge. The big coolers with drinks had been carried out earlier and Shane was offering everyone a drink.

As Amy hurried out with the hors d'oeuvres, Ivan came over, "Where's Laura?"

"Still laying down, I guess. Take these; I'll see to her."

When Amy knocked on Laura's door, she thought she could hear sobbing, but it stopped and a muffled answer came, "Yes?"

"Everyone is arriving, Laura. I thought you'd like to know."

"Yes, thanks. I'll be right out."

When Laura joined the party, she looked drawn and tired. Amy noticed right away, but Shane was having a blast and didn't seem to. Laura moved among all the guests and thanked them for coming. Amy kept her eye on her as she hurried around, getting more appetizers and seeing everyone had a drink. Then she headed to the kitchen to do the last minute preparations for the salads.

It wasn't long before Ivan fired up the barbeque and started some steaks. By the time all were fed, it was 6:30 PM. While Amy cleared away the food, Shane and Ivan got the music arranged. Soon there were young people dancing all over the lawn.

Laura was starting to look better. She helped with the clean up and later, when it was time for the cake, she was just like her old self.

With the cake cutting and gift opening out of the way, the dancing started up again. Laura even had a dance with Shane. He whirled her around until she was out of breath and laughing, told him to stop. Before Amy knew it, he had grabbed her and whirled her out on the lawn. She tried to object but he was having none of it.

"You're not too old; you don't look a day over … let's say … twenty-five!"

Amy punched him on the arm and he grinned, "So how do you like my friends?"

"They are a great bunch. Why don't you go dance with some of them?"

"I have danced with all the girls, except you, so that's why I grabbed you. Now I'm content."

Amy pulled away and he let her go. What a card! He did have a good sense of humor, like Ivan. Thinking of Ivan, Amy glanced around for him. He was leaning against the porch post, watching her. She smiled at him and he responded in kind, then pushing himself away from the post, sauntered over to her.

"Dance with her, Ivan," Shane yelled from over by the food table.

Ivan held out his hand. Amy hesitated, then took it. Why not, she thought. Everyone was dancing and having a good time. Why shouldn't we? She slid into Ivan's arms, just like it was meant to be. The music was slow and easy so it wasn't hard to move on the lawn. When Amy looked over at Laura sitting in her lawn chair, she gave Amy a 'thumbs up' and smiled. Ivan tightened his hold on her as they danced away over the lawn. He danced her right around the corner of the ranch house and into a corner by the lilac bush. He smiled down at her and then, very gently kissed her on the lips. She tried to pull away, but he held her fast.

"Now, that wasn't so bad, was it?"

When Amy shook her head, he continued, "That's my answer back for that sneaky way you kissed me out on the road."

Amy laughed, "I really don't know why I did that; just to see your surprise, I guess."

"Well, you sure did that!"

"Okay, now we're even. Let's get back to the party. Do you think everyone is having a good time?"

"The best, including me," Ivan gave Amy a little squeeze and then released her. I'd better not push my luck, he thought as he watched Amy scamper across the lawn. Things are good between us right now. We just need a bit more time.

Chapter 20

THE DAYS AFTER Shane's birthday party were a whirlwind of activity. Laura decided the barn and sheds all needed a coat of paint, so she commandeered Amy and Shane into getting the buildings ready. All of the old paint had to be scrapped off, and little repairs done before the new coat of paint could be applied. Ivan made himself scarce on the pretense he would be starting to swath the oats and barley. Shane was up early and out at the barn by 7:00 AM. He did the climbing up to the top part of the barn. Amy was grateful for that as she really didn't like heights. Shane's classes would be starting early in September so he was anxious to do as much as he could before he left. He was concerned about Laura, but was glad Amy would be there. Also Ivan was next door. Shane knew he could count on him. In some ways, Ivan had become a father figure to Shane in the years since his father died. He really hoped Amy and Ivan would realize they were meant to be together. He was sure Ivan knew it, but Amy seemed a bit skittish. From talking with Amy, he knew she had a bad experience with her first marriage so that was probably it. She seemed happy on the ranch though, so Shane hoped he could depend on her to stay with Laura.

Shane was worried about his Mom. Even though she told him she was fine when she had her check-up, he knew she picked up a prescription. When he asked her about it, she said it was just something to help her sleep. He had never known his mother to have trouble sleeping, so something wasn't right. He would have to keep an eye on things when he was home on the weekends. Maybe he would tell Amy and see what she thought. Shane pulled a bent nail from the plank and discarded it. He could see Amy coming from her trailer. She was dressed in jeans and T-shirt and carrying a pail. She had her gloves on and an old cap that once belonged to Ivan. Shane had to smile; she sure looked the country girl. Her hair was up in a ponytail and she had a good tan. No wonder Ivan was crazy about her, Shane thought. I would be too, if I was older or she was younger. Shane watched her saunter down the path to the first shed and start scrapping. I'd better mind my manners or I'll be in trouble with Ivan, Shane mused as he smiled at Amy.

"What are you gawking at?" Amy called over as she set her pail on the ground, "You won't get much scrapping done that way."

Shane laughed, "Just taking a breather. I've been at it since 7:00 AM. I don't sleep in like some one I could mention."

"For your information, I've already checked the ewes in the lower pasture, fed the rams and turned out the ewe with foot rot. Then I had my breakfast." Amy moved over closer to Shane.

"What time did you get up?"

"Around 5:00 AM. I couldn't sleep so thought I should do something constructive."

"If you can't sleep, maybe you should borrow some of Mom's pills."

"Does Laura take sleeping pills?"

"She never used to, but when we went to Lethbridge, the doctor gave her some. I'm not sure why. Do you think Mom looks a little tired out?"

"I have noticed she seems to tire quickly. But maybe it's her age. She will be sixty-one soon."

"You could be right. I'm sure glad you'll be here to keep an eye on things. You'll be able to manage all right with Ivan's help."

"Ivan has his own ranch to worry about, but we'll do fine here. I can handle the sheep with the help of Lad and Lady. You'll be home on the weekends so it will be okay."

Amy moved back to her shed and continued scrapping. She was planning to have a talk with Laura when Shane left for school, but now she was wondering if she should talk to her sooner. She hadn't forgotten about Shane's party, when she thought she heard Laura crying. Maybe she was just emotional about Shane turning eighteen and leaving home. Or was it something else? Amy planned to get to the bottom of it. If Laura was sick, Amy and Shane had a right to know.

≫ ≪

Ivan called at suppertime and asked if Shane could help him for a couple of hours. After he left, Amy and Laura cleared away the supper dishes and Laura then migrated to the porch and sat on her swing. Amy followed and took the stool by the planter.

Laura sighed, "I so love the late summer evenings. I guess I like to soak up as much sun as I can before the weather turns colder." She started rocking back and forth on the swing."

"It is a beautiful evening. Do you want me to get you anything?"

"I'm just fine."

"You didn't eat much supper. Are you not feeling well, Laura?"

"I get tired some days. It's nothing to concern yourself with."

"Laura, I think we are good enough friends for me to be concerned. Why are you taking sleeping pills?"

"Did Shane tell you that?"

"Yes, he did. He is worried about you."

"I don't want him to worry. I want him to go to school and get his first year in before he goes on his mission. If he thinks I'm sick, he won't go."

"Are you sick?"

Tears welled up in Laura's eyes. She wiped them on her apron and then looked at Amy.

"Yes, I am sick. But with care, I should be okay for a few years. Enough time for Shane to complete his mission and return here to the ranch."

"Can you tell me what you have?"

"I would prefer not to at this time. And the pills I'm taking are not sleeping pills. So don't worry about that. I sleep just fine."

"What can I do to help?"

"Just what you have been. Being a friend and helping us around here. That's the best gift to me." Laura reached over and patted Amy's hand.

Amy turned to Laura and blurted out, "Can I ask you a personal question?"

"Sure, fire away."

"When you adopted Shane, where did you adopt him from?"

"Well, it was a private adoption. We picked him up in Calgary, but that wasn't the mother's home."

"How did you find him?"

"You are asking personal questions. Why all this sudden interest in Shane?"

"I have my reasons. Be patient with me."

"Abe was contacted by his ex-wife. She told him his daughter had been an uncontrollable teenager and got herself in trouble. She wanted him to take the baby and raise it, because she sure wasn't going to. She told him it was about time he took some responsibility for his family. Well, unbeknown to her, this was no trial for us."

"I didn't know your husband was married before."

"Yes, he was married for three years to a woman from Medicine Hat."

Could it be? Amy was scared to ask, but swallowing the lump in her throat, she managed to say the words, "What was her name?"

"Oh, that's right. You're from Medicine hat. I'm sure you wouldn't know her, but it was Gladys Stump.....or Stem. No, it was Stern. Yes, it was Gladys Stern."

And with those words, Amy fainted.

Chapter 21

S OMEONE HAD APPLIED something cold to her face and was patting her cheek; it was bugging her, but she couldn't seem to get it to go away. She swatted at it and mumbled.

"I think she is coming around," she heard Ivan's voice say. She opened her eyes and gazed into Ivan's blue ones, which looked very worried.

"I'm okay; just quit with the patting and take that wet thing off my face."

"Oh yeah, she's coming back to normal. A guy tries to be nice and she gives him the gears."

Amy glanced over at Laura who was standing by the door with a glass of water.

"Here, drink this. Can you sit up?"

Amy struggled to a sitting position on the porch floor and took the glass.

"You sure gave me a scare," Laura said as she sat back on the swing, "One moment we were talking and the next, you were on the floor."

"I'm sorry. I'm okay; I just was a bit light-headed," Amy lied. "How did Ivan get here?"

Ivan gave Amy his hand and pulled her to her feet, "Laura called me on my cell phone. She couldn't get you to answer her."

"I'm okay. Just one of those things. Do you mind if I go lay down?"

"I'll walk you to the trailer, if you're sure you're okay?"

"I'll be fine. Don't be such a worry wart. I'll see you tomorrow, Laura."

Ivan saw Amy safely home. He kissed her on the cheek and told her to get some rest.

Amy headed into the bedroom and threw herself on the bed. So Shane really was her son! Somehow she knew it. Maybe it was motherly instinct. That part was easy to believe. The hard part was the fact that Laura's husband had actually been her father! A father, her mother told her was dead! All these years and she didn't know he was alive and now it was too late. One thing was for sure, Amy mused, her mother had a lot of explaining to do. Why would she tell me my father was dead? Was it a way of punishing him, or was she trying to control me? Maybe if I had known my father, I would have had a different childhood. Maybe in my teens, I could have lived with him. So Shane's adopted father was really his grandfather. Laura knew that too! I wonder if she ever told Shane? It probably never came up. Amy was sure Shane was so well adjusted, he wouldn't even think about questioning anything.

Now Amy had to decide what to tell Laura and Shane. Maybe it would be better to never say anything; not rock the boat, so to speak. Amy had never talked to Shane or Laura about her mother. Laura, Amy was sure, didn't know that Amy's mother and Abe's ex-wife were one and the same. Oh those family lies!!! One thing Amy was definitely going to do was face her mother up and get the whole story. She needed that for her piece of mind. Then she would decide what to tell Laura. Amy knew Stern was her mother's maiden name and she had never quizzed her about her married name. Amy had used Stern as her name until she married. Amy's mother had never asked her what the name of the ranch was where she worked. Who knows? Maybe she did know and that was why she didn't want Amy down at the ranch; was she scared she would find out? All these thoughts were whirling around in Amy's head, enough to give her a headache. Shane was Gladys' grandson, for Pete's sake. I guess that didn't mean anything to Gladys, Amy thought, as she propped herself up on her pillows. Well, maybe it's best if he never knows her. He sure wouldn't be able to please her anymore than I could. He would be 'tarred with the same brush' as the saying goes.

Amy decided morning would be time enough to decide everything. She suddenly felt very tired. She slid off the bed and headed into the bathroom, put on her nightie and took two aspirins. She had just finished brushing her teeth when she heard a knock on the door. She yelled "Come in" before she realized she was in her night clothes. "Who is it?"

"Just me, Shane. Mom said to check on you and see how you are doing and if you need anything?"

"I'm fine, Shane. I just felt light-headed for a bit. I'm okay."

"I think you are working too hard. Now, I forbid you from poking your nose out this door before 8:00 AM. Happy Cat, you see she stays here." Shane reached down to pet the cat.

Amy ventured out to the edge of the kitchen, "I'm not dressed Shane, but thank you. I'll try to sleep in a bit."

"Good. See you tomorrow."

"Good-night, Shane," and when he had closed the door behind him, Amy added, "My son."

Chapter 22

THE NEXT FEW days were busy with the barn and sheds as the painter was coming on the Saturday. Laura was looking good and was out in her garden whenever she had a chance. When Amy finished with the sheds, she got the lawn mowed and trimmed all the hedges. By Friday, everything was ready.

Amy then approached Laura about getting Saturday off so she could go to Medicine Hat. Laura agreed, saying, "I hope everything is okay?" to which Amy answered, "I just thought I should run home before Shane starts school."

"Yes, that's a good idea," Laura said, "You'll be back Sunday night?"

"For sure. Hopefully, I will come back to a freshly painted barn and sheds."

"I sure hope he shows up. It is ideal weather for painting."

"Laura, you will tell me if you have any special needs, right?" Amy questioned her.

Laura gave her a little hug and answered, "You'd be the first to know. Anyway, are you going to see Ivan before you leave?"

"Why? Do I need to?"

"I suppose not. Do him good to worry about you."

Amy laughed and patted Laura's arm, "So I'll leave in the morning. Tell Shane that ewe who is feeding the triplets seems to be getting foot rot. He might want to catch her. I could help him tonight."

"Shane is going to the movies tonight. I'll help him in the morning. Don't worry about it. Go and have a good time."

The first thing Amy did when she arrived in Medicine Hat was take her car to the garage for an oil change and check-up. It was due and a good time to get it done. Besides, the owner and his wife went to the same church as her mother so she was curious about what was being said.

She pulled into the lot and parked beside the service bay. Don came out and seeing who it was, gave her a big smile.

"Well, look who's here! What are you doing back here? Are you back to stay?"

"No way. I'm just bringing my car to the best service station in southern Alberta."

"Flattery will get you everywhere. Have you seen your mother yet?"

"No; I just pulled in. I'm heading over there after I'm finished here."

"I should warn you. Things have changed over there."

"What things?' Amy cautiously asked.

"Did you know your mother took in a boarder? An elderly man?"

Amy sighed, "Yes, I knew that and got told to mind my own business."

"Well, that's not all. Ed has persuaded your mother she should sell the house and buy one of those fancy new condos on the south side. He said he could still board with her and help her out, but things would be easier for her."

"Easier for her, or for him?"

"That's the big question. I'm glad you're here. I think Ed has absolutely too much control over your mother."

"Well, she won't listen to me. She never has so that's not going to change. I guess if she wants to sell her house, that is her business. I do appreciate your concern though. I just hope she doesn't turn the money over to Ed. I don't know him, but who knows?"

"He comes off as a decent, friendly, caring guy, but so do all con-artists. I just don't know what to think. Ester is having a fit he is living there at all, but you know my wife; really old fashioned."

"I think that is the best way to be," Amy responded, "Anyway, I'll talk to Mom and see what's going on. How long will my car be?"

"Give us an hour. Have you got somewhere to go?"

"If I can borrow a car, I'll just run to the Mall for a bit."

\>\> \<\<

As Amy approached her mother's house, she could see the porch steps had been fixed. So had the gate and the fence was all fresh painted. I suppose in preparation to sell, Amy thought. The old house looked pretty good. Then Amy noticed the Remax sign. It had a 'SOLD' on it.

"Well, I guess I'm a little too late," Amy shook her head and climbed out of her car.

Just as she opened the gate, her mother came from around the side of the house. She stopped short and stared at Amy, as if she didn't know her.

"Mom, how are you?"

"Well, that sure didn't take you long to dive in like a vulture as soon as the house is sold. How did you hear about it way down at your Godforsaken ranch?"

"I didn't know a thing about it until I arrived here. That's not why I'm here."

"Could have fooled me. Two visits in one month? That's not normal."

"So who did you sell the house to?"

"Why would you care? You never spend any time here."

"Only making conversation. Where's Ed?"

"He's gone to the Mall to get a haircut. Why?"

"Because I have something I want to discuss with you and I don't want any interruptions."

"So I suppose you are here about the money. Well, it's all spent. I purchased a condo over on the south side yesterday. I will only have a few thousand left. When I die, you can have the condo."

"I'm not here for the money. I have lots of money. I don't spend very much on the ranch and my housing is free."

"Well, if it's not money, what is it?"

"Can we sit down, maybe have a cup of tea?"

"I guess so. You'll have to excuse the mess. I've been packing."

Gladys led the way into the house. Amy headed to the kitchen to put the kettle on while Gladys went to wash up. Amy wasn't sure how to bring up the subject, but decided just to blurt it out.

They were sitting at the table, drinking tea, when Amy asked, "Why didn't you tell me my Dad was alive?"

Gladys' hand quit stirring her tea. She laid the spoon on the saucer and looked at Amy.

"Who told you such a cock-and-bull story?"

"Don't try to deny it, Mom. I know everything!"

"I don't know what you're talking about. Your father died when you were a baby."

"Why have I never seen his grave?"

"He didn't want one. He was cremated and we spread his ashes over the South Saskatchewan River."

"Where's his obituary card?"

"What is this, a third degree? I don't have to answer any of your questions and I don't have to listen." Gladys got up to leave the table.

"Sit Down!!" Amy ordered. Gladys stopped and giving a sigh, sat back down.

"Now, talking about a cock-and-bull story!! That was one if I ever heard one. Now I'll tell you what I know. Then see if you can deny it. First of all, my father didn't die when I was a baby. He died four years ago of a massive heart attack. He remarried to a lovely lady by the name of Laura. They ran a sheep ranch in southern Alberta. When I had my child in Calgary, you phoned my father and gave my child to him. He grew up to be a nice young man by the name of Shane Collins. And I am now working on the Collins Ranch."

As Amy spoke, Gladys' face grew whiter and whiter. When Amy finished, she got up from the table and headed into the living room. Amy waited, but when her mother didn't return, she followed her. She found her sitting on the sofa, holding a picture in her hand.

Gladys looked up and said, "I always meant to give you this picture, but I just couldn't seem to part with it, but now would be a good time."

Amy took the picture and gazed at it. It was her as a baby, her mother and what Amy assumed was her father. Her mother and father were smiling. Amy noticed she did look a lot like her father. No wonder Laura had commented on her hair when she had first arrived, and how she could pass for Abe's daughter. She was Abe's daughter.

"Are you giving me this picture?"

"Yes; I have no further use for it."

"Mom, aren't you going to comment on what I said?"

"You figure you have it all down pat. So what can I say?"

"Why did you say my father was dead?"

"What did you want me to say? That your father left me when you were a baby? That he filed for divorce so he could marry another woman? Would you have understood that?"

"I would have when I was older."

"It just never came up then. I thought things were better this way."

"You thought?? You sure didn't think of me. I was deprived of my father all these years."

"Well, I wasn't about to let some other woman have a part in raising you. Abe would have wanted visitations so this way, I could cut him off."

"Why didn't he ever come to see me?"

"Because I wouldn't let him. He did ask the first few years, but because he left me, he thought he had no rights."

"Why did he leave?"

"I guess he didn't want the responsibility of a family."

"That's not the way it sounded to me by the people who knew him down south. He worked hard and made something of himself, the ranch and cared for his family."

"I suppose it's in the blood, your love of the ranch. Abe always did talk of wanting to be out of town. I understand that new wife of his inherited the ranch so that's probably why Abe married her."

"They were married a few years before Laura inherited the ranch."

Gladys shrugged, "Whatever."

"Now to Shane. Why would you want Abe and Laura to have my son? Was it to punish my father?"

"Well, he had gotten off pretty easy. He didn't have to deal with you and all you put me through. I couldn't take care of the baby and I didn't want him going to strangers, so I thought of Abe. Served him right, having to raise a child when he was older."

"For your information, that backfired on you. Abe and Laura couldn't have children; they had filed for adoption, but they were considered a risk because of their age. So when you phoned, it was like a message from Heaven."

Gladys looked pained and answered, "Then you should be grateful I did what I did instead of condemning me. Your son had a good home."

"Yes, he did. I am glad for that, anyway."

"So does he know you're his mother?"

"Not yet. I'm not sure I will ever tell him and Laura. They are happy now. I don't want to rock the boat."

"I understand Abe joined THAT church, the Mormons, so he could marry that woman. I suppose your son is a Mormon, too?"

"Yes, he is. He is also graduated from school and going to college in Lethbridge this fall. Next year, he will go on a two year mission with his church."

"What a waste of time. A young man lollygagging his time away, preaching to people in those foreign countries, most which are heathens. Why bother with them?"

"You wouldn't understand." Amy replied, fingering the photo of her family.

The door opened and Ed walked in, all decked out in a new suit and was carrying a bouquet of flowers.

"Oh, you have company, Gladys. How are you, Amy?" Ed presented the bouquet to Gladys and taking one carnation out, he handed it to Amy.

Oh yeah, he was smooth, thought Amy as she accepted the flower. Her mother had risen and said, "I'll just put these in water. Amy, are you staying for supper?"

"Actually, I have to go, but I'll see you in the morning before you leave for church. Take care for now."

Amy grabbed her purse, and carrying the carnation and her picture, headed out the door. She decided to go to the Remax office and just see what was going on. Like Ron, she was really starting to not trust Ed. He was entirely too smooth and her mother was completely over her head. Look at his new clothes. Amy wondered who had bought them for him? Three guesses and the first two don't count. A true con-man, Amy thought. We'll just have to see what he's been up to.

Chapter 23

AMY PHONED HER friend Leslie from her cell phone and made arrangements to meet her for supper and stay the night at her place. She had met Leslie while working at the Dairy Queen and they struck up a friendship. Leslie and Frank had been married two summers before and Leslie was expecting a baby sometime before Christmas. Amy was thrilled for them. This was a second marriage for both of them and they seemed extremely happy.

As Amy walked in to the Remax office, she could see that she would be there a while. Everyone seemed very busy and there were several people looking at catalogues.

"Can I help you?"

Amy walked over to the receptionist who noticed her and she smiled at the young woman sitting behind the desk.

"I would like to talk to someone about the Stern property."

"Oh, I think that property was sold a week or so ago. I'll just check."

"I know it's been sold. I'm Gladys Stern's daughter. I would like to talk to whoever was in charge of the sale."

"That would be Dave. He's with a client right now. Can you have a seat for a bit?"

"I guess I have no choice," Amy replied and took the only available chair.

Twenty minutes later, the receptionist answered the intercom and then spoke to Amy, "You can go in now. Office # 3."

That's weird, Amy thought. No one has left. So she was cooling her heels while 'Dave' was doing 'God knows what' in his office.

As she entered #3, a tall, extremely large, dark haired man stood up. "Ms Stern? I'm Dave Watson."

"Amy Bacon," Amy corrected him as she took the proffered chair.

"Sorry; I guess I shouldn't assume anything, right?"

"Doesn't make for good sales relations," Amy smiled as she sat back in the chair.

"What can I help you with, Ms Bacon?"

"You were in charge of selling my mother's property?"

"Yes, I was. It wasn't on the market very long. A young couple from Coaldale bought it. The husband is with the oil and got transferred here. Your mother did well to get $149,000 for the property. It's an old house and in need of a lot of repairs."

For that house - $149,000?!?!? Well, Amy thought, Mom did okay for sure. I'm shocked. Housing must really be booming.

Amy looked at Dave and said, "Why would anyone pay that much?"

"Well, it's in a prime neighborhood, close to schools and shopping. The lot is worth a lot of money."

"Has the deal been finalized?"

"It sure had. Your mother was paid out the beginning of the week. The couple take possession on September 15th. Why? Is there a problem?"

"I'm only curious and I have some concerns about Ed, my mother's friend. What did he have to do with all this?"

"I'm sure I don't know. A gentleman was with her when she came in. He read all the contracts for her. I thought he was a solicitor or something."

"No, I think he said he was a carpenter."

"Really?"

"Did Mom buy her condo through you?"

"Yes, she did. That is a nice place she got. It will be easy for her as it's close to the Mall. There is a senior's bus service free from the complex to the Mall and downtown. She has security and everything."

"Can I ask how much condos sell for?"

"There are different rates and I can only tell you the rates. You will have to ask your mother what she paid. Client information and all that. You know how it is. I have probably told you more than I should."

"So what are the rates?"

The cheapest is $89,000. The most expensive; $129,000."

Amy stood up. "Thank you for your help." She said as she picked up her purse.

"You're welcome. If I can help you with anything else, let me know. Maybe I can sell you a condo?"

"I doubt that. I live in southern Alberta, but thanks anyway."

Amy glanced at her watch as she left the real estate office. Twenty minutes to get across town and meet Leslie for supper. Frank was out of town on business so it would just be the two of them. Amy was glad as she needed a friendly ear to vent to.

So why did her mother say she only had a few thousand left? Even if she purchased the most expensive condo, she would still have $15,000 to $20,000 left. What was her mother hiding? Amy planned to find out.

Leslie was running late so Amy had time to relax at the restaurant and have a coffee. She mulled over what she had learned at the real estate office. Why was her mother so secretive about selling the house and her plans to buy a condo? And what did Ed have to do with it? He sure did have some nice clothes for a man with no money. Buying flowers and all! Gladys sure was sucked in. If there was some way to find out about Ed. Where DID he come from and who was he, really? Amy didn't believe he was a carpenter by trade, or he would have been more anxious to fix things up around the house. The first time Amy had been home since he arrived was after he had been there over a month and nothing had been repaired.

When Leslie tapped Amy on the shoulder, she was so engrossed in her thoughts, she nearly jumped out of her skin.

"Wow! You were thinking so hard, I just about left again. But then I decided, it had to be a man! That's the only thing that makes a woman think that hard, and I want to know all about it," Leslie said as she slid her bulky body into the seat opposite Amy.

Amy laughed, "Good to see you too. You look great! When is the baby due?"

"December 9th. He sure is an active one. My girls were never so hard to carry. Maybe because I am older, it is harder for me."

"You're not old. Thirty-six isn't old these days. Women are having babies into their forties."

"I pity them. This is my last one, if I can help it. Frank agrees. He is so excited about the baby."

"That's great!"

"So what brings you to town? Is it something about the deep thoughts you were having?"

"Sort of. Let's order, then I will fill you in on everything."

Like the good friend she was, Leslie listened to Amy's story without comment. Then she reached over and took Amy's hand.

"What a sad story. I knew you had a baby while quite young, but for your mother to give it to your father, a father you thought was dead! That just plain blows my mind. How can you forgive her?"

"Well, I do know now that my son grew up in a loving, caring home. He is happy and well adjusted. I don't think I could have done as well raising him myself. I was a minor so my mother would have had control over both of us. I didn't have any say about my baby going up for adoption. I didn't even know if it was a boy or girl."

"Your mother never told you?"

"She said it was better I never saw the child. Easier for everyone. I don't think she saw the baby either. She wasn't there when I had the baby."

"So, are you going to tell your son….. What's his name……Shane? (Amy nodded) Are you going to tell Shane you are his mother?"

"I think in the best interest to everyone, I should just keep quiet. Laura is Shane's mother. I wouldn't want to take anything away from her. She has been very good to me, making me feel at home and treating me just like family which (Amy laughed) I guess I sort of am. Besides, I know Laura is not well. She won't elaborate, but I think it is terminal."

"You do seem happy, Amy. You look good. You have put on a bit of weight, all in the right places, of course, and look at that tan!"

"That's what wrestling sheep does for you."

"Well, it seems to agree with you. Now you said you had two stories to tell. Dare I ask what the other one is?"

When Amy told Leslie about Gladys and Ed, Leslie burst into peals of laughter.

"I didn't know the old girl was interested in men. Just goes to show, you never know."

Amy smiled and looked at her plate, "I don't think she is interested….that way….you know. I think she just likes having him to do things for her and keep her company."

"Can you see any man being content with just that?"

"If he has some plans, I do. Like maybe conning Gladys out of some money."

"She wouldn't be foolish enough to give him any power over her finances, would she? Gladys always seemed like a very sharp business woman."

"She has to be pretty good to get $149,000.00 for that old house."

"Frank says the real estate market is booming. A lot of people have discovered Medicine Hat and what it can offer. It's the little 'big' city of the south."

"That's what Remax told me. Gladys has bought a condo through them, but she has a surplus of cash and that's what I think Ed has his eyes on."

"How much are we talking about?"

"If she paid, say $119,000.00 for the condo, we're talking close to $20,000.00, but if she only paid $89,000.00; now that's something to aim for. Close to $50,000.00 is a good chunk of change."

"That should be your inheritance."

"I don't care about the money. I just don't want to see a con-man take advantage of a lonely senior. Oh, I know in some ways, it would serve Gladys right, but she is my mother."

"I know. Come on; let's get out of here. I'm anxious to show you my nursery. That reminds me, Frank is pretty good friends with some of the police force here. If you think Ed is a scam artist, maybe Frank could get them to do some checking."

"That would be good. Let's go see a nursery!"

Chapter 24

A s AMY DROVE into the ranch at 6:00 PM and got out of her car, Shane called from the ranch house.

"Mom says come up for supper. We're just going to sit down."

"Okay," Amy called back, "I'll be right up. She grabbed her purse and hurried up the walk and entered the house. Shane and Laura were already at the table. Amy quickly washed her hands in the porch sink. Ivan was no where to be seen, which suited Amy just fine. She wasn't ready to see him just yet. He had such a knack of reading her mind.

"Sit down; sit down," Laura said as she smiled at Amy, "It's nice to see you back. I cooked your favorite - my fried chicken. Of course, Shane's favorite, too."

"It sure smells good. Everything okay on the ranch? I see the painter arrived. The buildings look good."

"Everything's good. How was your trip?" Laura asked as she straightened the tablecloth.

"No problems," Amy answered vaguely.

Shane offered the blessing and they all dug into the scrumptious meal. Amy was glad to see Laura take a hearty helping of everything. Her color looked better and she seemed to be rested. Shane was busy shoveling the food in, until Laura commented, "I don't think it's the last supper..... again, Shane."

Shane stopped with a forkful halfway to his mouth; then he looked embarrassed and set his fork down. "Sorry; I guess I was thinking about the days ahead without your good cooking, Mom. No need to lose my manners, though. More chicken, Amy?"

Amy burst out laughing. Shane looked so embarrassed, it was hard to keep a straight face. Laura smiled and slapped Shane on the arm.

"You'd better eat up then. We don't want you to starve to death when away from the ranch."

Shane laughed too. "You know, the funny thing is, when I stopped long enough for my head to catch up to my stomach, or the other way around, I'm not hungry anymore. And I want to save room for that strawberry torte I saw on the cupboard."

The banter made Amy very glad to be home and assured her of one thing. She would never tell Laura and Shane who she was. No one down here, not even Ivan could ever know. Especially Ivan, in case he would blurt it out. This family had already lost one member. Amy wasn't going to upset the apple cart by bringing up past history. As Amy glanced around the dining room, she really noticed for the first time, a picture sitting on the side board. It was one of Abe, Laura and Shane when Shane was a baby. Now that she knew who was in the picture, she planned to have a good look at it when alone some day.

With supper over and the washing up done, the evening loomed ahead. Shane decided to run over to Ivan's and see what he was up to. 'Man talk' was the way Shane put it as he grabbed his cap and headed out the door.

Amy watched him go and then turned to Laura. "I thought Ivan would be here for supper. He usually comes on Sunday nights, doesn't he?"

"I think he was a little worried I would grill him. You see, Ivan showed up in church this morning. The first time in years. When he slid into the seat next to me, Shane and I were flabbergasted. Right after the sacrament service, he left. So we didn't get a chance to talk. I'm glad Shane went over there. Maybe he will talk to Shane.

"That's a good thing, isn't it….. Ivan going back to church?"

"It's wonderful if he's attending for the right reasons."

"What do you mean?"

"If he is only going because of outside pressures, it isn't the right thing to do."

"Do people pressure him?"

"Oh, like all churches, we have members that think they can solve all the world's problems. If they know a man holds the priesthood and doesn't remain worthy to exercise it, they can put some pressure on."

"Hold the priesthood? I don't understand. Was Ivan a minister or priest?"

"Amy, it's a long story and best explained by someone who holds it. Do you want Shane to explain it to you?"

"Not really. It's not that important to me. Well, I'd better go home and unpack my suitcase and say 'Hi' to Happy Cat."

Amy picked up her purse from the chair by the door and when she did, the flap opened and the photo her mother gave her, among other things, fell out on the floor. Before Amy could turn around and pick up the items, Laura had bent over and picked up the picture. She gazed at it then looked up at Amy.

"What is this picture of Abe and whoever, doing in your purse?"

Amy felt sick. She didn't want to tell Laura who it was, but how could she explain it? Truth is usually the best policy, so Amy swallowed hard and answered, "That is a photo of me when I was a baby. My mother just gave me the picture yesterday."

Laura stared at Amy, then looked down at the picture. Tears welled up in her eyes as she looked at the photo, then back at Amy.

"How dare you? Weddle your way into my home, my life and my world with full intentions of taking your son back. You've done a good job, Amy. Shane thinks you are perfect, Ivan is in love with you, and me; I trusted you, told you things close to my heart and all the time, you planned to steal from me."

"That's not true! I didn't even know my father was alive, much less his name until this last month. My mother hid it all from me. The first I knew is when you told me Abe's ex-wife's name."

"You expect me to believe that?"

"It's true!!"

"But you were quizzing me about Shane before? Why?"

"Because I found out from Ivan you adopted him from Calgary and he was born on the same day I gave birth."

"I don't believe you. Now I want you to get out of my house and off my ranch. I don't want you to say a word to Shane. He is happy here and has a good home. You can't offer him that."

Amy felt heartsick. She didn't want to leave the ranch. She expected a reaction from Laura, but not the one she got. How could Laura think she came there with the sole intentions of disrupting their lives? She didn't want to cause any pain to anyone. Why hadn't she been more careful with that picture?

"I'll leave, Laura, but you are wrong about me. I care about you and I care about Shane. You are a wonderful mother to him. I would never take that away from you both. But you need me here. I will stay in town for a few days. Shane leaves for college on Wednesday. If I don't hear from you by then, I will come back and pack up my things and leave. With Shane gone, it will be hard for you to manage here."

"I have Ivan. He'll help me. I don't need any traitors here."

Amy picked up her purse, and taking the picture from Laura's hand, turned and walked out the door.

Chapter 25

WHEN AMY ARRIVED in town she took a room at the B... motel on the highway. Laura won't have any trouble finding me here, she thought. She checked in, then washed up and put her nightie on. Her hands were shaking and she tried to calm herself down. She lay on the bed and closed her eyes. Then the tears started to flow.

"My life is such a mess," she spoke aloud. "What am I going to do now? I don't want to leave the ranch and Shane and Laura. Or Ivan for that matter. But Laura is so angry. Will she calm down and see that it's not my fault?" But Amy knew Laura was reacting out of fear. Her family was being threatened and she thought she had to protect it. The only way she could would be to make Amy leave. "I might react the same way," Amy guessed. "What a mess!"

Sleep finally overcame Amy, but then she had bad dreams. Shane was calling out to her and her mother was hauling him away in a wheelbarrow. Then Laura was there, fighting with her mother. Amy woke up in a sweat. She had a glass of water and laid back down. The traffic on the highway was starting to pick up, but she finally dozed off again, just before dawn.

The first thing Ivan noticed as he drove into the ranch was Amy's car wasn't there.

"Where's Amy? Didn't she come home?" he confronted Laura as she came to the door of the ranch house.

"I'm not sure," Laura answered as she turned away and added softly, so Ivan could hardly hear, "And I don't care."

"What do you mean by that?"

"Just forget her, Ivan. She's not for you."

"I think I'll be the one to decide that. What happened here?"

"Amy and I had a fight and I told her to leave."

"What!!! You can't do that. She's needed here. What did you have a fight about? Surely you can resolve it. You're too good a friends to not get over it."

"I'm not prepared to discuss it. She won't be back except to pack up her things."

"So she's still in the area? I'm going to find her and get to the bottom of this."

"Leave it alone, Ivan. I beg you. You will only make things worse. Shane's happiness depends on it."

"Why? What has Shane got to do with this? Did he fall for Amy, is that it? Amy would never reciprocate. Shane will get over it."

"Leave it alone."

"I'm going to find her," Ivan stubbornly announced and bolted out the door. "Tell Shane I'll be back in a while to work on that overhead door."

Laura let him go. She had no choice. She just hoped Ivan couldn't find her. If he did, would Amy tell him? She felt bad she had to lie to Shane when he returned last night. She told him Amy had a family crisis and had to leave for a bit. It wasn't really a lie as it was a family thing. Only Shane mustn't know he was the family. Laura returned to her kitchen and panning her buns.

Ivan drove straight to town and the first thing he spotted was Amy's car parked at the motel. *Good,* Ivan thought. *Now I'll get to the bottom of this.* He asked the desk clerk for Amy's room number and the sleepy clerk looked him up and down.

"I'm family." Ivan stated. The clerk then reluctantly said, "Room #204." Ivan darted out the door and walked over to the room. The curtains were drawn, but Ivan knocked anyway. No answer. He knocked again. Finally he heard some noises inside. Then the door cautiously opened.

When Amy saw it was Ivan, she tried to close the door, but he shoved it open.

"Ivan, I'm in no mood to visit."

"I know. You look like death warmed over. I can see you've been crying. Your eyes are all swollen. What is going on? I can't get a word out of Laura."

Amy sighed and sank down on the bed. She looked at Ivan and saw the concern in his eyes.

"I wish I could tell you, but that is up to Laura. She fired me last night."

"Why would she fire you? She thinks the world of you. So does Shane."

"That's the problem," Amy answered as tears welled up in her eyes again.

"Why? Has Shane been bothering you? I can't blame the guy if he fell in love with you, but he'd better get over it."

"No, no. You have it all wrong. Shane doesn't fancy himself in love with me. We're just good friends."

"Well, that's good. I wouldn't want to mess up his pretty face."

Amy tried to smile, but ended up crying. Ivan put his arm around her and she laid her head on his shoulder.

"Let it all out. Sometimes a good cry can make things a lot clearer and not so bad."

Amy snuffled and reached for a Kleenex. "I look a sight. You shouldn't be seeing me like this."

"Why not? You're beautiful to me, even when you're crying. You know how much I care about you. I don't like to see you unhappy. That's why we have to resolve this problem between you and Laura."

"It's not possible, Ivan. I can't explain it to you, but take my word for it. Laura won't back down on this one. If you get any explanation, it will have to come from her."

"So you don't think enough of me to trust me with this?"

"I made a promise, that's all."

"You always keep your promises?"

"I always try to."

"Good. I'll remember that. Now, why don't you go fix yourself up and I'll take you out for breakfast?"

"I'm not very hungry."

"Well, I am and I would like some company."

"Okay. It beats moping around here. Just give me a few minutes."

➤ ➤

When Ivan dropped Amy back at her motel with a promise to not leave for a day or two, he headed straight back to the Collins Ranch. Shane was waiting for him. Between them, they got the mechanism fixed on the overhead garage door.

Laura called them in for lunch. She kept glancing over at Ivan but he ignored her and focused on his lunch. After, Shane headed to the garage to tinker with his truck in preparation for his trip to Lethbridge and Laura started clearing the table. Once she was sure Shane was out of earshot, she asked Ivan, "Did you find Amy?"

"Do you want to know because you are concerned about her or do you want to find out what I found out?"

"So she did tell you! I knew she would be a traitor."

"For your information, she wouldn't tell me a thing. She said it was your story to tell. She looks terrible and she's hurting real bad. I'm worried about her."

"Don't waste your time worrying about her. She'll land on her feet. She's got you feeling sorry for her."

"I'm sorry for both of you. You've always been like a mother to me and I don't like to see you hurt. I'm positive Amy never meant to hurt you, if she did. She thinks the world of you and Shane."

"Oh, I'm sure she thinks a lot of Shane."

"She said Shane and her are just good friends. I thought maybe Shane had a crush on her."

"Heaven forbid. She's old enough to be his ...."
Laura stopped and turned away. She had nearly blurted it out. She would have to be careful.

"Old enough to be his mother? Hardly. She's only fifteen or sixteen years older than him."

"Yes, hardly." Laura turned and smiled, "Are you finished here today or should I expect you for supper?"

"I have a supper date, but thanks. I'll just go and say good-bye to Shane. You think about what I said. You need Amy. She's staying at the B........ motel, right on the highway. You can't miss it."

"Mind your own business, Ivan Johnson."

"I am. Anything to do with Amy is my business!"

➤ ◄

Thinking it was Ivan at the door and she wasn't ready yet, Amy opened it to find Laura standing outside.

"May I come in?"

"Of course," Amy answered as she stepped back to let Laura in. This was a surprise. Laura entered, then turning to Amy she abruptly said, "I'll make this short and sweet. First of all, I want to thank you for not telling Ivan about Shane. At least you seem to be willing to keep that a secret. Now, here's the deal. You come back to the ranch and we will proceed as before. I won't be telling you any heart-to-heart stories. We will be strictly employer and employee, understand? You will never tell Shane who you are until I'm gone. Can you live with that?"

"I don't know. I so enjoyed your friendship. I'm going to miss that. But I will accept your terms, mainly because I need the job and secondly, I love the ranch. Last, but not least, I'm hoping I can prove to you I did not come here with the idea of taking Shane away. It's the truth, so help me God. I had no idea when I arrived here that Shane was my son."

"So you say. Well, we'll see how well you keep your side of the bargain. Of course, that includes Ivan. He will work at you to try to find out, but he's too close to the family. He must never know."

"I promise. When do you want me to return?"

"When Shane leaves on Wednesday."

"I'll be there."

After Laura left, Amy sat on the bed and ran the conditions through her mind. She really was cutting Amy out of her and Shane's life. Well, at least she still had a job.

When Ivan knocked, she was ready to go. When she told him Laura had been to see her, he was overjoyed. She didn't tell him the conditions of her return.

Chapter 26

AMY RETUNED TO the ranch on the Wednesday morning. All was quiet at the ranch house. It looked like rain, so Amy decided to wait until the next day to check the sheep. Lad and Lady were overjoyed to see her as they cavorted around her and gave excited little barks.

"Well, at least you're both glad to see me," she commented as she ruffled the fur on each dog's shoulder. "Too bad some others don't feel the same way."

The days settled into a routine. Amy did her chores and waited for her instructions from Laura. Shane returned on Friday evening, all full of news about his classes and life in Lethbridge. He wondered why Amy wasn't having supper with them on Saturday night, but she assured him she had a date. Which was true, as she had talked to Ivan to be sure. Shane didn't seem to notice the coolness between Laura and herself.

Laura had her birthday on September 20th, and Shane and Ivan took her out for supper. Amy begged off, saying she had a headache. She was sure Laura would have a better time without her there. She had purchased a small gift of toiletries for her earlier in the summer, so left it in the porch for her when she returned from dinner.

As the weeks went by and the weather started turning colder, Amy was busy getting the fences repaired on the fall flushing pasture. When Ivan had mentioned to her they always put the ewes on the oat stubble late in the fall to flush them, she was a bit confused about what that meant. Then Ivan explained that the increased feed caused the ewes to drop more eggs per cycle, and they would produce more lambs.

Amy was intrigued. "Does that work with cattle, too?" she asked Ivan.

"I don't think so," he had responded, "One calf is enough per cow, anyway." He explained that the gestation period was approximately nine months for a cow, while sheep was only five months. I sure do have a lot to learn, Amy thought, as she prepared to head to the pasture.

Shane was home on weekends when he could. Laura seemed to like it better when he didn't show up. She encouraged him to take part in all the sports which often had matches on Saturdays. Anything to keep him away from the ranch and away from me, Amy mused. She still doesn't trust me. Maybe I would do the same.

One day, Amy got a call from Leslie. She had some news to report. First she said, "Do you want the good news or the bad news first?"

"Good first, always." Amy answered.

"Well, the good news is Frank talked to the police and they ran Ed through the system. He doesn't show up anywhere. He was actually born in Vancouver, an only child of divorced parents. His mother moved to Medicine Hat when he was young and raised him here. So he has lived in the Hat most of his life."

"Wow! The police found out all that?"

"Actually, no. I found out all the details. I made a point of taking your Mom a house warming gift and I got Ed talking. He told me he was born in Vancouver. He seemed very willing to talk."

"Okay, so what's the bad news?"

"You may perceive it as such. Are you sitting down? Gladys and Ed got married at City Hall three days ago."

Amy did sit down. Her mother and Ed? Married?

"Are you sure?"

"As sure as my eyes can see. There is an announcement in the paper."

"I don't know whether to be happy or worried."

"That's what I mean. If he really cares for her, it's the best news. But if he married her to get her money, that's another story."

"I wonder why she didn't invite me to witness it?"

"You know Gladys. Look how she withheld important facts from you before."

"That's true. Thanks for letting me know and for all the work you did. By the way, what's the condo like?"

"Really nice. Your Mom seems happy there."

"Good."

"How's things at the ranch?"

"Busy. We'll be weaning and shipping the lambs soon. I've been busy fencing and getting things ready for winter."

"Take care and we will talk soon. Please keep in touch."

After Amy got off the phone, she remembered she didn't know the address of the condo. She did have her mother's phone number so would have to call her. She assumed it would be the same number. But she would wait a few days and see if her mother called her first with the news.

One evening, while Amy was checking the sheep in the lower pasture, she came across a partly eaten carcass of a lamb. Lad and Lady sniffed at the lamb and circled around, smelling the ground and growling. Amy wasn't familiar with animal kills so couldn't identify the culprit. This called for an expert. She would have to get Laura out.

When she knocked on the door, it was a few minutes before Laura answered. She looked tired and was in her housecoat.

"Yes?"

"I just found a dead lamb in the south pasture. Something has been feeding on it."

"Did it die of natural causes or was it killed?"

"I don't know."

"I'll call Ivan to come over. I'm too tired to go out tonight."

"Okay. I'll wait for him by the barn."

When Ivan arrived, it was starting to get dark. Amy was worried about finding the carcass again.

"Feel like a camp-out?" Ivan said as he took a 30-30 rifle out of his truck and came over to Amy.

"What do you mean?"

"Put on some warm clothes. We'll locate that carcass, then find a place to hide up wind and see what comes to feed on it. With any luck, I'll get a shot at it."

Amy grabbed her warm jacket and gloves from the barn tack room and followed Ivan as he continued, "We'll walk so we don't scare anything away. Leave Lad and Lady home as the predator won't come in with their smell there."

The dogs were disappointed but obeyed the command to stay. Amy struggled to keep up with Ivan as he headed out. She managed to locate the carcass again, but Ivan said not to go near it. They circled up wind and found a place between some large rocks on the hillside. They settled down for the wait. Ivan put his fingers to his lips with the signal not to talk.

It was nearly dark when Ivan leaned over and whispered into Amy's ear, "Look to the left."

There, coming across the pasture was a large, dog-like animal. Amy thought it was probably a coyote, but it was really large.

"Wolf," Ivan whispered, "Get behind me."

Amy obeyed. Ivan slowly lifted his rifle, and then paused. The wolf kept advancing, stopping every now and then to smell the air. Amy held her breath. The animal was looking off toward the opposite hills. Ivan brought the rifle to his shoulder and with a quick squeeze, fired off a shot. The wolf leapt into the air and bolted for the hills, running right toward them! Ivan fired again, this time dropping the wolf only a few yards from where they were hiding.

Amy's heart was beating so fast, she thought she would faint. Ivan put his arm around her.

"Are you okay?"

"I never was so scared in my life. When you missed that first shot and it started running at us, I nearly died."

"What makes you think I missed the first shot?"

"Well, you did, didn't you? It was running toward us."

"I think you will find two bullet holes in that wolf. The first in the body, the last in the head."

"I'm just glad you got it. I'd hate to come out here and be alone if it showed up."

"Lad and Lady would protect you. You should always have them with you, just in case. I imagine it is an old wolf, pushed out from the pack so looking for easy pickings. It sure was a long ways east. Want to come have a look?"

"I think I'll just stay here, thanks."

Ivan went over to the wolf and poked it with his rifle, but it was dead.

"Yep; two bullet holes," he called back to Amy, "Let's get on home."

They walked back toward the ranch.. They could hear Lad and Lady barking, and Amy remembered the dogs had been doing a lot of barking at nights lately. She told Ivan and he agreed that probably the wolf had been around for a while.

"I wonder how many sheep he managed to get?"

"I haven't seen any other carcasses," Amy replied.

"We'll know pretty soon. You're weaning next week aren't you?"

"That's the plan. Shane will be home on Thanksgiving break then."

"Has Laura arranged for the trucks yet?"

"The trucks?"

"For taking the lambs out. She usually gets a couple of semi's in. With nearly one thousand lambs to go, you need lots of trailer space."

"She hasn't said, but I'm sure she has if that's the plan."

Laura decided they would move the sheep up to the pasture closest to the barns until weaning time. That way, the dogs would keep predators away. Amy thought that was a good idea. It would also save her some leg work.

Shane arrived home on the Thursday night as he had no classes on the Friday. He helped Amy do the final preparations on the corrals and runway on the Friday morning.

Saturday morning, they ran the ewes in and started sorting. Amy was amazed at the amount of work that needed done. First, they sorted off the lambs from the ewes. Laura kept a tab as they went through the chute.

"It looks like predators managed to snag about seventeen lambs," Laura said.

"That's not too bad," Shane replied, "Remember last year? That coyote family got away with about twenty-five."

"That's true," Laura answered, "I guess the wolf scared the coyotes off."

"I had no idea you could lost so many to predators even with watching the ewes closely," Amy said.

"Part of raising sheep," Shane closed the gate on the pen with the lambs, "Okay, let's have a lunch break, then tackle the ewes. Amy, can you bring the lambing charts when you come back from lunch?"

"Sure thing."

The afternoon was spent with sorting out the culls, vaccinating the ewes and treating for sheep keds. They also checked for foot rot and any other health problems. Any ewe whose udder didn't look normal was caught and checked out. If she had mastitis, she was culled out. Hooves were trimmed on any that needed it. Laura had hired two men from a neighboring ranch to help out and Amy was grateful for that. Along with Ivan, they were six altogether. It was hot, dusty work. There was a lot of racket as the ewes called for their lambs and the lambs were answering.

"Get used to it," Ivan laughed as he pulled Amy's pony tail. "You'll be hearing lots of it for the next few days. The truck doesn't come until Tuesday morning. These lambs will be heading to the states. Better market down there."

"What about the cull ewes? What happens to them?"

"I'm not sure. Probably go for dog food. I think they go to Calgary."

Laura had gone to the house to prepare supper for the men. As she walked past Amy, she told her to come up for supper, too. It was the first invite since their disagreement. Amy was hoping the door was opening up again.

Chapter 27

WITH THE LAMBS shipped out and the cull ewes gone, they turned the remaining ewes into the oat stubble west of the buildings. When they did the count while weaning, they found they had lost seven ewes during the summer. It was difficult to decide if they had died from natural causes or the wolf had killed them. It seemed unlikely he would pick a ewe over a lamb, but if the ewe was down, he would take advantage of that. They were just glad there weren't more sheep lost.

Shane was back to school and things were back to normal. Laura was still very distant, but she relaxed a bit and asked Amy to help harvest the garden root vegetables. Amy did all the heavy lifting as Laura just didn't seem to have the strength. Amy was worried about her, but didn't dare question her. She did mention it to Ivan one night.

"Why didn't you tell me sooner?" he demanded.

"Because I didn't want to upset Laura. I promised I wouldn't interfere in her family."

"That's not interference; that's showing concern. But don't worry. I won't let on you said anything."

"Thanks. I sure don't want to rock the boat."

"You and Laura still haven't buried the hatchet, have you?"

"I don't think that will ever happen. I just don't want things to get worse."

Ivan put his arm around Amy and grew her close. "You know, you could always move over to my place," he teased her, "then you wouldn't have to worry."

"Quit teasing. You would never move a woman into your house. You're too independent."

"I would if she was my wife."

"Is that a proposal? You'd better be careful. A woman might take you seriously."

"That's what I'm hoping."

Amy pulled away and laughed nervously. She really hoped Ivan wasn't serious. She wasn't ready for any commitment; maybe never with all her secrets. It's not good to start a marriage with secrets.

"You don't know when you're well off. The last thing you need is a wife to mess up your life."

Ivan grabbed her arm and pulled her against him. "When will you take me seriously? I want my life messed up as you put it. I love you, Amy. I don't find it easy to say the words, but I want you with me the rest of my earthly life. And I think you care for me too. You just won't let yourself go and admit it. You're even scared to kiss me with any feeling."

"I'm not scared."

"Yes, you are. You're scared of your own feelings and I'll prove it."

Ivan took her face between his hands and slowly lowered his lips to hers. Amy tried to pull away but he held her fast, and pressed his lips on hers. He lightly nibbled on her lower lip, then left a trail of kisses across her cheek to her ear lobe. A tickling sensation ran through Amy's stomach and her knees went weak. If Ivan hadn't been holding her, she was sure she would have fallen.

"Stop," she whispered, scared of the feelings she was experiencing.

"Why? Because you are feeling something?" Ivan murmured in her ear. "Let it go, Amy. Love me."

Amy put up her hand and entangled it in Ivan's thick blond hair. Ivan's lips were back on hers and she let herself enjoy the moment and respond to his kiss. When they broke apart, both were breathing heavy.

"Wow!! That was some kiss," Ivan remarked, "I could get used to that. Is that a yes? Will you marry me?"

Amy pushed away from Ivan, then turned to face him.

"I'm not sure. You have to give me some time. I have a lot of unsolved issues I need to deal with."

"Okay; you let me know when you're ready. Please don't make me wait too long. I don't think I could stand it. It's been six months since we met and every day I love you more."

"Oh, Ivan; there's so much about me you don't know."

"So tell me."

"I can't right now. Someday I will. I would never marry you with secrets between us."

"It's something to do with Shane, isn't it?"

"I can't say right now. I promise you, when the time is right, I will tell you."

"I remember you saying you always keep your promises, so I am holding you to it."

Chapter 28

I VAN'S BIRTHDAY WAS on October 14th, and they celebrated by going to a dinner in town and a movie. Shane was at school and Laura declined, saying she was tired and wanted to get to bed early. The dinner was delicious and the movie was a comedy and had them in stitches from laughing.. On the way home, Ivan declared it was the best birthday he had in all his forty-one years. He brought Amy home and walked her to her trailer, with the promise to be back in the morning to help move some feed around in preparation for winter feeding. It wouldn't be long before the ewes would have to have supplement feed as the growing season was long gone.

The first snow storm of the season hit with a bang. It was only late October, but the wind was howling and with the heavy snow, it turned into a real blizzard. The rams were due to be put out with the ewes in early November but they were still in their pen by the barn. Lately they had been doing lots of head butting, but the blizzard put a stop to the shenanigans for a day or two. Sometimes when they were fighting, Amy could hear the cracks from her trailer. She was worried about them hurting each other, but Ivan had laughed when she told him.

"They're just deciding whose going to be top ram. You know males; always have to get the girls."

"It seems a lot easier for the animal kingdom though, doesn't it?" Amy teased back.

"That's for sure. If I was like those rams, I'd just chase you around until you gave up."

"Isn't that what you're doing?"

Ivan made a grab for Amy's ponytail, but she dodged away and laughing, headed into the barn.

"I'll get you for that crack," Ivan called after her. Amy was sure he would. Ivan was always full of all kinds of tricks. He had a great sense of humor; that was one thing Amy loved about him.

"What did I just say? I love him? Well, I guess I do. I've finally admitted it. To myself anyway." Amy shook her head and spoke aloud, "I'd better be careful that Ivan doesn't find out."

"What can't Ivan find out?" Shane stuck his head around the corner of a stall.

"What are you doing here? I didn't hear you come home."

"I arrived a bit ago. You and Ivan were in the sheep pen, so I thought I would come in here and see how my little family is doing."

"Oh, the kittens? They're fine. Momma cat doesn't leave them very long. I've been feeding her."

"I can see that; that's good. So what's this about Ivan?"

"Nothing. I just don't want him to know all my secrets. He's too nosy."

"Can't blame a guy when he's in love," Shane answered.

"What do you know about love?"

"You'd be surprised. I'm not a baby, you know."

Amy laughed, "I know. Come on, want to come check the sheep with me and the dogs?"

Now this blizzard had hit. Ivan had phoned and told Laura and Amy the road conditions were bad so just stay put. If they needed anything, call him and he had a 4X4 so could get out.

Laura decided to do some sewing so she was occupied in the house. Amy was at loose ends, so decided to phone her mother. She had not heard from her about the marriage. She really didn't expect to, but it would have been nice to be notified.

Her mother answered on the first ring, "Ed?"

"No, it's Amy. How are you?"

"Oh, Amy. I thought it might be Ed. He's been away for a few days."

"Been away? Where?" Amy's heart gave a lurch. She sure hoped it wasn't what she thought.

"I'm not sure. He just didn't come home from his hair appointment. I'm worried."

"Mom, is it true that you and Ed got married a few weeks ago?"

"Who told you that?"

"It was in the Hat papers."

"I didn't think you'd get the paper out there."

"Is it true?"

"Yes, and don't you start on me. People seem to think I don't know my own mind. I've gotten along for years without all the help. Why do they care now?"

"I've always cared, Mom. Have you phoned the police about Ed missing?"

"They won't do anything for at least a week.. They seem to think we just had a fight, but that's not true. We get along great. Ed is wonderful."

"Mom, have you checked your bank account lately?"

"Why would I do that?"

"Just a feeling."

"Well, for your information, Ed insisted I leave all my money in my name. He can't touch it."

"That's good."

"If you have nothing else to say, hang up now as I want to leave this line free for Ed to call."

"Okay, Mom. Take care."

Amy hung up and called Leslie to tell her the story. Leslie was glad to hear from her, but had a meeting so had to run. She promised to call if she heard anything.

Chapter 29

NOVEMBER WAS A long month for Amy. She found the work tedious and the evenings boring. Ivan was busy getting his ranch ready for winter and Laura spent most of her days inside. She only ventured out once in a while to check on things. Shane made it home two of the weekends, but he was busy with his friends.

Amy checked the sheep every day, keeping an eye out for any problems. The rams had been turned in early in the month. She did a bit of clean-up around the yard and kept the snow out of the driveway. Since their early blizzard, there had been very little snow. The days were cool and it was freezing every night. Amy enjoyed the heavy quilt on her bed. Happy Cat would snuggle in with her, purring loudly. Amy was grateful for the cat's company.

Leslie had phoned early in the month to tell her the latest news. Yes, Ed had left and had cleaned out Gladys' bank account to the tune of $37,000.00. When Amy asked how he was able to take the money, Leslie said the authorities announced he had forged Gladys' signature. I guess he gave the bank a cock-and-bull story about purchasing a new car. There was a Canada wide warrant out for his arrest.

After Leslie's call, Amy had phoned her mother but got told to quit gloating and leave her alone, so that is what Amy did. She hadn't heard another word from Medicine Hat.

❧ ❦

One morning early in December, Ivan called. He said he had been talking to Laura. "Do you want to go shopping in Lethbridge? I thought maybe, with Christmas in three weeks, you might have some shopping you'd like to do."

"Is Laura going?"

"No, she declined. Said to take you."

"You're sure?"

"Of course I'm sure. Get your glad rags on. It's a beautiful day. I'll be there at 9:00 AM."

When Ivan hung up the phone, he headed to the bathroom to shave. He was looking forward to a day in the city with Amy. They hadn't spent much time together lately. Mostly, it was his fault as he had a lot of fall work to finish. He also thought it was good to give Amy a little space. Maybe there was some truth in 'absence makes the heart grow fonder'. He knew it sure worked for him. He couldn't get her off his mind. Maybe getting her away from the ranch would help her open up and talk to him. He sure wished he knew what the problem was between her and Laura, but both were tight-lipped. Laura just wouldn't say a word when Ivan had asked her again, what she had against Amy? He was told to mind his business and stay out of hers. So that is what he did.

He thought Laura was looking better. She didn't seem so tired. Amy had taken over all the outside work so Laura was free to pursue other things. Amy seemed to enjoy the outdoors and working with the animals.

"She sure will make a good rancher's wife," Ivan said to his reflection, "Now I just have to convince her to be this rancher's wife!"

When Amy hung up the phone , she wasn't sure she was doing the right thing. Was going to the city with Ivan giving him too much encouragement? Things had settled down on the ranch, but Amy was 'waiting for the other shoe to drop' so to speak. Laura still wasn't giving in and forgiving Amy. It's only a matter of time until she finds some excuse to fire me, thought Amy. I'm just going to have to work extra hard so she can't justify it. She seemed to want Amy to go shopping with Ivan. Why was that? Amy had gotten the feeling lately that Laura didn't want Ivan and Amy spending time together. Of course, Amy had to admit Ivan was just like a son to Laura so she would be protective of him. What happened to 'Amy, you and Ivan belong together. Amy, don't count Ivan out.' She was the same girl she was when she arrived.

Amy got up and headed into the bathroom. Well, today she was going to enjoy herself and forget all about the ranch. She jumped in the shower and lathered up her long hair. "I think I will leave it down today and, I'm going to shock Ivan and wear a dress." Amy had to smile. Ivan thought she was such a tom-boy! "Wait until he see me all dolled up! What was it Shane said; 'knock your socks off?'" That's what she was going to do. It would be fun to see the look on Ivan's face. It was time he got teased right back.

At 9:00 AM sharp, Ivan pulled into the ranch yard. Amy watched as he stopped at the main ranch house.

"Well, he can just come down here for me," Amy thought indignantly, "Just like a country boy!"

But Ivan was only a few minutes in the house and then he drove down to the trailer and parked behind Amy's car. When Ivan knocked on the trailer door, Amy did a last minute quick check in front of the mirror, then opened the door.

Ivan's eyes widened and he whistled, then said, "Wow! When Shane said you could knock a guy's socks off, he wasn't kidding!" Ivan reached down and checked his socks. "No, they are still there," he exclaimed and then he smiled and thought to himself. Boy, does she look good. She is some looker. I can't imagine any man letting her get away.

Amy had on a green silky blouse with matching skirt which was gathered at the waist and gave some fullness to the bottom. The blouse was long sleeved with pearl buttons down the front. She had left her hair loose and the flowing reddish brown curls accented the outfit perfectly. Ivan was starstruck.

"Are you going to stand gawking all day or are we going shopping?" Amy reached back for her jacket and purse.

"You look fantastic, Amy. Yes, let's go shopping, but I feel like a country bumpkin beside you. I just wore my jeans."

"You look fine. I just felt like dressing up for a change."

"You look good, even in jeans with sheep manure all over, but you are a sight for sore eyes today."

"Amy laughed, "What a nice, back-handed compliment. Sheep manure isn't my favorite perfume."

As they walked out to the truck, Amy could see Laura looking out her kitchen window. Ivan noticed her too, and gave a wave.

As they left the yard, Ivan commented, "It's too bad Laura didn't want to come. A day away might have been good for her. She gave me a little list of things, but it's not like picking your own."

"I don't think Laura cares to shop all that much. She is pretty frugal. Probably all those lean years when she and Abe were first on the ranch."

"Has Laura told you what her problem is?"

"No; I'd be the last person she would tell now. I was hoping you could tell me. Did you get a chance to ask her?"

"She told me to tend to my own business."

"Well, before all this other business, she did admit to me she was sick. She wouldn't tell me what specifically, but later made a comment about after she was gone."

"Gone? Gone where?"

"I assumed she meant, passed away......died."

"Are you sure?" Ivan demanded as he glanced over at Amy, "Are you sure you understood what she said?"

"Well, that's what it sounded like to me."

Ivan was silent for a while, mulling over what Amy had said. Was Laura a lot sicker than she was letting on? If so, Ivan had to find out. Why wasn't she getting some help, getting surgery if needed? He made up his mind; he was definitely going to find out. He owed it to Shane and Amy and to Laura herself. She needed help and was too stubborn to acknowledge it.

Ivan reached over and took Amy's hand, "We can't solve Laura's problem right now so let's forget about the ranch and enjoy our day. Where do you want to go first?"

Amy and Ivan had a fantastic day. Ivan turned out to be a great shopping partner. He was good at picking out the right items and while Amy was trying on some new jeans, he patiently waited for her and made her model each pair. He would make comments that had her in peals of laughter or annoyed with him.

"Too much of Laura's fried chicken for that pair," was one comment that had Amy punching him on the arm. Another comment of "too tight" related to his church upbringing, but Amy had to admit, when you're working with sheep, you didn't want your jeans too tight.

After Amy had made her purchases at the Ladies Wear store, they proceeded to Costco's where Ivan spent a lot of time in the electronics. They had Chinese food for lunch and hit a lot of different stores in the afternoon. Amy was totally exhausted by the time they left the Wal-Mart and headed to the truck.

"Do you want to stop for supper or just head home?" Ivan asked Amy as he stowed her packages behind the seat of the club cab.

"If it's all the same to you, I'm exhausted. Let's just head out. I do believe shopping is harder than wrestling sheep all day."

"You looked like you were having fun."

"I had a blast. Just because I'm tired doesn't mean I didn't have a good time. Thanks for all your patience. You make a great shopping partner."

"Just a shopping partner?" Ivan teased as he reached over and pulled a strand of Amy's hair around his finger.

Amy answered, "You always have to come back to that question, don't you? And I'm going to answer you. No, not just a shopping partner. I think you will make some lucky girl a wonderful life partner. I just don't know if I'm that girl."

"You don't have to know. I know enough for both of us. I would never do you any wrong."

"I know that, Ivan. It's just that I haven't resolved my past problems. To be fair to you, I can't marry you with these things hanging over my head."

"Does this thing have something to do with Laura?"

"Yes, partly."

"And you can't tell me?"

"I promised Laura. I will tell you this; it's something that happened when I was young."

"Laura didn't know you then."

"No; it's complicated. When Laura decides to talk, you will get the whole story from me. Then you will probably change your mind about marrying me."

"Never. I'm sure you're not an ax murderer, so I'm safe to say that."

"How can you be so sure?" Amy teased.

Ivan gave her hair a little tug and turned to the wheel and started the truck. "Knock-outs don't carry axes," he teased right back, "I just know you're too kind-hearted."

As they headed south toward home, Amy snuggled down in the seat and pondered Ivan's last statement. She wasn't sure she could remain kind-hearted if Laura didn't bury the hatchet soon. Amy laughed to herself.

Talking of ax murderers; had that made her think of hatchets? She drifted off to sleep and woke up when Ivan turned down the ranch road.

"Some company you are. Made me drive all that way without conversation. I was pretty lonely."

"I'm sorry. I was just so tired. You should have woke me up. Forgive me?"

Ivan reached over and took her hand, "Only if you make me supper."

"A deal," Amy retorted, "I hope you like scrambled eggs?"

"My favorite. Can I have toast with that?"

Chapter 30

S HANE WAS HOME the next week-end and on the Saturday, he took his
mother with him when he left the ranch. Amy was glad to see Laura
get off the ranch for a day. Maybe she would get her shopping done
with Shane's help.

Undecided about Christmas, Amy pondered if she should phone her
mother. She had heard from Leslie that Ed had completely disappeared and
the authorities thought he was probably overseas somewhere. So Gladys was
out the money. Leslie said Gladys had tried to sue the bank for cashing the
cheque, but it didn't look too promising. Amy wondered how her mother
was making out financially. She could give her some money if Gladys would
accept it, but Amy doubted it. Maybe she would phone, just to see what
kind of a reception she got.

The phone rang several times, but no one answered. She must be out,
Amy thought, as she replaced the receiver. She would try later.

Amy was sure Ivan would have an invitation to the ranch house for
Christmas day, but she doubted she would. Not to embarrass the family,
Amy thought she would plan to be away, even if it was only into town. They
wouldn't know the difference. She would leave her presents for them the
night before.

Amy dressed up and headed out to the barns. Shane had fed the ewes
before he left, but she wanted to check on the cat family and fill the water
trough. The rams had plenty of feed so they were okay.

While out there, she decided to clean up the tack/lunch room. Over the summer it had gotten totally neglected. The fridge needed cleaned and the floor scrubbed. Amy stripped off her jacket and put the kettle on to heat some water while she swept up. She cleaned the fridge first, then grabbed a mop and pail and got at the floor. She was busy scrubbing away and humming to herself. All of a sudden, she felt someone watching her. Before she could react, the mop was taken from her.

"Just what do you think you are doing?" Ivan demanded, "You'll freeze your hands doing that."

Amy grabbed her mop back, "Mind your own business, Ivan Johnson! You are entirely too bossy. They are my hands and I'll freeze them if I want to!"

Ivan grinned and grabbed Amy's hand. "See! I told you they are freezing. Don't you have enough to do without making work?"

Ivan's big warm hands covering hers did feel really good. Her hands had been cold but she was determined to finish the job. "If you're so worried about my hands, why don't you finish mopping?"

"Do you think I'm crazy? A good way to develop arthritis in my hands. No thanks. Come on; leave it. It will only get tracked up again. Are the chores all done?"

"Yes, Shane fed the ewes before he and Laura left. Do you know where they went?"

"I'm not sure. Shane said something about Laura getting her hair cut and then some shopping."

"Good. I'm glad she went for a change."

"So what are your plans for the rest of the day?"

"I haven't made any; why?"

"How about supper and a movie? Romancing the Stone is showing in town."

"I've heard that is a good movie. Sounds good. Can you give me a while to clean up?"

"I'll be back at 4:30. That way we can have an early supper and catch the first feature."

Ivan headed out the door, carrying Amy's bucket. I guess that ends my cleaning, Amy thought to herself as she put the mop away. I'll just have to get to it another day.

≫ ≪

Over supper in town, Ivan asked Amy what her plans were for Christmas. Amy hedged a bit, then admitted she didn't have any.

"I've been trying to get hold of my mother, but she's not answering. I don't know if I should be heading to the Hat or not. She wasn't very friendly the last time I talked with her. But I know if I don't make an effort, she will be mad, so what is a person to do?"

"Why don't I take you home for Christmas? What would your mother say?"

Amy started to laugh, "I know exactly what she would say; Where did you snag him? He's way too good for you."

Ivan puffed out his chest, "See how special I am?"

"Seriously," Amy sobered, "Laura will expect you to spend Christmas with them."

"She hasn't asked me yet. So first come, first served."

"I would never want to interfere in Laura's plans especially if she isn't well."

"I guess you're right. Why don't we go to Medicine Hat before Christmas?"

Amy thought about that, then said, "If Laura will give me next weekend off, okay. But Shane would have to be home. Let's clear it with Shane first."

"Sounds good. We'd better hurry now or we will miss the start of the movie."

The movie was great. Amy and Ivan thoroughly enjoyed themselves. Ivan had his arm around her and they shared a bucket of popcorn. Amy was sad when it ended. They walked out holding hands. The night was cold and the stars were clear.

"It's going to freeze hard tonight," Ivan commented as he unlocked the truck.

The trip home took no time at all. Amy had snuggled next to Ivan to keep warm and when they parked in front of Amy's trailer, she was reluctant to leave the truck. Ivan killed the motor and put his arm around her. She next thing she knew, they were locked in a tight embrace. Amy ran her fingers through Ivan's hair and he held her tight against him. He tipped her face up to his and very slowly traced her lips with his thumb. Little thrills went through Amy's body. She started to feel weak in the knees again and was glad she was sitting.

"Ivan, stop; you're making me crazy."

"I'm making you crazy?! You've been driving me crazy since I first met you. I want to kiss you and hold you, and make love to you. Please don't ask me to stop." and with that Ivan lowered his lips on to hers. Amy responded. It felt so good to be held and kissed by Ivan. He was a good kisser. But things had gone far enough.

"Okay, okay!" Amy gasped as she came up for air, "We'd better slow down or we'll be doing something we can't back out of."

Reluctantly, Ivan sat back. He sighed and put both hands on the steering wheel. "You're right. It's just so hard to hold myself back from you. You'd better make up your mind pretty soon. For now, you'd better get out of this truck before I ravish you. Do you want me to walk you to your door?"

"Don't be silly. It's only six steps. I'll see you soon." With that, Amy reached over and squeezed Ivan's arm, then slid out of the truck and ran to the trailer. She paused before opening the door and looked back. Ivan was watching her. He raised his hand and started the truck and backed away. Feeling devilish, Amy blew him a kiss, then went inside.

Happy Cat greeted her with a meow and started rubbing against her leg.

"Did I forget to feed you? I'm sorry, you poor cat. I'd better get my head straightened out pretty soon, or we'll all suffer. What do you think? You like Ivan, don't you? But then, you like anyone who will pay attention to you and feed you."

The cat purred and headed to the cupboard. Amy had to laugh to herself. Nothing was on that cat's mind but food!

Yes, she wished she could just tell Ivan the whole story and 'let the chips fall where they may'. He might consider her damaged goods and not want to take a chance on a wife who probably can't have children. She knew Ivan loved kids so he probably wanted some. Then a thought struck Amy. She could tell Ivan about her past; she just didn't need to tell him the child she had grew up to be Shane Collins. That way, if he accepted her after knowing she had a teen pregnancy, he shouldn't be too upset when he finds out about Shane.

The more Amy thought about it, the more sense it made. She wasn't going to be able to hold Ivan off that much longer. He as a strong, virile man and wanted a wife. She was having a hard time resisting the urge to throw caution to the wind and tell Ivan she would marry him. It just wouldn't be fair to Ivan not to tell him about her past.

After her marriage to Raymond, Amy wasn't sure she really knew what love was. She was smitten with Raymond and his good looks and personality and look where it got her! Well, she knew it wasn't Ivan's good looks; he was not exceptionally handsome. He had a strong rugged look to him, but his nose was too big, He did have a strong chin. Amy had to smile. What she liked most about him was his sense of humor and his head of thick blond hair. He kept it closely cropped on the sides, but it was thick and full on the top. She also loved the way he teased her. So, did that constitute love on her part? She just didn't know.

Yes, before they went to Medicine Hat, she would tell him about her past. Then if he accepted that, she would accept his marriage proposal.

Chapter 31

AMY FINALLY TALKED to her mother the next day. When she asked her how she was doing, Gladys responded, "Why do you care? You haven't seen fit to call me or worry about me before."

"That's not true, Mom. I have tried to call you and I think you remember, the last time we talked, you told me to quit gloating and leave you alone."

"Well, you were gloating. You warned me and I wouldn't listen, so you were right. Satisfied?"

"Oh, Mom, you know I only want what's best for you. How are you doing? Financially and otherwise? I can help you out with funds."

"No need. I sold the condo."

That was news to Amy. Leslie hadn't kept her informed of that, but she and Frank were expecting any day.

"Where are you living?"

"I've moved in with Edith. She offered me a place to stay until I decide what to do. I put the furniture into storage."

"That's good you have someone. But how have you got the same phone number?"

"Edith let me install a phone line in my room. I might be here a while."

Amy laughed to herself; 'Nosy Edith' to the rescue!

"So what are you doing for Christmas?"

"Oh, Edith has a large family. So her daughter has invited us over there to Brooks. You never come home and I don't want to spend Christmas by myself."

"Well, you sound like you're all settled in. Actually, I was thinking of coming home the weekend before Christmas for a day or so."

"Don't feel you need to. I'm doing okay."

"I need to. I have someone I want you to meet."

"What? Not another man? When will you learn? Men are all pigs."

"I can understand you are feeling that way now, but Ivan is special. You'll see."

"You can't stay here. There's no room."

"I know. We'll stay at Leslie's or take hotel rooms. Bye for now. I'll see you soon."

After Amy hung up, she called Leslie's. Frank answered the phone. He told her Leslie had given birth to a seven pound, two ounce boy the day before. They were calling him Dylan Paul. Leslie would call her when she got home in a day or two.

There, Amy thought as she hung up the phone. It looks like I'd better get my act together. Everything is coming to a head and time is running out.

She checked out the window, but Shane and Laura hadn't returned from church yet. She imagined Ivan had gone too. As she sat down at the table, she mulled over her situation. She was going to have to decide about the religion issue if she was going to marry Ivan. Abe and Laura had been married for 'time and all eternity'; wasn't that what Laura said? That sure backfired for Laura. She was spending lots of time here without her husband. Amy wasn't sure she believed in all that. It wasn't that she didn't believe in God. It was just so many people were like her mother; heading to church on Sunday, like that gave them a license to do what ever they wanted the rest of the week. She realized her mother was probably not the best example, but she had shied away from any church since she grew up. Raymond didn't believe in any church and said he was an atheist. Ivan was practically raised as a Mormon and was now attending church again, so he would want to be married by his church. Amy wasn't sure she was prepared to join that church. She had heard from other people that the Mormons expected a lot from you when you joined them. They also had some kind of Bible that wasn't a Bible, but they said it was the word of God and had only been discovered recently. That was a bit hard to believe, Amy thought. Maybe she should get a copy of that Bible and read it. She would ask Shane for a copy. If she asked Ivan, he might get the idea she was more interested than she was. She would read the book, then make up her mind about the church.

When Shane left for Lethbridge that evening, Amy went to see Laura. She wanted to tell her what she had decided about Ivan.

When Laura answered the door, she looked surprised to see Amy, "I wasn't expecting company. What's on your mind?"

"I need to talk to you; about Ivan and me."

Laura stepped back and motioned for Amy to come in. "Well, talk. I'm tired and plan to go to bed early."

"Can we sit?"

Laura nodded and they both took chairs at the table. Amy glanced around the room. She missed coming over and she missed Laura's company.

"Laura, as I'm sure you know, Ivan and I have been seeing each other for some time. Ivan has asked me to marry him, but I can't accept until some things from my past are revealed. So this is what I have decided to do. I'm going to tell him I had a child when I was young. I just won't tell him that child is Shane until you say it's okay to tell him."

Laura sighed, "I'm not surprised about you and Ivan. In spite of our differences, I think you will make a good wife for Ivan. He's madly in love with you. He has dated a few other girls since Cindy, but he never seemed too impressed. I know you have to tell him about your past. Do you really think you should marry him, until you can tell him the whole truth?"

"I don't think Ivan is willing to wait that long. I don't think I am either."

"It won't be as long as you think. I told you I am sick. When I'm gone, you can tell Shane."

"Don't you think the story should come from you? He's a lot stronger than you think, and you will always be his Mom."

Tears welled up in Laura's eyes, "You're probably right. I want you to know that I misjudged you. I have had a long time to think things over and I remembered Abe telling me that he doubted his daughter even knew he was alive."

"So why didn't he try to find me after I grew up?"

"He did, but couldn't find any trace of you. He figured you had probably married, but Gladys wouldn't give him your married name. So he decided to let it go. By then, Shane was a good sized kid and Abe and I were worried if you came into the picture, it would disrupt all our lives. Who thought it would happen now?"

"I'm sorry. The last thing I want to do is cause you pain. If I could change things, I would."

"I know, I'm sorry too. I need friends right now. Can you forgive me?"

Amy got up and went to Laura. She put her arms around her and said, "Of course. I miss our friendship."

"Me, too," Laura was weeping quietly. Amy just held her until Laura finally pulled away and wiped her eyes.

"Can you tell me what your problem is?" Amy asked.

Laura stood up and walked to the counter. She turned to look at Amy and said, "I don't want Shane to know, but I have cancer. When I was in Calgary, they did a biopsy and found it was too far advanced to operate. They want to do treatments, but then Shane would have to know. I don't want that."

"But Laura, it could prolong your life. Can't you get the treatments in Lethbridge?"

"Probably, but that's a long ways."

"Ivan or I could take you. Don't you think you owe it to Shane to try to fight this thing?"

"He doesn't know I'm sick."

"I think you should tell him. But that's your decision. We could take you for treatments during the week before Shane gets home."

"I'll think about it - after Christmas."

"Please don't wait too long. You were diagnosed in August and it's now December. The cancer will have advanced a lot in that time."

"I have been praying. God will help me to get through."

"God helps those that help themselves. He wouldn't want you to be foolish."

"I appreciate your concern, but I'm tired now and have to get to bed. Thanks for listening, Amy. I hope you and Ivan settle things. How do you feel about Ivan being a Mormon? Are you okay with that?"

"I'm not sure. I was going to ask Shane for one of your bibles, but I'll ask you."

"Sure," Laura went over to the shelf by the cupboard and picked up a book, "Keep it, Amy. When you're ready, we can discuss it if you like."

"Thanks. Please take care. I've missed our chats. I'm so glad we're friends again."

"Me, too. I realized I was only hurting those I care about, but I didn't know how to break the ice. I'm so glad you came over tonight."

"See you tomorrow and thanks for the book."

Chapter 32

AMY BROKE THE news about Laura to Ivan the next time he was over. He took it really hard and Amy held him until he could get his feelings under control. Amy liked the fact that a strong, sensitive man could let his feelings show.

When Ivan could talk, he said, "What a stubborn woman! If she had only told us, we could have been getting her to treatments for the past months." Ivan sat down at Amy's table, "I guess one good thing about all this is Laura and you are talking. How did that come about?"

"I decided to go over to the ranch house and talk over a few things. Laura admitted she was wrong about me and asked me to forgive her. I think she missed me as much as I missed her."

"I'm really glad. Two of my favorite people shouldn't be estranged."

"So what are we going to do about Laura? Do you think we can persuade her to start treatments right away?"

"I doubt it. It's only a little better than a week before Christmas. Let's let her have that, then get on her case right after the New Year when Shane is back to school."

"Oh, oh, I forgot to ask her about this weekend. I told my mother I was bringing someone," Amy told Ivan about her conversation with her mother.

"It looks like she knows how to land on her feet. I hope she didn't take too much of a loss on the condo."

"She didn't say and I didn't ask or she will think I was just interested in the money."

Ivan stood up, "Well, I'm off to the ranch house. I want to have a chat with Laura."

"I have to get out and do the feeding anyway. I'll see you later."

Laura answered the door as soon as Ivan knocked. "I figured you'd be up shortly, when I saw you go to Amy's this morning."

"You figured right. What? Am I not a good enough friend or trustworthy enough to confide in?"

"Oh, Ivan; it's not like that. I hadn't planned to tell anyone, but it just sort of came out last night."

"I'm not upset about you telling Amy, for heaven's sake. I'm upset because you didn't tell us sooner, so we could help you through this. You should have been having treatments a long time ago. Is that the sole reason you went to Calgary?"

"No. I wanted to see my sister, too. The doctor in Lethbridge sent me up there and scheduled me for the biopsy. I am terminal, but with the pills I've been taking, the doctor in Lethbridge is amazed at how well I'm doing. They are experimental but seem to help. I take them for four days, then quit for four days. I find they make me really tired and I have no appetite, but no other side affects."

"So will you start treatments after the New Year?"

"We'll discuss it then."

"I'm holding you to it."

Laura laughed and said, "You always were bossy. But I love you. Talking of love, things are heating up between you and Amy, I hear."

"Oh? What did she tell you?"

"That you asked her to marry you."

"What did she say about that?"

"Now, that's private, but you know how I feel about you both. I know I said some things, but I was upset. Amy will make you a great wife."

"I know it and you know it, but she is still holding out."

"Amy has some issues to work out. But she asked for a Book of Mormon when she was here."

"She did?!"

"Oh, she called it that other bible, but I think that is a good sign she is interested. You should ask her to come to church with you."

"I'm not sure I want to do that just yet. I don't want anything to jinx my chances with her."

"Amy loves you. I don't think you should wait too long to get married if she agrees. The worst that could happen is you will have to be sealed later if she joins the church. I want to see you two married, even if it's just a civil ceremony."

"Tell Amy that. Well, I have to go feed my cows. You rest and if you need anything from town, Amy or I will get it for you."

Laura came over and gave Ivan a hug. "You always were like a son to me. I have two sons and now, maybe I will gain a daughter."

"From your lips to God's ears," Ivan answered as he headed out the door.

Chapter 33

S HANE WAS COMING home for the weekend and when Amy asked Laura if she could go to Medicine Hat, Laura was happy to let her go. When Ivan was mentioned, Laura asked if it was a good thing for Ivan to meet her mother. Amy had laughed and said that Ivan was a good judge of character and could make his own opinions.

On the Thursday night, Amy asked Ivan to come over to the trailer for supper. She cooked a little roast and put some vegetables around it. She even made an Apple Crisp for dessert. She wanted the evening to be special, because she had decided to tell Ivan about her past. If he accepted that, then she would tell him she would marry him.

She dressed up with her nicest dress and put on a little perfume. She left her hair loose and hoped it wouldn't get in the food. While waiting for Ivan, she made a salad and put it in the fridge.

Ivan wasn't there at 6:00 PM. Amy turned the oven off and hoped he wouldn't be too late. Good practice for a rancher's wife, she thought. Things do come up.

Ivan arrived at 6:30 PM, all apologetic. One of his cows had slipped and dislocated her hip, so he had to get her into the vet. Things were very busy there and by the time he got home and cleaned up, it was already late. To make matters worse, the battery went dead on his cell phone so he couldn't call her.

"No problem," Amy said as she kissed him and led him to the table, "Just sit down and I will get everything on the table."

"Something sure smells good in here and I'm not just talking about the food."

Ivan couldn't take his eyes off Amy. She was beautiful. Her hair was loose and her cheeks were flushed from the oven. She had on a dress that accented her good figure. Ivan wondered what all this was about. Amy didn't often invite him to the trailer; he usually just showed up. When Amy set the bowl of vegetables and plate of beef on the table, Ivan caught a scent of 'Evening Musk' perfume.

Amy sat down, then looking at Ivan, asked him to bless the food. Surprised, he looked across at her, then obliged.

"There, let's eat," Amy said as she passed the meat to Ivan, "I'm famished."

The food was good and as they ate, they chatted about ranch business. Ivan explained about his cow and how the vet fixed it up. He said he would probably ship her after this summer, as these injuries don't usually just go away without complications. Amy mentioned the preparations she had helped Laura with for Christmas. Since their reconciliation, Laura had asked Amy and Ivan to join her and Shane on Christmas day. Amy had only agreed if Laura would let her help. So today, they had made shortbread and some pies. Laura seemed grateful for the help, Amy told Ivan.

Ivan ate the last of his Apple Crisp and sat back. "Now, that was a meal fit for a king. So what are you fattening me up for? Should I be worried?"

"I hope not," laughed Amy, "I'll get this mess cleaned up, then we can relax."

"We'll get the mess cleaned up. You wash, I'll wipe." Ivan stood up and took his plate and Amy's, "You put the food away; you know where it goes."

With everything cleaned up and Ivan relaxing on the sofa petting Happy Cat, Amy was reluctant to start, but the whole plan for the evening was to come clean so she cleared her throat and said, "I invited you here tonight for a reason."

"Come sit beside me," Ivan patted the sofa and moved Happy Cat to his knee.

"No, it's better I say what I have to say standing. You may not want me sitting beside you after that."

Oh, oh, Ivan thought; here it comes. She's going to kiss me off; fatten me up, then kiss me off.

Amy looked at Ivan and saw the stricken look on his face. I'd better get on with it before he gets the wrong idea, Amy thought, so she spoke quietly, "You remember I told you I wouldn't accept your proposal of marriage before I could come clean and tell you about my past?"

"I remember," Ivan responded.

"Well, I have decided to tell you. You may withdraw the proposal after if you wish."

Ivan didn't say anything so Amy went on, "When I was fifteen years old, I became pregnant from a one night stand. My mother couldn't deal with it, so sent me to a home for unwed mothers in Calgary. I gave birth there and the baby was put up for adoption. I never knew if I had a son or a daughter. I had to return to my mother as I was a minor. When I was eighteen, I took out a student loan and went to beauty school in Calgary. You know the rest of the story, except for the fact my ex-husband and I could never have children. I realize it was for the best now, but it was probably my fault. The specialists think having a child when I was so young and having a difficult birth could be the reason. So I probably will never be able to have a child."

Ivan hadn't said a word while Amy was talking When she finished, he set Happy Cat on the sofa and got up. Amy was sure he was leaving, but he come over to her and took her in his arms.

"You poor kid. You did have a rough time. Having a child and having to give it up. Did you ever try to find it later?"

Amy snuggled into Ivan's arms, so happy he was taking this so well, "Yes, I did a time or two, but it's pretty hard." She couldn't tell him she had found him.

"When we are married, we'll look for your child," Ivan stated as he drew her closer, "You will marry me?"

"If you still want me, knowing all this."

Ivan beamed, "Of course, I still want you! What kind of guy do you think I am? Your past is your past. I have one too." He bent down and kissed her boldly on the lips, "Yahoo!! You just made me the happiest guy in all Alberta! When can we get married?"

Amy pushed him away a little and laughed, "I'm glad you're happy. I'm happy, too. But we have a few things to discuss before we set a date."

"Anything is fine with me. You set a date and I'll be there. Oh, except try not to make it during calving. I want to be able to spend time with my bride."

"And it can't be during lambing, so it will have to be before or after."

"I start calving the middle of February. So looks like it will have to be a New Year's wedding. I don't plan to wait until May!"

"We have to discuss other things, too; like Laura and her treatments and where we'll be married."

"I've been doing some thinking about Laura. I have a good friend in Lethbridge that I went on my mission with. I'm sure Laura could stay at their place while taking chemo. I'll check with them and Laura. As to where we get married, I'll leave that up to you. We haven't really discussed my church so it's your choice. Laura did tell me you got a Book of Mormon from her."

Amy nodded, "I've been reading it, but there's a lot I don't understand. While we're going to Medicine Hat, you can explain some of it to me."

"That's a deal. Now, let's go tell Laura the good news. I know she'll be happy for us."

Laura was indeed happy and gave both Ivan and Amy a hug. She was even more happy when she found out they planned to marry right away.

"How about a New Year's Eve wedding, a private affair, right here at the ranch? Bishop Lang could do the service."

Amy objected, "That's too much work for you, Laura. Besides, I don't know if I want to be married by your church. I thought we'd get a Justice of the Peace."

"You wouldn't be making any commitment, Amy. Only if you are married in the Temple. Our bishops are licensed, just like a Justice of the Peace, so you would be married by the laws of Alberta."

Ivan nodded, "That's true."

"Okay," Amy agreed, "but I don't want Laura doing any extra work. Couldn't we be married at your ranch instead?"

"Nonsense! This is a much bigger house. Shane will be home over the holidays and he will help. He will be so happy for you two. He thinks the world of both of you."

Amy and Ivan finally agreed. Ivan phoned Bishop Lang to see if he would be free on New Year's Eve, so it was all settled when he said he was. Laura told them to make up a guest list, but no more than twenty people, which suited them just fine. Other than Frank and Leslie, she really didn't have anyone special to ask. She had asked Laura to stand up with her and Ivan planned to ask Shane to be best man.

Laura seemed to really perk up as they made plans. Maybe this is what she needs, Amy thought; something to look forward to.

It was getting late, so everyone headed home with the promise to get together soon to make final plans.

Chapter 34

THE TRIP TO Medicine Hat was wonderful. Amy and Ivan had a good discussion about many issues, the church being one of them. Amy agreed to go to church with Ivan to see what she thought. Spending three hours in church on a Sunday seemed a bit much to her, but she was willing to give it a try. If Ivan thought it was important, she could deal with that. Ivan in turn, promised not to pressure her into anything.

The visit with her mother went better than she expected. Gladys was trying her best. She was full of talk about the new minister at her church. He was very young and so good-looking. She told Amy she should be 'back in the city where she could snag some young executive instead of wasting time on that ranch. She was no country girl.' Amy was embarrassed, but Ivan spoke up.

"Mrs. Stern, I beg to differ. Amy is a model country girl. She can wrestle sheep, deliver lambs, stack bales and drive any tractor on the ranch. Before long, I suspect she will be helping me deliver calves. Yep, she's no delicate city girl, our Amy."

Gladys had sputtered and then said, "I wasn't putting you down really; I just thought Amy would be happier back in the city."

"I'm perfectly happy," Amy had answered, "Ivan is exactly what I want in a husband. He's kind, gentle, funny and he loves me."

"Hey, don't give me a swelled head," Ivan had responded.

"So you are planning to marry this guy?" Gladys had turned to Amy and asked.

Ivan spoke up, "I love your daughter, Mrs. Stern. After we are married, we would like you to visit the ranch. We're really quite modern."

"That won't happen," Gladys had answered abruptly, "and I won't be at your wedding. I can't travel that far. So I'll give you your wedding present now."

She got up and went to her room, and came back with a box which she presented to Amy. Inside was a set of Royal Albert china. Amy recognized them.

"Mom, you don't want to part with these. You've had them as long as I remember."

"Your father gave them to me and I no longer have any use for them. Maybe you can use them, if you ever entertain out there at the ranch."

"Thank you, Mrs. Stern. We'll take good care of the set," Ivan had answered.

"Call me Gladys," Amy's mother had answered.

They had left Gladys around 5:00 PM with the promise to see her in the morning before church. Ivan had made a 7:00 PM reservations at a fancy restaurant so they went to the hotel and got freshened up. They also made plans to see Leslie and the new baby on Sunday before they headed back to Milk River.

It was at the restaurant, between the main course and dessert that Ivan gave Amy an engagement ring.

"When did you have time to shop for this?" Amy had asked him and he had replied, "I've had that ring since my trip to Montana. That's how determined I was to marry you."

"Well, I'm glad it wasn't Cindy's," Amy had teased him, to which Ivan had retorted, "I wouldn't do a sleazy thing like that." They had both laughed and then Ivan said, "Besides, it would be a bit hard to find it. I threw it away in one of those coulees behind the Collins ranch."

They had a quick visit with Leslie on the Sunday. Leslie was thrilled for Amy, but scolded her for holding out. "She never said a word," she informed Ivan.

Ivan was busy holding Dylan. He looked so natural with the baby in his arms. Amy wondered if she was doing the right thing, depriving him of the chance to have children. Maybe she should start praying for a miracle.

Chapter 35

CHRISTMAS EVE WAS Amy's birthday and Ivan hadn't forgotten. He took her out to a fancy restaurant and presented her with a lovely watch. He also apologized for not having a birthday party for her, but had run out of time. Amy didn't mind. There was just so much going on with the wedding in a week's time.

Christmas Day was the best ever for Amy. Laura was feeling good and Shane was full of mischief. He was so excited about the New Year's eve wedding and took advantage of the opportunity to tease Amy and Ivan at every turn. They loved the attention and were both happy to see Laura looking so well.

Laura gave Amy a beautiful sweater and Shane gave her a nice pair of gloves. From Ivan, she got a set of earrings and necklace to match. They were gold with tiny heart-shaped diamonds on them.

"Ivan, you shouldn't have. That's way too expensive."

"Don't you like it?"

"It's beautiful, but I don't want you buying me expensive gifts. The ring was enough."

"I want you to wear those at our wedding."

Amy agreed and then thought, she still had to shop for a dress the next week.

She gave Shane a briefcase for his schooling and to Ivan, a heavy denim jacket for doing chores. In the pocket, she had tucked a watch. For Laura she gave a warm chair comforter for the evenings. Laura said it was just what she needed when the evenings were cool, watching TV. Amy was thinking ahead to the days when Laura wouldn't be well.

The week between Christmas and New Year's was the busiest ever. Shane was home so he took over all Amy's chores so she could concentrate on getting ready for the wedding. Laura felt well enough one day to accompany Amy to Lethbridge to shop for dresses. Amy finally purchased a peach-colored ankle length dress with long sleeves and a heart shaped neckline. The skirt was A-line. It was made out of silk and draped beautifully. Laura thought Amy looked like a dream.

"What do you plan to do with your hair for the wedding?" she asked Amy.

"I don't know. What do you suggest?"

"I have a friend who is a hair dresser. She could do your hair. It would be my treat."

"Thank you. Now let's get your dress. What do you have in mind?'

"Something elegant, but simple. Nothing low-cut for me."

"Okay, let's get shopping."

Amy didn't see much of Ivan during the week before the wedding. He had stopped over a couple of times and said he was working hard to get all his chores caught up so he would be able to spend time with her after they were married. They had discussed plans for a honeymoon but decided they were both needed at the ranches so would put that off. Amy was glad Ivan had agreed with her as she didn't want to leave Laura with the burden of the chores and everything. Amy knew Laura was trying hard, but she would see the strain the activities had on her. Amy would be glad when the wedding was over and they could get Laura for treatments. They had told Laura they would be staying around after and she seemed relieved. Their plans were to move to Ivan's ranch after the wedding and return everyday to do the chores and whatever needed done. Ivan said they could work together which Amy was happy about. Ivan had a way of making the time so much more fun. They discussed lambing time with Laura and she agreed that Ivan and Amy could move back to the trailer for the duration and Ivan would drive back to his ranch everyday to feed and check things.

The 'soon-to-be-newlyweds' hoped they had everything worked out. Now they just had to convince Laura to start her treatments. Ivan had talked with his friends, the Mullek's in Lethbridge and they were only too happy to help. They said they would take her to the clinic every day for her treatments. Ivan and/or Amy would drive her up Monday morning and pick her up Thursday afternoon after her last treatment. The treatments would be in three sessions a month apart. Laura had checked with her Doctor to find out the schedule, but hadn't committed herself any further.

Laura had hired a girl from her church to help her and plans were progressing nicely for the wedding. The girl, Sarah had vacuumed, dusted and then put up decorations. The sofa, chairs and accent tables had been moved to one side. In their place would be chairs that Ivan had borrowed from the church. The guest list was 23 people including the bride and groom. Amy's side of the list only included Leslie and Frank but they had called to say they wouldn't be able to make it as the baby was having some breathing problems. They promised to come out to visit after things settled down in the New Year. Of course, Amy knew her mother wasn't coming so all the guests would be friends of Ivan and Laura That didn't bother Amy at all. She wasn't even thrilled at having a wedding. She would have been just as happy going to the Justice of the Peace and being quietly married; but Ivan and Laura seemed to want this so she went along. She would just be really glad when the day was over.

The day before the wedding, Amy and Laura, with Sarah's help, were busy cooking and baking. The kitchen smelled wonderful and Laura's cheeks were flushed from the oven heat. Worried that she was overdoing it, Amy made her sit once the pies were in the oven. Sarah had finished the salads so all was ready. Since she had plans for the evening, Sarah left early. Amy was glad as she wanted to talk with Laura.

Wiping her hands on the towel, Amy turned to Laura, "How are you holding up?"

"I'm okay. I took a pill this morning and they always make me tired. I'll be better by tomorrow."

"I hope so. I don't want you doing anything tomorrow. The girls Ivan hired to serve and look after things will arrive by noon. With the wedding at 4:00 PM and the reception at 5:30 PM, they have lots of time to prepare everything. With the salads and desserts all made, they should have no problems.

If they do, Shane, Ivan or I will handle it. You'll be able to rest for a while in the afternoon. What time is our hair appointments in the morning?"

"Angie said to try to be there by 11:00 AM. She will do my hair first and while I'm drying, she will work with yours and let you see different styles."

"I'm sure whatever she does will look great."

"Oh, and while we have a chance to talk, I wanted to tell you, I have decided to take the treatments. There are three sessions so I should be done in time for lambing."

Amy hugged Laura, "I'm so glad you decided to take the treatments. You know Ivan has made plans for you so with any luck, Shane doesn't need to know."

"That's what I'm banking on. I know my son and if he thought I was sick, he would drop out of school and come home."

"Well, we can't let him do that. Everything will work out, you'll see."

Chapter 36

N EW YEAR'S EVE dawned cold and clear. The temperature had dipped down to -20 degrees Celsius, but the sun was shining. Ivan called at 9:00 AM to say good morning and to see if Amy had any last minute doubts.

"Not on your life; you're stuck with me, Ivan Johnson!"

Ivan laughed, "That's music to my ears. I can hardly wait until 4:00 PM. I want to be able to say, 'Meet my wife, Amy Johnson. Sounds good, doesn't it?"

"Not half as good as; 'Meet my husband, Ivan Johnson."

"Keep that thought and I'll see you soon."

The night before, they had a brief rehearsal and Laura had served punch and cookies after. The Bishop seemed very nice and had welcomed Amy and invited her to attend church with Ivan. Amy had already decided to go with Ivan. She wanted to check things out for herself. The wedding ceremony would be very precise and not one that Amy felt uncomfortable with.

After Ivan's call, Amy finished dressing and tidied up the trailer. She already had her suitcase packed for spending the night at Ivan's. She laughed to herself. She was going to have to learn to call the ranch her home soon. For some reason, it just didn't seem a reality yet. Maybe after she moved in she would be more at ease with the thought. In a day or two they would come back to the ranch and move some more things. They would have to do chores anyway, as soon as Shane left to go back to school. Amy planned to keep an eye on Laura. The next Monday was the day she started her treatments. That was only three days away and she didn't want Laura making any excuses not to go.

Shane was busy doing the chores when Amy and Laura left for the hair-dressers. Laura's color wasn't the best and Amy kept glancing at her as she drove. She prayed Laura would be okay.

The hairdresser, whose name was Susie, was waiting for them and after the introductions, she started on Laura's hair, while chatting away to both of them. She handed Amy a magazine and told her to be looking through it for any style she might have in mind for her hair. Amy laughed, "I'm not too smart about what looks good on me. I think I will have to leave that up to you, but I will look anyway."

"You have gorgeous hair. The only other person whose hair I cut that was that color was your husband, Laura. He had such thick auburn hair. He always wanted me to thin it out and it was such a shame."

Amy glanced at Laura, but she was taking it well and replied to Susie, "I know. He always wanted to look like a scalped chicken and we argued over that. I liked his thick hair. Amy is fortunate to have such nice hair. I wish mine was a little thicker. If it gets any thinner, I will be bald!"

"Oh, you're not bald yet, Laura. You still have enough hair to get all fixed up. You'll be a knock-out."

The morning went quickly and when the two women left the salon, they were both quite happy with their hair. Amy had elected to leave the back flowing down her back, and Susie had swept the sides up and cascaded the curls down the back. She had inserted flowers and ribbons in the sides and top and let the ribbons flow down the back. They were the same color as her dress. She also handed Amy a small bouquet to match for her to carry. It was just perfect in Amy's mind and Laura thought she looked just beautiful. And so much like her Dad, it brought tears to Laura's eyes.

As Amy was going to dress for the wedding at the main ranch house, she hurried down to the trailer and picked up her dress and cosmetics that she would need. She grabbed a quick sandwich, even though she wasn't hungry, but she didn't want her stomach to start growling in the middle of the ceremony. When she arrived at the main house, she could see the girls had arrived and were getting things set up for the reception. Laura had retired to her room to have a rest. Amy sat on the sofa and mentally started going over the list to be sure nothing had been forgotten. In about two hours, the first guests would start arriving, so she wanted everything to be ready.

Shane came in from outside and grabbing a sandwich from the kitchen, came into the room. He spotted Amy on the sofa and migrated that way.

"So, are you all ready, or are you running scared yet?"

Amy laughed and punched Shane on the arm, "Do I look like I'm running away? I was just going over everything to be sure we haven't forgotten anything. Maybe you had better check on the groom. He's the one that might have second thoughts."

"Not on your life. Ivan would never run out. He's been waiting too long for the right woman. And you are that woman. Actually, I'm heading over there right now. I have to help the groom get dressed, just in case he has forgotten how."

"Boy, you are lucky Ivan isn't here or he would punch you out, inferring he doesn't know how to dress. Maybe he is coming in his jeans and western shirt."

"I doubt that. Even he can get away from the ranch for a bit," Shane replied, "I bet he will be so dolled up, you won't know him."

"That's no good. I want a man I can recognize," Amy teased back as she got up from the sofa. "I think I will just head to the spare room and make sure I have everything I need. You be sure the groom isn't late for the wedding."

"You can count on me," Shane responded as he headed out the door, "See you at 4:00 pm."

The guests started arriving at 3:30. Laura was up and dressed and had helped Amy with her dress. She persuaded Amy to stay in the bedroom until time for the ceremony. She and Shane were greeting the guests and getting everyone seated. Amy couldn't hear Ivan's voice, but she assumed he must be there or Shane would have said something.

Amy looked at her reflection in the mirror. She did look good. The dress she picked was a perfect match for her coloring. Her hair magnified the color and made her cheeks glow. Or maybe it is all the excitement and hustle.

"I sure hope I am doing the right thing," Amy spoke aloud to her reflection. "I feel a bit remorse, not being able to tell Ivan the whole truth. I sure hope Laura decides to tell Shane soon so I can clear my conscience."

Biting her lip, Amy picked up the bottle of musk perfume she had brought over and dapped a bit on her neck. It was nearly 4:00 PM and Laura would be back at any minute.

"Dear God, I pray I am doing the right thing. Help me to be a good wife to Ivan and helpful to Laura in her trials."

When the knock came, Amy was ready and joined a smiling Laura as they walked out to the living room.

A gasp ran through the room as Amy appeared in the doorway. Her eyes searched the room and finally spotted Ivan. Amy couldn't believe her eyes. He was indeed dressed to the nines. He had on a charcoal grey suit with a white shirt. He also was wearing a tie that wasn't a western one. He did look good and he was staring at her. Then he winked and smiled.

The music started and Amy walked slowly down the aisle between the chairs, following Laura. When she reached the front where Ivan and the Bishop stood, Ivan reached over and took her hand. He leaned over and whispered in her ear, "Wow!"

Amy blushed and dropped her eyes. Shane was grinning from ear to ear. Amy felt very special at the moment and grateful to have so many people care about her.

The ceremony was short and concise and when the Bishop announced them husband and wife and told Ivan to kiss his bride, the guests all cheered and hollered. Ivan took Amy's arm and turning her to face him, gently kissed her on the lips. He gave her a squeeze and said, "You are the most beautiful bride, and now you are my wife. I am the luckiest man in the world!"

Amy smiled up at Ivan and replied, "You're not so bad yourself."

By this time, the guests were crowding around. Laura and Shane were introducing each one to her when Ivan was occupied. One elderly gentleman kissed Amy on the cheek and told her, "I thought that old confirmed bachelor was never going to get married, but here he had you hidden all this time. He was holding out on us."

Amy laughed and shook his hand, while others were gathering around. Everyone was friendly. Some were from Ivan's church and some were close neighbors. A surprise to Ivan was the arrival of his friend Ace and his family from Montana. It was a wonderful afternoon. Ivan was very attentive to Amy and made sure she knew everyone. Laura looked happy and was holding up well.

At exactly 5:30 PM., the girls announced that the reception was ready and everyone sat down to a scrumptious smorgasbord of good cooking. Shane gave a toast to the bride and groom, and Ivan's friend gave a bit of a roast to Ivan. It was all in good fun and the house resounded with laughter. Laura was thoroughly enjoying herself, but Amy could see she was tiring. After the meal was cleared away, she whispered to Ivan and he stood up and replied to the toasts and roast and then thanked everyone for coming. He welcomed them all to visit at the ranch when he and Amy got settled in.

Soon people started leaving and Amy headed to the kitchen to thank the girls for the wonderful job they did. They blushed and told her it was their privilege to serve at the wedding. They commented on how nice she looked and she thanked them. The girls were ready to head out the door. Amy was glad they had cleaned everything up so Laura wouldn't have to.

As the last guest left, Ivan closed the door and returned to the living room. He moaned as he looked at all the chairs and furniture to be returned to normal. Shane noticed and came over and poked Ivan in the arm.

"Hey, you newly-wed. Get your bride and get out of here. This is my job. Jack is coming over in the morning and he will help me get everything back to normal. You two get out of here."

"Thanks, old buddy. You are a life-saver. Thanks for all your help these last few days. It gave Amy and I time to get other things done. Where's your Mom? I want to thank her, too."

"The last time I saw her, she was heading to her room. Probably to change. Do you want me to call her?"

"No, I'll check on her. She's probably tired after all the excitement."

Ivan hoped that was all that was wrong. He had glanced at her several times during the reception and she seemed to be okay, but Laura was good at hiding how she felt. As Amy came out of the kitchen, Ivan strode over to her and together, they headed to Laura's room. At the knock on the door, Laura told them to come in. She was sitting on the bed and had her housecoat on.

"What are you two still doing here? You should be on your way."

"We just wanted to check on you and to thank you for everything. The wedding was just beautiful. You are a wonderful hostess," Amy said as she sat beside Laura, "How are you feeling?"

"I'm a little tired, but very happy. You two were meant to be together. You are such a handsome couple. I feel like you are my children."

Ivan came over and kissed Laura on the cheek, "Well, in some ways, we are your children. You were always like a mother to me. I love you dearly."

"Okay, okay, enough mush. You two get out of here and enjoy your honeymoon, even if it is just at the ranch."

Ivan laughed, "We're leaving. Shane said he and Jack will clean up the living room in the morning, so you just rest. We will see you tomorrow. Remember, you and Shane are coming for supper. It's New Year's day and we don't want you working."

"You and Amy need some time to yourselves. You don't need us over there tomorrow."

"We have the rest of our lives to have time to ourselves. You are family, and family spends special holidays together, so don't argue."

"Okay."

Amy kissed Laura and wished her a good night. Laura squeezed her hand and hugged her back. Amy felt a lump coming in her throat so she quickly turned and followed Ivan out the door.

Chapter 37

THE SUN STREAMING in the bedroom window awoke Amy and she stretched and rolled over. When her eyes opened, she wondered where she was for a moment, then remembered. She glanced over to the other side of the bed, but the pillow was empty. "I wonder what time it is?" Amy mused aloud. "I didn't even hear Ivan leave." She sat up on the side of the bed and grabbed her housecoat and slippers and moved over to look out the window. She could see Ivan down by the barns. He was in the corral and it looked like he was checking cows. Amy smiled to herself as she remembered the night.

When they had arrived at the ranch, Ivan had insisted on carrying her over the threshold. He had kicked the door closed with his heel and carried her all the way into the living room before he set her down. "Just in case you decide to bolt, you are further from the door," he had said. He then told her to stay there while he headed up the stairs. A few moments later, he came back down and beckoned to her to come. A wonderful surprise met her when she walked into the bedroom. Candles were glowing softly on the dresser and in their glow, she could see rose petals strewn around the bed and on to the floor. A single red rose lay on her pillow. On the nightstand was a bottle of non-alcoholic apple cider and two glasses. "For a toast to each other" he had said. Amy had been very touched at his romantic gesture.

Ivan turned out to be a very gentle and compassionate lover. Amy couldn't believe how happy she felt. No one deserves to be this happy, she thought as she turned from the window and headed down the stairs.

In the kitchen, she found a note on the table with a rose laying beside it. As Amy read it, she had to smile again. It was a beautiful poem, thanking her for being his wife. As she read the poem, smiles turned to tears. She wiped them away and then she noticed something written on the back. It said, "Breakfast is ready; just pop it in the oven and I will be in shortly to eat with you. Love, Ivan."

Amy opened the fridge and found a dish on the shelf. She recognized Laura's hand in the Wife Saver Casserole. She realized she was very hungry. After she put the casserole in the oven, she scurried back upstairs and headed to the shower. She wanted to be dressed and in the kitchen when Ivan came back in.

Shane and Laura arrived at 5:00 PM and they all had a wonderful time together. Amy had cooked roast beef with all the trimmings. Laura had brought dessert that was left over from the wedding. Shane was very talkative and had a great time teasing the newlyweds. On one trip to the kitchen, Laura cornered Amy and asked her if she was happy. Amy turned and hugged her.

"I think you can see how happy I am. I don't know why I waited so long to say yes. Ivan is wonderful. He treats me like I am a Queen."

"Well, you are the queen in his world. Be good to each other and everything else will fall into place. I pray you will always be as happy as you are today."

"Me too. I was so worried I would disappoint Ivan."

"Just be yourself and you will never disappoint him."

The evening went quickly and soon Shane and Laura headed home. Amy was cleaning up the kitchen when Ivan came in and took the towel away from her.

"Enough work for my bride. I want her all to myself."

Amy grabbed the towel back, "Hey, mister, I'm not finished with that. Are you trying to boss your new wife around?"

Ivan grinned, "And it's not working, is it?"

Amy reached up and gave Ivan a kiss. He put his arms around her and drew her close. As he kissed her on the ear, he whispered, "Our bed is waiting for us. The kitchen can wait."

Amy whispered back, "What are we waiting for?"

Chapter 38

S HANE LEFT FOR school on the Sunday afternoon. Amy and Ivan went to the ranch to see him off and assure him they would be looking after the chores and checking on Laura to see if she needed anything. Of course, they didn't tell him that Laura would be heading to Lethbridge herself the next day. Ivan and Amy both planned to take her up and see her settled at Ivan's friends. One of them would pick her up on Thursday after her last treatment.

Shane and Laura had attended church that morning, but Ivan thought he would give Amy another week to settle in before he broached the topic of going to church. Officially, they were still on their honeymoon.

After Shane left, Amy and Ivan headed down to the trailer and picked up a few things to take back to the ranch. Amy planned to leave all her chore clothes at the trailer as she would be continuing to do the chores. Calving would start at the Johnson ranch in February so she would have time to move things later if she wished.

Happy Cat was purring loudly when Amy opened the door. She scooped her up and cuddled her.

"Did you miss me, you crazy cat? I miss you too. You were always there when I needed you." Amy checked her food bowl and water and refilled them both. Ivan watched her and a light bulb went on. 'That's what I can get for her! I wanted something special that she would take to. And I know just where to find one. I'll try to sneak away some day.'

Laura invited them for supper, but she looked tired so they declined, telling her they had some unpacking to do and wanted her rested for her trip the next day.

The trip to Lethbridge was uneventful and they got Laura settled in. Amy really liked Ivan's friends, the Mulleks. She had met them at the wedding and they seemed to be a loving, caring family. They welcomed Laura with open arms. They all had an early lunch together as Laura's first treatment was at 2 PM. Laura didn't eat much, but did seem to like the family, especially the young girl. Amy guessed her to be about ten years old. She was curious about Laura and why she had to get some yucky needles and Laura found that very endearing. She hugged the little girl and explained as best she could.

Amy and Ivan left right after dinner as they both had chores to do back at the two ranches. They hugged Laura goodbye and assured her that everything would be okay at the ranch so not to worry. Amy just hoped that Shane didn't call during the week. He usually didn't unless there was a problem. He would be home Friday night as usual, and Laura would be back on Thursday, so Amy hoped they could pull it off. Shane wasn't dumb and she really hoped Laura didn't get too sick. The treatments affected people differently.

Everything was fine at the Collins' ranch so they did up the chores and headed home. Amy was ready to help Ivan with his chores, but he shooed her off to the house, telling her he could handle it, if she wanted to start supper.

"Say, what is this? All of a sudden, I'm chief cook and bottle washer and you are the chore guy? I thought this was a partnership? We did everything together!"

Ivan laughed and pulled her close and hugged her. "You are so cute when you get your dander up. No, I don't think you are only my cook and housekeeper. I just thought you might like to have some time in the house to get things the way you want them. Remember, I was just an old bachelor with no idea to what goes with what. You have more decorating talents. The cows are not calving yet so it's just a matter of checking them and giving them a few round bales. I should only be about an hour. I can make supper when I get in if you want."

Amy hugged Ivan back, "Don't be silly. I was just trying to get you riled. I am quite happy to get into the house and start supper. Suddenly, I feel quite famished and am looking forward to a nice supper and relaxation with my husband later. So get your chores done!"

Ivan kissed her and whispered in her ear, "How could I get so lucky, to convince you to marry this old bachelor?"

Amy whispered back, "I was the lucky one!"

Amy and Ivan awoke to the sounds of banging and screeching. Ivan jumped out of bed and looked out the window. Amy glanced at the clock. It was 12:00 AM! What on earth! Ivan turned from the window and groaned, "Get your clothes on, Amy. Those crazy fools are chivareeing us."

"Chivaree? What's that?" Amy grabbed her housecoat and headed to the window.

"When a couple gets married, the neighbors wait until the newlyweds are in bed some night, then they all sneak over to their place. At the time when the house seems to be really quiet, they start making all kinds of racket. I can't believe they managed to sneak in here without the dog barking. He really is getting old."

"How long does the noise go on?"

"Until we open the door and invite them in."

"You're kidding!"

"Nope, so get dressed. I'll see you down stairs."

When Amy got to the living room, it was full of people. Amy recognized an odd one from the wedding, but most were strangers. Ivan started introducing them to her, but there was just too many to keep track of. Amy had never seen anything like it. The women had brought mounds of food, and the men had brought their own refreshments. Knowing Ivan was a Mormon, they had stuck mainly to pop and light drinks. Everyone came over and congratulated the couple and wished them many happy years together. Even though it was the middle of the night, Amy was starting to really enjoy herself. She had never known caring like Ivan's neighbors had for the other neighbors. Chatting with some of the other wives, she found out where they lived and about their families. They all invited her to come and visit them when she was settled in.

Several asked about Laura, as they had phoned her place to invite her to come but didn't get an answer. Amy had replied that Laura was away visiting for a few days.

The food was some of the best Amy had ever tasted. They had brought cabbage rolls, perogies, Chinese food, pizza, casserole dishes, and all kinds of desserts, from pies to cakes, and all the trimmings.

The women insisted on cleaning up everything before they left at 4:00 AM. They left all the extra food, saying a newlywed shouldn't have to be cooking when she had a husband to entertain. Amy had blushed and everyone had laughed. There had been a lot of good fun, with teasing and tormenting Ivan, but it was all in jest and Amy could tell they all thought a lot of Ivan. She was honored that they seemed to accept her so readily. One young woman came over to Amy and hugged her and said, "You must be something special to catch our most eligible bachelor. Many women have tried, me included, but he just wasn't biting. What is your secret?"

Amy had laughed and said, "Playing hard to get." which made everyone laugh.

When the last person went out the door, Ivan closed it and turned to Amy, "I'm sure glad that is over. I hope you didn't mind too much."

"Mind! I had a blast! Your neighbors are wonderful. I just know I am going to love this place."

"How about loving your husband? He sure could use a cuddle."

Amy went over and snuggled into his arms. "So all the women were chasing you but you wouldn't tumble, eh?"

"Don't believe everything you hear. There were only ten or twelve."

Amy playfully punched Ivan in the ribs, "Ten or twelve! How did you ever have time to talk to me?"

"Oh, that was all before you came on the picture. From the moment I laid eyes on you, all other women disappeared from my line of vision."

"That's nice; and you just keep it that way!"

"You can bet on that. I love you beyond reason. Let's try to get a bit of sleep before the morning comes."

Chapter 39

J ANUARY TURNED OUT to be very mild, making life easier on the two ranches. The cows would start calving in early February so Ivan was hoping the good weather would hold. With the weather moderating, the cattle were not consuming as much hay. Over at the Collins Ranch, the ewes were just on maintenance feed. Sometime in early March, a bit of grain would be added to the feed. When a ewe carries twins or triplets, Ivan had told her, the little rascals crowd her stomach something awful, so she needs more nutritious food as she can't consume as much. Amy was grateful for Ivan's experience with the sheep, as he could teach her all the extra things she needed to know. That way, she didn't have to bother Laura with all the little details.

Amy had started attending church with Ivan and found the people to be very friendly and welcoming. Ivan was reading the Book of Mormon with her, which is what his bible was called. She had learned a great many things about his church in a short time. She still wasn't sure she believed what his church believed, but she couldn't see any harm in going. At the present time, she was still trying to get settled in and adjusted to her new life on the ranch. Dealing with things from the church were the farthest from her mind. Ivan had been called to teach a class in Sunday school and that was fine with Amy. He loved being with the kids.

Shane was studying hard at school, and so far, Laura seemed to be doing okay. Shane was usually so full of his news from school on the weekends and helping Amy with the chores, he didn't seem to notice that Laura didn't

154

come out to the barns. Amy had been baking for Laura during the week so there was lots when Shane came home. Otherwise he would wonder why his mother had quit baking his favorite recipes.

One afternoon in late January, Ivan was gone for a few hours from the ranch. Amy was busy with the laundry and didn't think too much about it, as Ivan did go off once in a while, probably to the neighbors, or to check things in the pastures.

Ivan arrived home shortly after 5:00 PM. Amy was busy fixing supper when he walked into the kitchen.

"Supper will be a bit yet. I didn't get the laundry finished until a few minutes ago. I hope you don't mind."

Ivan came up behind her and kissed her on the neck, "I don't mind. You know I would wait forever for one of your delicious suppers."

"Flattery won't get you anywhere. What will get you somewhere is setting the table!"

Ivan laughed and playfully pinched her cheek. He headed to the cupboard and took down a couple of plates and two glasses. Heading into the dining area, he commented, "It sure was a beautiful day today. I decided to head over to Swartz's to check out that new bull he is so proud of. But, you know, Amy, I still think I have the better stock. So far, I seem to have a lot less trouble with calving, etc."

"What kind of cattle does he have?"

"Well, he started out with Herefords, like a lot of people did here on the range. Then twenty years ago, he imported a Limousin bull from France. It crossed well with his Herefords, but the disposition wasn't that good. Later, he incorporated some Simmental blood. Now he has bigger, hay-burning cows with poor dispositions. So now, finally he went out and purchased a red Angus bull. It will be interesting to see what he gets from his mixture."

"I can't even imagine that many breeds crossed up. I don't know anything about cattle, but are they like sheep; stronger and bigger when the breeds are crossed?"

"I would think they wouldn't be too delicate." Ivan set the dishes on the table and reached over and turned on the light. When he did so, the funniest noise came from his vest pocket.

"What on earth was that?" Amy exclaimed as she turned from the stove.

"Maybe you should come and look," Ivan responded as he started grinning from ear to ear.

"What are you up to? I don't like crazy surprises. And if you think I am going to put my hand in your vest pocket, you have another think coming!"

"Oh, don't be silly. I would never do anything to hurt you. Come here." Ivan stretched out his hand and Amy walked over and took it. Again she heard a faint snuffling noise, then a plaintive cry from the vest. Curiosity got the better of her and she reached out and pulled the pocket open. Immediately a little white and black head popped up and looking around, gave a big "Meow!"

"Oh, Ivan, it is just the cutest thing!" Amy reached into the pocket and removed the little kitten carefully. It immediately stuck it's claws into her hand and hung on for dear life. Amy cuddled it close to her chest, and the kitten nestled in tight and started purring.

"What are you going to name it?" Ivan asked.

"Is it for me?" Amy questioned as she stroked the little head.

"My gift to you," Ivan answered. "I know how much you like Happy Cat so I thought maybe you would like to have your own here on the ranch."

Amy felt tears running down her cheeks. She wiped them away and turned to Ivan and gave him a hug.

"Hey, hey, what's all the tears for? Aren't you happy with the kitten?"

"Of course I am. I'm crying because no one has ever been so nice to me. I never had a pet when growing up."

"So you deserve it. Now, you haven't answered my question. What are you going to name your kitten?"

"Is it a boy or girl?"

"I don't know. Let's have a look" Ivan picked up the kitten and tipped it over. "Looks like a little girl to me."

"I'm going to call her Cuddle Cat, Cuddles for short."

"Okay, sounds good to me. Now, maybe you can put Cuddles down and salvage the dinner that is burning."

Amy pushed the cat back into Ivan's arms and made a dash for the stove and pulled the pan off the heat.

"It's not too bad. I think we can eat it."

Ivan put the kitten in the veranda and closed the door. He headed to the bathroom to wash up. Amy got the food on the table and sat down. As she waited for Ivan, she mused over what had all happened in the last few days and wondered how she could be so lucky. She also wondered if all this happiness would last.

Chapter 40

I T WAS A Thursday evening in late January when Ivan and Amy got a surprise visit from Shane. They had just finished supper when the knock came on the door. When Ivan opened it, Shane pushed his way in and slamming his cap down on the table, turned to face them.

"So just when were you going to tell me about Mom, or were you planning to never tell me?" Shane demanded.

"Calm down, Shane," Ivan said as he put his hand on Shane's shoulder.

Shane slapped the hand away and glared at Ivan, "I will not calm down. Do you know how it would feel to have some girl at school come up to you and tell you your Mother is taking treatments for cancer and is staying with her family. Do you know how humiliating that is?"

Amy spoke up, "Shane, it was your mother's idea to keep it from you. She thought you would not go to college if you knew. She wanted to spare you all this."

Shane's face crumpled and he dropped into the chair and put his face in his hands.

"I don't know what to do. I can't lose Mom too. She is the only thing I have left. She has always been so strong; I guess I took her for granted." Big sobs racked Shane's body.

Amy moved over and put her arms around Shane. "Let it all out. It does good to let your feelings go. Remember, Laura wouldn't want you to do anything drastic. She depends on you to do the right thing. And the right thing for now, is to just go on as we have. Your mother finished her first set

157

of treatments today. She sees her doctor in three weeks and then she will know if she will need more treatments right away. It would be better if she didn't know that you found out. This way, she will try harder; try harder to keep it from you, which in turn keeps her spirits up. Do you understand what I am saying?"

Shane wiped his eyes and cleared his throat. "I guess so. It will be hard to keep it from her, though. She is very attuned to my thinking."

Ivan agreed, "It will be hard, but I'm sure you can pull it off. If she gets through these next few months, maybe she can lick this thing. We can only hope and pray. Now that you know, we will put her name on the prayer list at the temple. We didn't before in case you found out."

Shane stood up and gave Amy and Ivan a hug. "I will do my best. But one thing for sure, I will be home every weekend from now on. If Mom questions me, I will say I found playing football was interfering with my studies and I want to pass with good marks. She will buy that."

Shane left and Ivan and Amy watched him drive away. "He sure is upset. I hope he can pull it off. I wonder what he will tell Laura is the reason he is home tonight and not tomorrow. But he's a smart kid and will figure something out." Ivan smiled and headed out to check on the cows. Amy started cleaning up the supper dishes. As she worked, she thought about Laura's decision to not tell Shane. Somehow, it just didn't seem right, but she certainly wasn't going to interfere. She had learned her lesson on that one.

Chapter 41

FEBRUARY CAME IN with a bang. The first week dumped a large amount of snow in the valley and on the hills. Ivan was kept busy watching the cows as calving was about to begin. Amy took over the chores completely at the Collins ranch. True to his word, Shane was home every Friday night and he took over for the weekend. This gave Amy time to get caught up on her work at home.

Cuddle Cat had been growing like a bad weed and had taken over the house. She was mischievous and loved to play with anyone's stocking feet. She tried climbing the drapes and got strongly reprimanded for her efforts. Whenever Amy had to be away, she locked the kitten in the veranda where there was less for her to get into.

At times Amy was sure Ivan regretted giving her the kitten, as she seemed to take great pride in annoying him. When he sat in his chair, she climbed up the back and played in his hair. When he sat at his desk to do his books, she played with his feet. He finally had to close the door to get any peace. Amy found when she did the dishes, Cuddles would be climbing up her pant leg. Amy tried to convince herself that the kitten would grow out of all the pranks. She had better, or she would be banished to the barn! But Amy found her so endearing when she would settle down and cuddle next to her on the sofa. She would purr loudly and wash Amy's hand or whatever she could reach. Who couldn't love such a cute little creature?

Laura had been doing well since her treatments. The middle of February she went to see her doctor and had some tests done. He told her to come back in a month; sooner if she wasn't feeling well.

After the storm, the weather turned mild and Laura even ventured out to have a look at the ewes and offer some advice to Amy. Amy was excited to have her back out in the barn. Laura was impressed with some of the improvements Shane and Amy had done. The dogs danced around her all the time she was out.

"Okay, you dogs! You are making me dizzy. Quit with the bouncing. I missed you guys too." Laura reached down and petted each dog. They whined and pushed against her. Laura laughed, "Boy, does it feel good to be out and about."

Calving was in full swing so Amy tried to be home as soon as she could to help out. Laura understood and urged her to get along home. "Things are all fine here. I will check on the rams and let down some feed if they need it."

Amy headed home. During the drive she mulled over the changes in her life. She found that all were for the better. She called her mother every week or so, but her mother never seemed to want to talk very long. She was always rushing off to some thing or another. To date, she had made no effort to come and visit Amy and Ivan at the ranch. Amy wasn't surprised. Her mother had a lot of bad memories to deal with concerning the ranches in southern Alberta. Amy was convinced her mother had never stopped loving her father. That was why she was so mad at him. Well, life goes on and she has to accept things, just like the rest of us, Amy mused as she drove up her driveway and parked by the house.

Chapter 42

L AURA WAS DOING well by the end of February. She was taking an interest in the ranch again. Amy was happy to see this as it gave her more time to be with Ivan during the calving. She couldn't get over how Ivan seemed to understand each cow. They would let him come in and check the calf, though at the same time be very protective. When Amy showed up on the scene, it was a different story. Immediately, the cow would circle her calf and become very aggressive. Amy found it best to stay out of the way and just run errands for Ivan. Sometimes there would be a cow having trouble calving that he had to get into the barn. For this he used the horse and his trusty rope. There he could help the cow out. Amy didn't feel as secure around the cows. They seemed to be such big critters. Sheep were more her size, she thought.

Amy was thoroughly enjoying her life on the ranch. She never believed she could be so happy. With Ivan as her steady companion, there was never a dull day. If he wasn't teasing her, he was educating her about the ranch life and how things were done. Amy was an eager learner. She wanted to be able to pull her weight. Of course, Ivan told her she was doing more than her share, but she didn't feel that way. She felt she could never have too much education.

➤ ◄

One morning toward the middle of March, Ivan came stomping into the porch and called out to Amy, "Say, helper, come on out here. I have a job for you."

Amy wiped her hands on the towel and set the cake she was mixing up back on the counter. "What's up?"

"Just come and see," Ivan prompted.

As Amy stepped into the porch, she was greeted by a sight she would never forget. Ivan was covered from head to toe with mud and it looked well mixed up with something a little stronger. He was a sight!

"What happened to you? Did you fall?" Amy asked as she tried to keep a straight face.

"Don't you laugh or I'll rub it all over you. I was checking the lower pasture as I seem to be missing one of my young heifers. I was riding Scamp and we went through a dip and I guess he lost his footing and down he went. I didn't want to get my leg caught so I bailed off. I picked the worst spot of all. I slipped as I hit the ground and went for a slide down the bank into the mud."

"You do look pretty funny. Are you sure that is just mud?"

"I wouldn't guarantee it, coming from the cow pasture. Can you come outside and hose me down? Then I will strip my clothes off. I sure don't want to bring all this mud into the house."

"You'll freeze if I hose you. Couldn't we just strip them off and I could hose them off?"

"Whatever. Let's get it done. I'm starting to get cold."

Amy and Ivan stepped outside and Amy proceeded to get the clothes off Ivan and spread them out on the ground. As she worked, she asked Ivan, "What did you say about missing a heifer?"

"I'm sure I am missing at least one heifer. I just hope we don't have another predator problem with lambing coming up at the Collin's Ranch. Yesterday the cows with the calves seemed very spooky. It could be a bear coming out of hibernation."

"Have you had bear problems before?"

"Not since I've been ranching, but my dad did a couple of times. It was usually in the spring. I've been thinking maybe I should invest in another cattle dog. Rover is too old to be much of a guard dog now. Most times he doesn't even bark when people come. Remember how the chivaree-ers were able to get to our door before we knew they were here?"

"Whatever you think we need, I am in favor of. Now, get into the house and into a warm shower. I will hose off these clothes."

"You're an angel; did I ever tell you that before?"

"No, and you had better remember it, Ivan Johnson. Now get!"

Ivan headed into the house and Amy took the hose and tried to get the worst off the jeans and jacket. As she worked, she thought about the possibility of a bear being around. She would have to be careful when she went for her walks. Rover really was no protection. She couldn't even coax him to come with her. She would just have to be watchful.

As Ivan hurried into the house, his mind was on many things, but uppermost was the possibility of bear trouble. He sure hoped he was wrong. Amy loved her walks and if there was a bear around, Ivan may have to see that she was safe. One thing he had not got around to showing her was how to fire a rifle. Maybe the time was now. It would be a good thing for her to learn if he ever was away and she had trouble at the ranch.

Ivan marveled at the way Amy was so eager to learn everything. He just could not believe his luck - to find a wife so attuned to his needs and to the ranch. He wished she would show more of an interest in the church, but Ivan hoped that would come in time. Right now, she was learning all she could. He was glad she was friends with Laura again. Being ranch women, it was nice to have the companionship. He realized a ranch life can be a lonely time for a woman if there is no other women close by. Several of the ranch neighbors had stopped by and welcomed Amy to the district, but to date, she didn't seem inclined to go visiting. "I will have to urge her to do that," Ivan mused as he stripped off the rest of his clothes and stepped into the shower.

Chapter 42

I VAN WAS MISSING three heifers from the lower pasture, but by the end of March, there appeared to be no more casualties. Ivan had been talking with some of the other ranchers in the area and two of them were missing calves. They could find no sign of a predator either, but they all agreed it could be a bear and every one was on their guard. Ivan had taken time to teach Amy to fire the rifle and, just as a precaution, asked her not to walk in the hills for the time being.

Shane was through school the first part of April so was home in time for lambing on the Collins Ranch. Laura had taken another series of treatments in March and was doing better. She still hadn't told Shane about her condition and Shane had managed to keep it from his mother that he knew. Now that he was home for the summer, Amy didn't know how Laura could take any more treatments without Shane knowing. Maybe Shane would have to be away for a week or something so Laura would go back. They would have to sort that out later. Now they were in the process of getting set up for lambing. Ivan and Amy were going to stay at the trailer during lambing. Ivan would go back to the ranch every day and check on things and feed the cattle and look after Cuddle Cat. Amy planned to lock her in the porch while they were gone. She would miss her, but didn't think she would get along with Happy Cat.

➤ ◄

Lambing started early in April with a bang. Laura took it upon herself to be chief cook and bottle washer. She also planned to take a shift out in the pens. Amy insisted she only work for a few hours at a time, and it seemed to be working out. Because of Ivan's obligations at their ranch, he was only able to be in the pens later in the day. Amy enjoyed those times. They sent Shane off to sleep and Laura to do whatever and they worked together. At midnight, Shane would come out and Amy and Ivan would get some sleep. Then Ivan would be back out at the pens at 6:00 AM while Amy got ready for the day.

One morning, as she sat up and put her feet on the floor, she immediately felt nauseous. She laid back down and it subsided. As she sat up again, she had the same sensation. What now? She thought. What did I eat that disagreed with me? She headed to the bathroom and only made it in time. As she vomited in the toilet, she started thinking, Could it be? No!! Impossible! The Doctor said I couldn't have any more kids. But it sure feels like it. Amy went to the sink and wiped her face. She looked pale. Maybe she was just working too hard. She decided to let the boys handle things for a bit. She wouldn't say a thing to Ivan. There was enough sickness around for them all. Hopefully, she would feel better after her shower.

The next morning the same thing happened. She had felt fine the evening before. Now she was sick to the stomach again. She took a sip of water and nibbled on a cracker. She sat for a few minutes and things started settling down. Amy wanted to feel excited, but she was scared to hope. What if it was a false alarm? She couldn't remember when she had her last monthly. Was she overdue? Just let me get through this lambing, then I will go see a doctor and confirm or not, Amy mused. If it was true, then all her prayers would be answered.

She could see Shane and Ivan working together in the sheep pens. What a surprise for them both if it is true. And Laura will be so happy. She felt so blessed to have this family as her family. If she was having a child, Amy thought, she would have to make a decision about the Mormon church. She had been attending church on Sundays with Ivan and was finding it a peaceful way to spend the day. She missed her Sunday jaunts into the hills, but enjoyed spending the day with Ivan and usually Laura and Shane. Laura was still trying to have Sunday suppers at her place and with Amy's help was managing very well. Anyway, she was sure that Ivan would want his child raised in the Mormon faith. Whoa, Amy chastised herself, you are putting the cart before the horse. It might not be that I am pregnant anyway. Don't get your hopes up, girl!! First, she had to get through this lambing and then time would tell. One thing was for sure, she wasn't going to say a word to anyone until she was sure. She didn't want to jinx anything.

Chapter 43

LAMBING PROGRESSED VERY nicely. With the extra full time help of Ivan, and Laura feeling good enough to be in the pens for several hours each day, the lambing seemed to be so much easier to Amy than the year before. She thought maybe some of it was the fact she was better at her job. She couldn't believe she had been away from Medicine Hat for a year. She heard very little from her mother. She had invited her several times to visit them on the cattle ranch, but her mother always had some excuse. Amy just hoped she was doing okay. She did seem depressed at times when Amy phoned her, but it was hard to tell After lambing, Ivan and Amy planned to take a quick trip to the Hat to see Gladys.

"I have made a decision," Shane announced to Amy one day when they were in the pens.

"A decision about what?"

"I have decided not to go on a mission. Mom needs me here. You and Ivan have your own ranch to take care of; you don't need the extra work of this one."

"Have you told your mother?"

"Not yet. I think I will wait until later in the summer. I don't want to upset her right now."

"She's not going to be happy. Her fondest wish was for you to go on a mission. I don't understand a lot about your church, but going on a mission seems to be very important to everyone."

"Well, yes, it is important, but so is my mother. I could not just take off on a mission and leave her, knowing what I know about her health. Our church teaches that family is important and my mother is very important to me. She is the only family I have left. I was never lucky enough to have brothers and sisters. You didn't either, did you?"

"No, I didn't. I often wished I had a sister to talk to and confide in, but it wasn't in the cards."

"Well, you have family now. We are all part of your family. Ivan is like a father-brother figure to me. So you are like my sister."

"Thank you," Amy answered and turned away. She had a lump in her throat as she thought, "not sister, Shane; mother". Someday he would know the truth, but today was not the day. She was concerned about Shane's news, though. Laura would not be happy about his decision, but Amy was going to stay out of it. Shane didn't turn nineteen until August, so there was time for him to change his mind. According to Ivan, the young men didn't go on missions until the age of nineteen.

Amy was convinced she was pregnant. The last week or so was much better; not much vomiting but her body felt different. She never realized that even your thoughts changed when your body changed. She found herself thinking about baby things, like preparing a room and picking names. She knew it was foolish to think such things before she was sure, but she couldn't seem to help herself. Right after lambing, she was going to see a doctor. She would find some excuse to go. Amy was grateful for Shane's help on the ranch but didn't want him to jeopardize his future. His church meant a lot to him and to his Mother. When he talked about family, she was so tempted to blurt out that maybe he did have a brother or sister. That sure would have been a mistake. IF she was pregnant, Ivan had to be the first to know. Then she would tell Laura.

Chapter 44

LAMBING FINISHED UP on the last day of April. Except for a few stragglers, the main flock was all lambed and out on pasture. The weather was nice and warm and the grass had been sprouting for a while.

Amy loved the spring time most of all. With all the new life popping up everywhere, it made the countryside seem so much refreshed. She took the time to take another walk with Lad and Lady up into the hills behind the Collin's ranch, just for old times sake. As she walked along, she thought back to the time Ivan had met her at the old cabin. She smiled to herself. Yes, he had been sneaky about stealing into her heart, but she was sure glad he did. It was almost sinful for one person to be so happy, she thought. Ivan and her were soul mates and enjoyed all the same things, even down to the kind of movies they watched. If she was having his baby, she was sure he would be excited. He often said he loved kids. Of course, he didn't expect to have any of his own. They had talked of adopting some later. Yes, the first order of the day, now that lambing was over, was to see a doctor.

"Yes, Mrs. Johnson, I would say you are about two months along. We will run some more tests, get some blood work done and get you on a good pre-natal vitamin. How old are you?"

"I'm thirty-five," Amy answered absently as she let his words sink in. She was pregnant!! "You are sure?"

"I'm sure," Dr. Allan answered, "Is this your first child?"

Amy sat up straight and looked at the doctor, "No. I had a child when I was only sixteen. Is that going to be a problem? Other doctors told me I could never have another child."

"It's not a problem, but we will keep a close watch on you. Was it a difficult birth? Is that why they said you couldn't have anymore?"

"Yes, I guess it was. It was so long ago and I think they must have put me out as I don't remember much of it."

"Well, we will take good care of you; don't worry. I imagine Ivan is excited. Have you told him yet?"

"No, I wanted to be sure."

"Well, now you are sure. Go home and tell the lucky father."

Ivan was late coming in for lunch. He had started some of the spring work and wanted to finish spraying the forty acres to the east of the pasture before he shut down. The wind was down and a good time to do it. As he washed up, Amy got the food on the table. Ivan was talkative and spoke to Amy between mouthfuls.

"I should be finished with seeding by the second week in May. How would you like to take our long awaited honeymoon after that and before haying starts?" he asked Amy as he took another sandwich.

"That sounds wonderful. Where would we go?"

"How about to the mountains, maybe to the coast? Have you ever been to the west coast?"

"I haven't been out of Alberta," Amy answered, as she cleared away the plates and set the pie on the table, "I don't know much about traveling. Is it hard on a person to travel a lot?" Amy mind was running in circles. Should she agree to a trip at this time? Would it be hard on the baby? She had heard the first trimester was the most crucial time. She sure didn't want a miscarriage. She had planned to tell Ivan right away, but somehow the words just wouldn't come out. Maybe she was afraid talking about it would jinx everything. No, it was best to tell him now.

"Ivan spoke just then, "I find traveling very exciting. You see new things and new places. Sometimes you even make new friends. I would find it a pleasure showing all that to you."

"Ivan, before we make any plans, there is something you should know."

"What's that? You're not scared of the mountains and traveling, are you?"

Before Amy could answer, the phone rang. Ivan picked it up. As he listened, his expression changed and he said, "We'll be right there."

He hung up and picking up his plate and some of the dishes from the table, said to Amy, "That was Shane. He just took Laura to the hospital in Milk River. He admitted to her that he knew about her sickness. She is now asking for us."

Amy felt like a rock had fallen on her. Laura had been doing so well. She must be devastated that Shane knows, Amy thought as she grabbed the food off the table and got things squared away. Her news could wait. Laura was the most important now.

Ivan broke the speed limits on their drive into Milk River. They didn't have much to say on the drive as each was deep in their own thoughts. As they pulled into the parking lot, Shane was waiting for them. He looked terrible. Amy gave him a hug and he clung to her and big sobs wracked his body.

"It's okay, Shane. We are here. Everything is in God's hands. Your Mom would want you to be strong now and take the reins. We are here to help you."

"I know," Shane mumbled as he wiped his eyes, "It is just so hard to see her like this. I have never seen her in this much pain. I thought she was doing better, but I guess she was just trying really hard so she could keep it from me. I wish I had let her know I knew before today."

"When did you tell her?"

"I came in from fence building for breakfast and she said she had a bit of a cold and was going to lie down this morning. So I went back to work. When I came in at 11:00 AM, I couldn't get a response from her for a while. I finally called 911. She came out of it before they got there. That is when I told her I knew and the ambulance was on it's way. She was pretty upset that I knew, but has accepted it now. She is stable and asking for you guys."

Amy wasn't prepared for what she saw when she went into the hospital room. Laura looked so small and fragile in the bed. Her color was not good. Ivan went over to her and gave her a hug.

"What are you trying to do, scare us all to death?" he teased as he held her hand.

Laura smiled and answered, "You're too big to scare easy. Amy, my dear, how are you?"

Amy moved closer and took Laura's other hand, "I am fine. But why didn't you phone us when you knew you were sick?'

"I did really think I just had a cold coming on. I guess I misjudged. I am sorry that Shane found out though. How long has he known?"

Shane walked in just then, "Shane has known since the first time you took a treatment in Lethbridge."

"Why didn't you say anything?"

"Because I thought if you didn't want me to know, you must have a good reason, so I would just be quiet."

"I love you, Shane; and I love you too, Ivan. Amy came into our lives and my love extends to her too. I wanted you all here today for a reason. I have something to tell all of you, if you will bear with me."

Amy could sense what was coming and she wasn't prepared for it. She stroked Laura's arm and pleaded, "Maybe this isn't the right time. Why not wait until you are feeling better and at home?"

Laura looked at Amy and then glanced at Ivan and Shane, "It has to be now because I may not get another chance to clear my conscience. You have been so good to me through all this and complying to my wishes. It is only fair to you that I be honest now."

Ivan was looking from Laura to Amy and over to Shane, "What are you talking about? You are the most honest person I know. Whatever it is can wait."

Laura was adamant, "No, it can't. So everyone draw up a chair. I have a story to tell."

When everyone was seated, Laura continued, "Nearly nineteen years ago, Abe and I had a phone call from Calgary about a baby that was up for adoption. We had always wanted children, but I was unable to conceive after my first two miscarriages. This was like a sign from heaven so we adopted the baby boy, whom we named Shane. Shane, you always knew you were adopted. We never hid that from you. What we did hide from you was the man you called Dad was actually your biological Grandfather."

"What?!? How can that be?" Shane blurted out.

"Let me finish. The woman that called us about the baby was Abe's ex-wife. I know....you didn't know Abe was married before, but he was. He also had a daughter by that marriage. When that daughter was fifteen years old, she got pregnant and was sent to an unwed mother's home in Calgary. The ex-wife didn't want strangers getting the baby, but she wasn't prepared to let the daughter keep it and help her raise it. So the baby was taken away from the mother and given to us. The mother had no say in any of it."

Now Ivan spoke up, "Well, I for one, think Shane was very lucky to have a home with you and Abe. You were always like parents to me. It's too bad the daughter had no say, but it could have been worse. You have nothing to be sorry for or confess to. Now you had better get some rest."

"No, Ivan. There is more. Over the years before Shane was born, Abe tried to see his daughter, but his ex-wife would never allow it. So he finally gave up. Later he often remarked that maybe if he could have helped raise his daughter, she wouldn't have made some of the mistakes she did. Granted, we were always grateful to have been given the chance to raise Shane. There seemed no reason to tell you, Shane, that Abe was really your grandfather. Maybe we were worried you would go looking for your real mother; I don't know. Then Abe died.

Now we come to the second part of the story. We needed help on the ranch and a nice young woman from Medicine Hat applied to our ad. From the first moment she stepped onto the ranch, I could feel she was something special. I sensed a familiarity. We quickly become fast friends and she was a Godsend to us." Laura looked over at Amy and took her hand and continued, "Then one day, Amy came back from Medicine Hat from visiting her mother and a picture fell out of her purse. It was a picture of my husband Abe with a woman and a little girl. When I asked her who was with my husband, she admitted it was her and her mother. Well, you can imagine my shock. My first thought was Amy had lied to us and wormed her way into our lives so she could take her son back. So I immediately fired her. Shane, you didn't know any of this because I didn't want you to become suspicious. So you see, Ivan, I had to keep my reason for firing Amy to myself. I had second thoughts later and re-hired her, but it took me a while to come to terms with everything. For the record, Amy didn't even know her father was alive, let alone was raising her son. She didn't even know her baby was a boy. So to make a long story short, Shane, Amy is your biological mother. Ivan, I begged Amy not to tell you about Shane until I was gone, so don't blame her. But now I know I am dying. I don't know when, but it is soon. I want you all to pull together as a family. I am not scared to die as I know I will be with my Abe, but I am sad to leave all of you."

Amy was quietly crying in her chair and Shane had big sobs shaking his body. Ivan had his head down and when he looked up, Laura could see he was shaken to his core. He let go of her hand and stood up. Glancing over at Amy, he left the room.

"Amy," Laura gently poked Amy on the arm, "I think you had better go after Ivan right now."

Drying her tears, Amy got up and followed Ivan's route out of the room, but when she got into the hallway and the waiting room, there was no sign of him. She went out to the truck, but he wasn't there. She had no choice but to return to Laura's side. There she found her sleeping and no sign of Shane. As she sat beside Laura's bed, she couldn't help feeling a sense of doom. Why did things have to be so complicated? It would have been so much better if she could have told Ivan and Shane when she found out. But she had to respect Laura's wishes, didn't she? She only hoped Shane and Ivan would understand.

Chapter 45

As Laura slept, Amy held her hand and thought about what had all been said. She was glad it was all out in the open finally. She was sure it was a great weight off Laura's mind. She only wished she knew how Shane and Ivan were taking the news.

She was deep in thought when she sensed someone looking at her and glanced up to see Shane standing in the doorway, staring at her. Immediately she stood up and crossed over to him.

"Are you okay?"

"I will be. I just have to get this all straight in my head. The man I called Father for all those years was also your Father?"

"Yes, he was. I never knew my father as my mother told me he died when I was a baby. She didn't want me to have anything to do with him and his new wife. I believe my mother never stopped loving him. But I want you to know from me, I did not know any of this when I took the job at the ranch. It was just a coincidence I picked the Collin's ranch."

"Didn't the name ring a bell with you?"

"No, my mother didn't use her married name. I grew up as Amy Stern. She hid all the pictures so I didn't even know what he looked like."

Laura stirred, so Amy took Shane's arm and said, "Let's go talk in the lounge."

"Okay," Shane agreed, "That is a good idea. Mom needs all the rest she can get. Where did Ivan go?"

"I don't know. It is probably hard for him to digest all this news too. He probably thinks I lied to him, but I didn't. I knew you were my son when I married him, but I had promised Laura to keep quiet. I did tell Ivan I had a child when I was young. So I didn't lie; I just didn't tell him all the truth."

"I'm finding it hard to believe you are my mother. You don't seem old enough."

"Well, I was only sixteen when you were born. I didn't even get to see you at the time."

"That is really sad."

"You know, Shane, maybe it was a rotten thing for my mother to do, but I do believe you had a better home with Abe and Laura. If I had raised you with my mother, you would have had the same life I did, which was not good. My mother was controlling and manipulative. She would have controlled every aspect of your life."

"Who was my father?"

"It doesn't matter. I never saw him again."

"It does matter to me. As you know, we do family history and we keep track of our ancestors."

"I can tell you his name, but he will deny having a son. It is Dave Knight. He lives in Regina."

"Is he married and has he family?"

"The last I heard, which was quite a few years ago, he had a daughter by his first wife, but no children by his second. I don't know if he is still married or not. He works for the city of Regina."

"Why do you think he will deny having a son?"

"Because when I found out I was pregnant, I told him, and he said it wasn't his baby. He has never tried to contact me at any time to see if I kept the baby or aborted it or anything."

"He sounds like a winner."

"Just remember, you have Abe's blood in you and he was a special man from what I can see. I am very proud of the man you have become."

Shane changed the subject, "What do you think of Mom's chances of beating this thing?"

"Oh Shane, I really don't think she will. I am no expert, but she doesn't look good. Maybe if she hadn't waited so long for treatments.......I don't know. I think we had better be prepared."

Tears build up in Shane's eyes. He reached over and squeezed Amy's hand. "I will pray every day for God's mercy for her. His will be done. I am so glad I have a strong faith because I know she will be with Dad......er, Abe after she leaves here."

"I wish I had your faith. It would make things so much easier for me."

"You can. Just read the Book of Mormon and follow the promptings of the Holy Ghost. It will tell you the right way."

"Thank you, Shane. Now maybe we should get back to Laura."

Laura was still sleeping and there was no sign of Ivan. Amy was starting to worry about him. Shane said he was going to stay with Laura so if Ivan's truck was gone, take his to go home.

"I think you had better go and find him. Maybe he needs to talk, too."

Amy agreed. When she got to the parking lot, she could see that Ivan's truck was indeed gone. Unlocking Shane's, she slid the seat forward and started the engine.

She was getting worried about Ivan. Why did he not stay around to talk to her? Had she underestimated him? He seemed so understanding about her having a child when she was young. Was it such a big sin, not to tell him about Shane?

When she drove in to the ranch, she could see Ivan's truck parked at the barn. Rover was laying in front of the door so she thought Ivan was in the barn. Opening the door, she quietly called his name. No answer. She called again. She checked out the stalls, but there was no sign of him. Returning to the door she glanced around the yard. Then she spotted him down by the feed yard, sitting on a rock.

Ivan glanced up as she approached, then went back to studying the ground in front of him.

"Ivan?"

"What?"

"Why did you leave? Don't you want to talk?"

"Talk about what? Is there something we should talk about?"

"You know there is."

"Really? You think I am now trustworthy enough to divulge important information to?"

"Don't be like that."

"Like what?"

"Don't blame me for being a friend to Laura and honoring her wishes. She didn't want you to know because she thought you might slip and say something to Shane because you two are close."

"I understand Laura's point. I just don't understand yours. You had lots of opportunities to tell me. You know me well enough to know I would NEVER say or do anything to harm Laura or Shane."

"So you think I should have ignored Laura's wishes?"

"Yes."

"Well, you are wrong."

"So I guess I know where I stand. Your friendship with Laura is more important than I am."

"Ivan, don't be an ass!" Amy was starting to get really annoyed. What was the matter with him? Was he actually jealous of her friendship with Laura?

Ivan jumped to his feet and stomped away, flinging words over his shoulder, "Well, if I'm such an ass, maybe this isn't the right place for you!"

As Ivan moved away, Amy sank down to the ground. What had she done? Well, he was being an ass. Couldn't he see her side of this? If she had told him and Laura found out, Amy would have lost Laura's friendship for good. Now it looked like she lost her husband. What should she do? Maybe he just needed to cool off.

Amy got to her feet and headed back to the house. She would pack a bag and take Shane's truck back to him and stay in town tonight. Maybe by tomorrow Ivan will feel differently.

There was no sign of Ivan as Amy left the house and got into Shane's truck. Ivan's truck was gone from the barn. Amy had packed a small bag and left Ivan a note on the table. She told him she was staying in town that night. She hoped she didn't run into Ivan at the hospital. Right now, he was the last person she wanted to talk to. It was hard to believe she could feel so angry with him. Ivan was usually so easy going. Why was he so pig-headed about this? It wasn't like she had deliberately deceived him. If he had not known about a child at all, Amy would understand more, but he did know. What difference if it was Shane or another child? Was this a man thing? Maybe she just didn't understand men.

When Amy pulled up to the hospital, there was no sign of Ivan's truck. Good, she thought. No more confrontations today.

Laura was awake and talking with Shane when Amy entered. Laura smiled and patted the chair beside her "Come sit down, Amy. Did you find Ivan?"

"Yes, I did."

"How is he?"

"That is hard to tell. He is angry with me, that is for sure."

"He will come around. I will talk to him."

"I will, too," Shane spoke up, "There is no way he should blame Amy for all this."

"I brought your truck back, Shane. When we leave here, you can drop me off, okay?"

"Sounds good. The doctor was in and checked Mom. He said if all goes well, she might be able to come back home tomorrow."

"That's wonderful, Laura. Are you feeling better?"

"I feel really tired, but the pain is gone. I know I will rest better in my own bed."

Shane stood up and reached over and kissed Laura, "So I will say goodnight then. Take care and sleep if you can. I will be here in the morning."

"Okay. You both look like you could use some sleep. I'll be fine."

Amy kissed Laura and followed Shane out of the room. As they strolled out to the truck, Shane asked about Ivan.

"I didn't want to say much in front of Laura, but he is really ticked at me. Then I got mad and called him an ass. That didn't go over very good."

"Well, he is being a bit of an ass, if I do say so. I'll talk to him."

"Thanks, but I think I had better fight my own battles. Could you drop me at a motel for tonight and pick me up in the morning to go get my car?"

"Things are that bad?"

"He told me, maybe the ranch wasn't the right place for me."

"So what do you plan?"

"I thought I would let him cool off for a bit."

"Why don't you stay at the trailer?"

"I never thought of that. That's a good idea. Do you think Laura would mind?"

"Mind! She would love having you close for a bit. During lambing we are too busy for visiting so this would be good for her."

"I will take you up on that. Thanks, Shane."

Chapter 46

IVAN STOOD BESIDE his truck and gazed down the long coulee into the
meadow below. The grass was coming good, he thought. With the warm
weather and the spring rains, the hay was really coming along. It looked
like a record crop. He kicked a dirt clump in front of his foot as he thought
back to his quarrel with Amy. She just could not see his side of the argument at all. Couldn't she see he felt betrayed? There is something called
trust in a marriage and Amy just didn't seem to have that trust. Possibly, it
stemmed from her previous marriage, but she was going to have to get over
it. She probably thinks I should apologize, Ivan mused, but I don't think I
have done anything wrong. SHE should apologize to me. So she thinks I am
an ass, does she? She doesn't even know what an ass is. I think I have been
very good to her, and I thought she loved me enough to trust me completely.
Well, she can sulk if she wants. I will wait for her to come to me.

Ivan jumped back in the truck and headed back to the ranch. As he drove
down the driveway, she could see Shane's truck was gone. She probably went
back to visit Laura, Ivan decided. Good. Now he could grab something to
eat and finish entering his costs in his ledger. When Amy got back later, they
could thrash this all out.

Taking off his boots in the porch, Ivan entered the kitchen. It was spot-
less, as usual even though they had left in a hurry. Then he noticed the note
on the table. As he read it, he could feel anger welling up inside. So she
just runs out. At the first sign that she didn't get her way, she just runs out.
Even Ivan knew this was no way to deal with a problem. Why couldn't Amy

see that? Well, let her pout. He wasn't going to run after her again, like he did the last time she stayed in town. If that was what she was hoping for, it wasn't going to happen. And when she comes home tomorrow, Ivan vowed, he was going to be no where around.

Shane dropped Amy off at the trailer and told her to have a good night and he would see her in the morning. Taking her suitcase and opening the door, Amy was greeted by Happy Cat. She reached down and petted the cat, "Hello to you, too, you pretty thing. I'm glad to see you too. It's too bad that people can't be as uncomplicated as cats, don't you think?"

Happy Cat meowed and rubbed up against her leg. Amy set her suitcase down on the floor and checked out Happy Cat's dish. As she took the food from the cupboard and filled it, she wondered what Ivan was up to. Had he found her note? He probably went rushing off to town to drag me out of the motel like last time, she smiled. Won't he be surprised when he can't find me. Serve him right. If he wasn't being such an ass, we could have solved this whole thing earlier. I, for one, am going to have a good night's sleep and worry about things tomorrow. Maybe I will just stay here for a few days. I can be here when Laura gets home and help her out. I'm sure when Ivan thinks about all this some more, he will realize I did the only thing I could. I could not betray Laura at this time in her life. She was just too fragile.

Amy checked out the cupboard for something to eat and found some crackers. Taking them and opening the fridge, checked out the interior. There was some cheese on the shelf among the salad dressings, mustard, and ketchup. Not much, she thought, but enough for tonight. Tomorrow I will stock up on some things.

Laura come home in the morning. She looked very frail and her color wasn't good. Shane and Amy got her tucked into bed and Amy set about making lunch for them all. Laura managed to eat a bit of soup, but was too tired to try anything else. When Amy checked on her a little later, she was sound asleep.

There had been no word from Ivan. Laura had asked about him when they picked her up, but Shane just said he was busy getting ready for seeding. Laura was happy that Amy was staying in the trailer for a day or so. She wasn't happy if there was a problem between the love-birds, but she was happy to see that Amy was standing her ground. Ivan was not being fair. In this, she was on Amy's side. After all, it was Amy's loyalty to me that caused this problem, Laura thought. I will see Ivan one of these days and get this straightened out.

Shane made sure Amy and Laura had everything they needed, then he headed over to Ivan's. This quarrel was ridiculous, as far as Shane was concerned. He's the one that should be upset, if anyone needed to be. He was the one that was adopted and raised by a grandfather, whom he thought was his adopted father. He's the one that hadn't been told that Amy was his mother when Amy and Laura found out. It really didn't concern Ivan that much. Why was he being so irate about everything? Shane vowed to find out.

He found Ivan working on the drill down by the barn. As Shane approached, he just grunted.

"Good morning to you too," Shane responded, "What are you working on?"

"Oh, some of these drill feeds are plugging, so I need to replace them."

"Can we talk?"

"What about?"

"About you and Amy."

"If she sent you here to talk to me, she can just forget it."

"She doesn't even know I am here. She is at the house with Mom. Mom came home from the hospital this morning."

"I'm glad Laura is home. How is she feeling?"

"Really tired. I am worried about her. She seems to have given up."

"We knew that would happen when she found out you knew. She was trying harder because she wanted to keep it a secret."

"So you are saying I shouldn't have said anything? How would she have explained this relapse?"

"No, I'm not saying you shouldn't have told her. I was against her not telling you in the first place. I'm just saying that is probably why she feels the way she does. She also unburdened herself of her secret so now she feels the pressure is gone."

"Talking about her secret, why are you so bent out of shape about it?"

"You wouldn't understand."

"Try me."

"I don't like being lied to."

"I don't see that. Nobody lied to you. You just weren't told the whole truth."

"To me, that is one and the same thing."

"It affects me more than you and I'm not upset."

"You don't mind that Amy is your mother?"

"Why should I? She is a friendly, hard-working woman, who made a mistake when she was young. She had regretted it ever since."

"See; I knew you would not understand."

"What I do understand is you are being stubborn about all this. Amy did not intentionally keep something from you. She was not at liberty to divulge the information, through her obligation to Mom."

"You can believe that if you want, but I know differently. I would never have intentionally hurt you or Laura and Amy knew that. She just didn't want me to know. When I think back on it now, when she told me about having a child when she was young, I mentioned that when we were married, we would look for the child. She changed the subject right away. She could have told me then."

"No, she couldn't. She had promised Mom."

"Have it your way."

"Amy was right; you are being an ass."

"If you are finished, I have work to do, as I'm sure you do."

"I'm leaving. I just thought you would like to know, Amy is staying at the trailer. She wants to be close to help Laura for a bit."

"It doesn't matter to me. When she is ready to apologize, she knows where I am."

Shane shook his head and turned away. Boy, Amy was right. Ivan had his mind made up. He wasn't going to give an inch. Shane had never seen that side of Ivan before. Was it his pride that was hurt, or what was the problem? Maybe it was time to call in the big guns. Maybe he would listen to Bishop Lang. It was time Ivan was made to see how wrong he was about the whole thing.

Chapter 47

I N THE DAYS that followed, Shane and Ivan got busy with the seeding and Amy was left to care for Laura. Everyday, Laura improved some and was eating better. Ivan had been over to see her a few times. He ignored Amy and vise-versa. Amy planned to be just as stubborn as he was. Laura had tried to talk with him, but he just shrugged it off and told her not to worry. Things would work out eventually.

While Ivan was in the field, Amy went home and checked on Cuddle Cat one day and picked up some more clothes and her car. It looked like she was going to be away for a while so wanted to be prepared. Laura really did need her, so it was a good excuse to be there. She thought of taking Cuddle Cat, but wasn't sure how Happy Cat would respond, so left her with a promise to be back to see her often.

Amy was no longer having morning sickness and she was grateful for that. Her body was changing and she was sure she would soon need bigger clothes. She didn't know when she would tell anyone, but there was no hurry. She wouldn't start showing until around four to five months into the pregnancy. She wanted to keep fit, so each day, when Laura was down for her nap, Amy went for a walk into the hills with Lad and Lady. They were thrilled that Amy was back and yipped and bounced all around her when they started out.

"Yes, you crazy dogs; I am glad to go walking with you, also. Things sure made a lot more sense back when we went regularly. Why do humans have to make everything so complicated? Why can't we just be like dogs? Happy with the simplest things and very forgiving." Lad whined and licked Amy's hand. "I do believe you understand what I am saying, Lad," Amy reached down and caressed his ears, "Do you miss Ivan like I do?"

When Amy went to check on Laura, she found her up and dressed.

"Are you feeling well enough to be out of bed?"

"Well, I am tired of just laying around, doing nothing. I thought I would venture out and sit on the porch, if you think it is warm enough."

"It is a beautiful day. Lad and Lady will be glad to see you. They are missing you being out."

"I miss them too, and I miss Ivan coming around more. Have you two not solved your problem?"

"Our only problem is Ivan's stubbornness. If he would just admit he is wrong, we could get on with things."

"And he probably thinks you should apologize to him, right?"

"That is what I understand, but what do I have to apologize for? The fact I made a mistake as a kid? What kid didn't, though a lot didn't make as drastic a mistake as I did. Some kids were just lucky. I don't see where that has anything to do with Ivan. I didn't know him then."

"Somehow, he has the idea you betrayed him and didn't trust him. I am sorry I asked you to keep my secret because it is causing trouble for you now. Can you forgive me?"

"You haven't done anything for me to forgive you for. At the time, you thought it was for the best. I guess we both know we were wrong, but that is water under the bridge. We can't change what has happened. Someday, Ivan will see my side of it. Until then, I am content to stay in the trailer, if you don't mind. I like being close so I can help you out."

"I love having you here, but I don't want to be the cause of a break-up between you and Ivan. You two love each other too much for that. One of you is going to have to pull in your horns and make amends."

"We'll see. Right now, let's get you out to the porch and I will see about starting supper. What are you in the mood for?"

Ivan filled the drill with the last of the barley seed and checked the boots for problems. If the weather held, the barley should all be in by tomorrow.

Then they would start on the oats and mixed feed. This year, Shane had decided to plant mixed feed instead of wheat. This way, it would already be mixed for the ewes. Ivan fed mostly barley to his herd when the need arose, but the sheep needed the wheat for the selenium content. It helped prevent certain diseases in the lambs.

Shane hadn't mentioned his mission again. Ivan was pretty sure he had decided not to go because of Laura. He would have to talk to him. Going on a mission with the church was one of the best things he had done and he didn't want Shane to miss out on the experience. The last time Ivan had been over to see Laura was a few days before and she was fading away. Ivan didn't think she would be with them that much longer. Then what excuse would Amy have for not coming home? She didn't say two civil words to him while he was there. But he didn't have much to say either. He really missed her but wasn't ready to give in on this. He was convinced he was right. Why couldn't she see that? It didn't help that Laura and Shane had taken her side. Was he being unfair? Somehow, it was hard now to come forward and ask her to come home. You would think she would want to come home, if she really cared. We'll see, Ivan mused as all these thoughts went through his head as he worked.

The seeding was finished the third week in May. Amy had planted a small garden for Laura and got the yard work caught up around the ranch. She was anxious to go back to her home and get her yard in order, but Ivan had made no overtures toward her returning, so she waited.

One afternoon after Laura had her nap and got settled on the porch, she called Amy to come and sit with her. Amy was glad of the break. She had been weeding around the flower beds and ready for a drink.

Bringing out two glasses of lemonade, she said to Laura, "Do you think I should have transplanted some of those columbines to a different area or just weeded some out? They are getting pretty thick."

"They could be thinned out, I guess. I love them so, as the hummingbirds are attracted to them. Come, sit by me. I have a question I want to ask you."

"Okay. What's up?"

"When are you going to tell Ivan?"

"Tell Ivan what?"

"That you are carrying his child."

Amy stared at Laura, "How did you know? Did the doctor blab?"

"No. I just happen to be able to tell when a woman is expecting. You have that glow about you. When are you due?"

"Sometime in November, I guess."

"I am sorry I won't be here to see the child, but I am really happy for you and Ivan. You are happy, aren't you? You told me once you didn't think you could have any more children."

"That's true. That is what the doctor said when my first husband and I didn't have any children. Yes, I am happy about it, but at first I was scared to say anything in case I jinxed it. Now, I don't know how to say anything to Ivan. He will think I am using it to get back to him. Maybe he won't want children with me, a woman who betrayed him."

"Nonsense! Ivan loves you and he loves kids, so he will be thrilled. You should tell him."

"Not yet. I want him to come to me first."

"Do you think that is ever going to happen?"

"I don't know. But now I am going to ask you to not divulge this information."

"Mum is the word. I can keep a secret. But don't be foolish like me and keep it too long."

Chapter 48

MAY TURNED INTO June and Amy was still at the trailer. The men had started haying so were gone long hours. When Ivan was gone, she headed home and puttered around her yard and got things in shape. She also planted a small garden. Then she would head back to the trailer.

Amy had taken over checking the sheep and rotating the pastures while Shane was busy haying. One day, as she was checking fence lines, she found an area where the ground was a bit swampy. The fence was flattened down and there were tracks everywhere. Amy was not good at identifying tracks, but these were big and could only be made by a bear. Lad and Lady were smelling the ground and their hair was standing up along their backs. Suddenly, Lady took off over the rise. Amy tried to call her back, but she kept going. She wished she had her rifle with her now, but had no choice but to follow the dogs. Topping the rise, she could see the two dogs circling a spot on the ground and then Amy saw it. It looked like a fair sized sheep. As Amy got closer, she could see it had been partly eaten, then partially buried. Calling the dogs, she hurried back to the house. This was a job for the guys.

Telling Laura about the kill, she jumped into the truck and headed to the hay field.

➤ ◄

Ivan was the first to spot Amy coming across the field in the farm truck. Thinking it must be about Laura, he quickly got the haybine stopped and putting the tractor in neutral, jumped down and ran over to the truck. Amy rolled down her window and said, "We have a problem in the lower pasture. Something killed a sheep and ate part of it and tried to bury the rest. I think it is a bear."

"Oh, that's all? I thought it would have to be Laura to bring you out here to talk to the enemy."

"You know what, Ivan? You are still being an ass! If you aren't concerned about a predator on the loose, I guess I shouldn't be either."

"Were there any tracks?"

"Lots of tracks. They come from the swamp at the lower end and lead right to the ewe. The dogs tracked it."

Ivan sighed, "Okay, I'll tell Shane. We'll have to check into it. Meanwhile, don't go walking for a few days."

"How do you know I go walking?"

"Never mind."

"Have you been spying on me?"

Ivan just waved and headed back to the tractor. Amy stuck her tongue out at his receding back. As she started the truck and headed out of the field, she thought about what he said. How did he know she was walking in the hills again? He had to be spying. Did that mean he still cared? He sure didn't act like it at times. Well, like Laura said, I guess one of us is going to have to get off our high horse and make the first move. But why does it have to be me, Amy mused? I really don't feel I should apologize. I'll wait until haying is over, then make up my mind.

That evening, Ivan and Shane checked out the bear tracks. The carcass of the ewe was gone, but there were tracks everywhere. Undecided what to do, they did nothing that night. Ivan phoned some of the neighbors but none of them had seen a bear or had any problem. Shane suggested that maybe the ewe had died and the bear took advantage of a free meal and Ivan was inclined to agree. They would keep a close eye and see what transpired. It would seem likely the bear would take a lamb instead.

At home, Cuddle Cat greeted Ivan at the door and immediately tried to climb up his leg. "Cut that out, you varmint. You will get banished to the barn if you don't stop with the leg climbing. What's the matter? You hungry or do you miss her too?"

Ivan got so he hated coming home. Before Amy was in the picture, he was very happy and contented with his house, but now everywhere he looked, he could see her hand in things. She had a flair for decorating and the place looked so cozy and comfortable, but to Ivan, it looked sterile without her there. Shaking his head, Ivan headed to the kitchen and checked out the fridge. Nothing looked appetizing. Slamming the door, he headed to his office. As he marked down the acreage hayed and the weather conditions, he let his mind roam back to the day he first brought Amy to the ranch. She was so interested in his office and what he did there. She had an infectious way of getting under a person's skin, Ivan lamented. Why can't I get her off my mind? Probably because you love her, his subconscious mind retorted. Oh man, will the hurt ever go away, he moaned as he closed his eyes? He wanted her back, in his life and in his house, and yes, in his bed. He ached to hold her close and whisper love words in her ear and make love to her. Man, he sounded corny, even to himself, he thought. Why can't I just go over to her and tell her this? Because of stupid male pride; right? Right. Well, haying was almost done. He would finish that, then see what happens.

Chapter 49

I T STARTED RAINING on the 25th of June and rained for a week straight. Ivan and Shane were glad they had all the hay baled that was down. When the rain stopped, they would be able to start again. It was a beautiful rain and much needed for the thirsty crops. Because work outside was curtailed, Amy took the opportunity to do some housecleaning at the ranch house. Laura was spending most of her days in bed, but did manage to come to the supper table and eat a few bites. She had no appetite and was so thin. When she was awake, she spent most of her time reading the Book of Mormon. Several ladies from her church had come out to see Laura and had offered help to Amy. Amy thanked them, but told them everything was under control. They didn't ask about Ivan, so Amy was sure they knew about their separation. Though Shane still went to church on Sundays and asked Amy to go with him, she always declined as she knew Ivan would be there. She wasn't quite ready to meet him on his turf yet.

One rainy evening, Ivan showed up to see Laura. Amy was just finishing up the dishes and as soon as she was done, she headed to the trailer. This way, Ivan could visit without her interrupting. She also had some things she needed to do when she had a free moment.

Ivan knocked on Laura's bedroom door and was bade enter. When Laura saw it was Ivan, she said, "Ivan, how thoughtful of you to come over. I have been missing you."

"I've been missing you too. I am glad we got the hay up before this rain, though. Things are sure wet out there."

"Shane said it is a bumper crop this year. That is always nice to hear."

"Yes, there should be no shortage of feed this year. We still have around three hundred acres still standing and it is coming along nicely. Do you remember when Abe and I went down on the flat and I got lost in the hay field?" Laura nodded. "Well, this crop is even higher than that one."

"Enough about farming. How are you?"

"I'm getting along. I have enough to eat and a roof over my head. What else does a guy need?"

"How about his wife home where she should be."

"Well, that is up to the wife, right?"

"Not really. Maybe that wife feels she isn't welcome back there."

"That is just an excuse."

"Okay, Ivan; I am going to treat you just like my son, which you are anyway. Why don't you just get off your high horse and admit you are wrong, and go down to that trailer, apologize to that lady and then take her home!"

"So you are saying that I am the one at fault here? Is that what you are saying?"

"No, I am the one at fault and have caused this awful mess. If I had never asked Amy to keep her secret from you, none of this would have happened. Now I feel terrible about all this. Before I die, I want to make amends and have you two back together where you belong. Amy is miserable without you. She loves you so much and wants to be a family."

"Why would she feel she isn't welcome at home?"

"She said you told her, it wasn't the place for her, which she took as meaning she didn't fit in there."

"That is ridiculous. I have never stopped loving her. I was ticked that she didn't tell me the whole truth at the beginning; then I was ticked because she ran off and didn't stay and argue it out. Then as time went on, it sort of became a game; who is going to give in first. Last Sunday, Bishop Lang had a talk with me. He is concerned about us. I think Shane blabbed to him, but he meant well. I wasn't perfectly honest with the bishop. I told him, Amy was staying with you because you needed her. It is the truth, but I didn't mention the rest of the problem."

"You know Ivan, two wrongs never will make a right. You both are being stubborn so one of you will have to take the first step. I think it should be you. Don't you agree?"

"Actually, I am getting tired of my own cooking."

"Oh, you!! You are a good cook."

"I do love Amy and I agree with you. It is now time to get this settled. But I won't go to the trailer tonight. I will set up something in my own way."

"Just so you get it done soon. I can't go to my grave with you two on my conscience."

Ivan stood up and leaned over and kissed Laura on the cheek. There were tears in both their eyes when he straightened up.

"Oh Laura, how will we ever get along without you? You are like a mother, a sister, a confidant, and very dear friend. I can only let you go, knowing you will be with your beloved Abe. Maybe he needs you more now than we do."

Laura squeezed Ivan's hand, "I can go in peace because I know you and Amy will be there for Shane. Be sure he goes on a mission. I know he is thinking about the ranch and that he is needed here, but some arrangements can be made. He will never regret his duty to the church."

"I know. I will see that he goes."

"Thank you. Now, go and let me rest. Come see me again soon."

"I will."

Ivan gently closed the door and headed out to his truck. He glanced over to the trailer, but there was no sign of Amy. Good. He would have to think about things and decide how to get things back to normal.

Chapter 50

A MY WATCHED IVAN drive away out of the yard. He had stayed a long time with Laura, so that was good. Laura missed Ivan. He was the son of her youth that she didn't have. Amy thought it was too bad that Ivan wasn't raised by Abe and Laura. But he had the next best thing. Amy finished up her work and put on her shoes. Now that Ivan was gone, she would go and see if Laura needed anything. Shane had gone to town to see a movie with his friends, so Laura was alone.

As she entered the house, Amy noticed the silence. Tip-toeing to the bedroom door, she listened. No sound. She cracked the door, and saw that Laura was sleeping peacefully, her Book of Mormon still in her hand. Amy gently closed the door and headed to the kitchen. She decided to make a cup of herbal tea and wait for Shane to come home.

As she sat down at the table, she thought about Ivan's visit. He always seemed to make Laura more peaceful. So far, she seemed to have her pain under control this week. The doctor had increased her medication and it was making her tired, but at least the pain was tolerable. Amy shuttered as she thought about the devastation caused by cancer. Why, if there was a God in heaven, would he let a wonderful woman like Laura have such a painful disease, Amy wondered? Was there a big plan, that certain people had to suffer and others didn't? Laura had such faith in her church and her bible, the Book of Mormon. Were the answers in that book? Amy had tried to read the book but found it very confusing. Ivan had started to explain some of it to her, but then they got side-tracked with this misunderstanding. IF they got back together, she would have to get him to explain more to her, Amy decided as she took a drink of her tea. Maybe things would clear up in time.

Ivan let himself into the house and turned on the light. Cuddle Cat was sleeping on the sofa and only looked up and stretched when she saw Ivan.

"You lazy cat. You haven't even got the energy to say hello, do you?" Ivan remarked as he sauntered over and rubbed the kitten's ears. Cuddle Cat was really growing and had finally learned not to get on the counters or climb the drapes. She still liked to climb Ivan's leg when he was in the kitchen, but it was getting better. "You miss her too, don't you? Maybe someday soon, she will be back where she belongs; then we will both be happy, right?"

Cuddle Cat meowed and set off purring loudly. Ivan laughed and headed up to bed. Tomorrow, he had some plans to put into effect.

Shane arrived home around eleven and was surprised to find Amy still sitting at the kitchen table, and it appeared she was reading the Book of Mormon. She glanced up as Shane entered.

"Hi. Glad to see you are home safe. I will now scuttle off to my bed."

"You didn't have to wait up for me. I am a big boy, you know."

"I know. I just thought I would stay here if Laura needed anything, but she has been sleeping ever since Ivan left."

"Ivan was over?"

"Yes. He had a long visit with Laura. I am glad, as she misses him."

"Did he talk to you?"

"I wasn't here. I went to the trailer while he visited."

"Running away won't solve the problem. You should talk to him."

"I know. Maybe I will one of these days."

"Make it soon."

Amy stood up and took her cup to the sink. She flicked Shane on the arm as she passed him on the way to the door and remarked, "Yes, boss."

Shane laughed and retorted, "And don't you forget it!!"

When Amy arrived at the main house the next morning, Laura was already up and dressed. She informed Amy that Shane had a phone call early and it had awakened her. Amy helped her into her chair in the living room and brought her breakfast there. The chair was situated where Laura could see out the window. She could watch the birds at the finder and see her flower garden. On nice days, she always wanted to sit on the porch. But it was still raining slightly and the day was starting out very gloomy.

Laura managed to have a bit of oatmeal and a piece of toast, before she pushed her tray away.

"I just seem to have no appetite anymore. I know I have to eat something, but it is a real effort."

"As long as you eat some. You have to keep up your strength. You have to keep fighting."

"You know, Amy, I am just about through fighting. The Lord is calling me to the other side. My Abe is waiting for me. I am ready to go."

"Oh, Laura, I wish you wouldn't talk like that. I am not ready to let you go. Neither is Shane or Ivan. We need you here."

"Shane and Ivan know. They know that Abe is waiting. I wish you knew that too."

"I wish I had been raised with your kind of faith, but I wasn't. I don't know what to believe. I have so many feelings tugging me every which way. I go from hating God for putting you through this, to wanting to have your faith, so I will know you are going on to a better place. I can't understand why you have to suffer so much with this terrible cancer. Why you?"

"No one knows why we have to suffer some things. They say in the Bible and the Book of Mormon that our trials will make us stronger. I think of Job and what he suffered to prove he would not be swayed from his faith in God. I haven't suffered at all when I think of Job."

"So you truly believe you will be going to join Abe?'

"Yes, I believe that with all my heart. And when his time comes, Shane will also join us. Families can be together forever. Shane has been sealed to Abe and I in the temple."

"My understanding of heaven is everyone lives in the same place and you love everyone equally. That is what my mother said."

"Oh, you love everyone, but you know who is your family."

Amy thought about that for a bit, then said, "You know, I like that idea. Is there anyway Shane can be part of my family, too?"

"I'm sure there is. But I am starting to feel a bit tired. Can you help me back to the bed. I think I will lay down for a bit."

After Amy helped Laura back to her bed, she went to the kitchen to clear up the breakfast dishes. Shane had eaten early and headed out to check on the sheep and repair some fences. He mentioned that Ivan was heading to Lethbridge to do some business. Laura seemed to be fine and Shane would be back by noon, so Amy thought she would take the opportunity to head home and check out things there. With Ivan away, she wouldn't take the chance of running into him.

She made up some sandwiches and put in the fridge and left a note for Shane.

She then checked on Laura and found her sleeping. She left a note by her bed so she would know where she went. Amy then packed her sandwich in her bag and grabbing her coat, headed out to her car. She was eager to see how her little garden was doing and to check on Cuddle Cat.

Chapter 51

I VAN FLICKED THE straw off his pants and settled down on the bales near the loft doorway. He wanted to be where he could see Amy when she arrived. He smiled to himself when he thought about what waited for her inside the house. Personally, he thought it might be the thing to bring her back home. He just hoped it wouldn't backfire on him. Not knowing what frame of mind Amy was in could cause a problem. Laura said she was pining for him and wanted to come home, but Ivan had not seen any sign of that. Well, he would know soon enough. If she wanted to come home, she would follow the maps and end up out here, Ivan assured himself. If she didn't, she would get in her car and drive away.

As he glanced at his watch, Ivan settled more securely on his bale. He might have a long wait. It was already ten o'clock and no sign of her. Shane said he made sure she thought he was going to Lethbridge for the day. Amy usually came to the ranch when she knew he was gone. Why would today be any different? Probably because I am so anxious, she will take her time coming, Ivan complained to himself. Maybe I am assuming way too much. Maybe Laura is not well this morning and she has to stay with her.

Ivan slapped his knee and shook his head. "Quit with the self-guessing!" he said aloud, "Worrying isn't going to bring her any sooner. Maybe I will just lay back and relax. That should make the time go faster." And with that, Ivan propped his feet up on the neighboring bales and closed his eyes.

➤ ◄

As Amy drove into the ranch yard, she looked around for Ivan's truck, but there was no sign of it. Good, she thought, I have the place to myself. She slid out of the car and sauntered up the path to the house. She could see her flowerbed needed weeding and the grass needed trimmed. Maybe I will have time for a clean-up, she mused as she opened the door into the porch.

Cuddle Cat heard her coming and met her as she stepped inside.

"Well, hello you pretty kitty. Have you missed me as much as I've missed you?"

Cuddle Cat purred loudly as Amy reached down to pick her up and cuddle her. As she did, she noticed a collar on the cat with something attached to it.

"What the.....why do you have a collar?" Amy wondered as she tried to remove what appeared to be a note. Cuddle Cat wasn't being very co-operative as she wanted all the attention and kept twisting around to lick Amy's fingers. Amy finally managed to remove the paper. She set the cat down and opened the note. As she read, tears welled up in her eyes and she had to keep wiping them to be able to read.

Ivan had written to her and it said,

> To Amy:
> I love you because of all the things you are
> And because of all that I am
> When I'm with you....
> I love you because you have shown me
> In hundreds of beautiful ways
> What love means.
> Please forgive me???
> (Follow map to next clue)

Clutching the note, Amy sank down on the floor and wept quietly. Cuddle Cat climbed up into her lap and she absently stroked her fur. Amy didn't know how to react. Where was Ivan? Was he gone to Lethbridge and knew she would be here, so left the note. It was a very sweet gesture, even if a bit chicken. He apologized, but not in person. But the poem was beautiful. She would cherish it always.

She stood up, then she remembered. At the bottom of the note it said, follow the map. As she looked at it, she could see it went into the kitchen, so she headed that way. At the doorway, she stopped short. There on the table was a huge bouquet of roses, with a card propped up beside it. Eagerly now,

Amy went to the table, took a smell of the roses and then picked up the note. Inside was another poem:

How happy are the days
When two people together
Find the hours they share
Bring all that makes life worthwhile.
They have learned to share their love
And care about one another.
Promising to give their love
All their life through.
How happy the life where two people
Share the same dream.
We share the same dreams;
Let's make those dreams come true.
I love you.
(Have you forgiven this ass yet? If not, follow the map)

Amy started laughing, then crying. What is all this? This is just like a treasure hunt. I wonder what I will find at the end of the hunt? She studied the map. It looked like it headed out the door and across the yard to the barn. Now what would be in the barn? Did Ivan get her a pet of some kind? Maybe he got the new puppy he was talking about earlier. Amy loved all animals so she hurried across the yard in anticipation of what waited for her now.

As she slipped through the door way into the barn, all was quiet. Not a sound came to her ears. She glanced around and then she saw it. Attached to a stall post was what looked like another note. As she opened it, she read "For a personal apology, go to the loft." Amy started to smile. So Ivan hadn't gone to Lethbridge after all. Boy, he was sneaky. Just for the devil of it, Amy thought about just leaving the barn and heading back to the house to see what Ivan would do. But then she thought better of it. He was offering the olive branch and trying to patch things up. Maybe it was her turn to apologize. He sure is quiet if he's up there, Amy thought as she started up the ladder to the loft.

Poking her head up through the hole into the loft, Amy looked around for Ivan, but couldn't see him. Light coming in through the open loft door made everything hard to look at. Then she saw him. He was laying on a bale with his feet propped up on another bale, his hat over his eyes and he was sound asleep. Amy continued on up into the loft. Standing and brushing the straw off her pants, she studied Ivan's sleeping figure. Poor guy, she thought.

He must not be sleeping very well at nights to be able to sleep so soundly during the day. She approached him quietly and stood looking at him. It was then that Ivan seemed to sense something different. He grabbed his hat and sitting up quickly, glanced out the window of the loft.

"Oh, no!" he moaned, "She came and I didn't see her. I wonder……"

"What do you wonder?"

Ivan nearly fell off the bale, he turned so quickly, "Oh Amy, I didn't see you there."

"That's obvious. You were sound asleep, snoring so loudly, I could hear you over at the house."

"What? I don't snore…….. do I?

"Just kidding; but you were really asleep. You didn't even hear me come up the ladder."

"You've been in the house?"

"Of course."

"Then you got my notes."

"I did."

"So what do you think?"

"I think I climbed up this ladder to the loft to get what is promised to me."

"What is that?"

"A personal apology."

Ivan stood up and walked over to Amy, "I really don't know where to start."

"You already did, with the beautiful poems you wrote to me."

"I have to confess; I didn't write those poems. I found them in a poetry book by some lady from Saskatchewan, but they reflect exactly how I feel about you. And yes, I was being an ass and I hope you will forgive this old rancher and come back home."

Amy reached out and took Ivan's hand, "I accept your apology and now I want to apology to you. I had no idea you would be so upset about Shane and would take it the wrong way. So I should apologize for not telling you what you wanted to know."

"No, you were right. You couldn't betray Laura's trust. She is feeling very badly that all this has caused a rift between us. She wants us to make up so she can die in peace."

"I know. I don't want to cause her any unnecessary pain. I also don't want you to suffer any more. Can you forgive me?"

"I forgave you a long time ago. It was just male pride that kept me from apologizing and begging you to come home."

"Then we are okay? There is nothing else you wish to talk about?"

"All I know is, if Shane is your son, I am privileged to have him as a step-son. I always looked on him as a son anyway."

"Good; then let's kiss and make up."

"I thought you would never ask."

A little while later, Ivan and Amy descended the ladder and headed across the yard to the house.

"I'm so hungry, I could eat a horse," Ivan remarked, "You didn't. by any chance, bring something good in your lunch bag?"

"Well, I really didn't expect anyone here so I only brought my sandwich. You are welcome to share, but surely we can rustle up something in the kitchen."

Ivan gave her a squeeze as they walked along and laughed, "I was just hoping for some of your good brownies."

They entered the house and Amy turned to Ivan and said, "I must phone right away and see how Laura is doing, okay?"

"You do that and I will see what I can find for us in the fridge."

Laura answered on the first ring, "Amy, is that you?"

"Yes; are you okay? Is everything okay?"

"I'm fine, but I was worried about you. Where are you?"

"I'm here at the ranch.........with Ivan."

"Shane told me what Ivan was up to and I was concerned for you both. Is everything okay now?"

"I think so. We're talking anyway. Will you be okay for a bit?"

"Sure thing. Shane is here and he said he will be around the yard all after-noon, so take your time. By the way, have you told him yet?"

"Not yet. I will this afternoon."

"Don't wait, I beg you."

"I won't. Bye for now."

While Amy was on the phone, Ivan had set out the lunch on the table. He had managed to find some ham and cheese, dill pickles, cucumber slices, and cantaloupe.

"What do you think? Will that fill the gap?" Ivan asked as he took Amy's hand and set her down at the table.

"You don't have to treat me as a guest. I used to live here, remember?"

"I know; how could I forget? The best months of my life were when you were here with me."

"Mine, too. How could we let something so silly tear us apart? Let's make a pact right now that we will always talk things through, no matter how angry we are, or how hurt our pride, okay?"

"I think I have learned my lesson. Male pride should never stand in the way of true love. And I do love you, with all my heart and soul. I think families are so important. I consider Laura and Shane part of that family. I am glad you are close to them."

Amy took a bit of the ham on her plate and picked up a pickle. She then reached across the table to Ivan and took his hand, "Let's seal that pact with a handshake."

"I would rather seal it with a kiss," Ivan responded and stood up and came around the table. Pulling Amy to her feet, he gently kissed her on the lips. Amy responded in kind, running her fingers up his cheek and into his hair.

"Whoa back; we had better finish our lunch before we get carried away here," Ivan took her hands and kissed them, than set her back down, "Eat your lunch, woman."

Amy laughed and picked up her fork and continued to eat. During the remainder of the lunch, they talked about Shane and Laura and how they could best help them at this time. They decided that Amy would continue to be with Laura during the day while Shane was busy on the ranch and at nights, she would come back to this ranch. Ivan would join them at the Collin's ranch for suppers. Amy thought that should work out for now, until Laura needed more full time care.

"I am so glad we are back together. I don't think Laura is going to be with us much longer. It is going to be very hard to let her go. She seems so resigned and ready. I notice she is reading her bible at lot these days. I wish I had her faith. She is convinced she will be joining Abe."

"I had a talk with Laura last night. I know she is ready to go and she begged me to get off my high horse and get this thing solved between us. We have made her very happy by making up. It has made me very happy too."

"So you two were talking about me, eh? My ears should have been burning."

"Laura thinks the world of you. She had only good things to say about you."

"I wasn't talking about Laura."

"Who? Me? I never said anything against you. I admitted to Laura that I was being a stubborn fool. To give me courage to do what I did today, Laura told me that you were still in love with me and pining to come home, so I thought, what could I lose? Go for it. I'm so glad it worked."

"You sure did surprise me. I never imagined you would give me poetry and set up something like this........and the roses are beautiful, thank you. How did you manage to get them on such short notice?"

"I already had them. I was just trying to figure out a way to give them to you."

"And Laura told me Shane was part of all this. He made sure I thought you were going to Lethbridge today."

"He's a good kid. He wants us back together as much as Laura does."

"Shane is special to you. You will make a good father."

"Yes, I hope someday we can adopt a couple of children. I have always liked kids and you do too, don't you?"

"Like I said, you will make a great Daddy."

"Someday."

"Sooner than you think."

Ivan was finishing his melon and he glanced up, "What do you mean? Have you already checked into adoption?"

"We don't need to adopt."

"We don't need to ....what are you saying?"

"I'm saying I hope you are ready to be a dad, because we are going to have a baby."

Chapter 52

I VAN WAS SPEECHLESS. It was the last thing in the world he expected. He just sat in the chair and stared at Amy. He stared so long, she started to get nervous and wonder how he was really taking it.

"Ivan? Are you okay?"

Ivan shook his head, and spoke, " You are sure? We really are going to have a baby? How do you know?"

"I just know, but I have been to a doctor and it is true."

"Well, we've been apart for a while, so you must be…….. How far along are you?"

"We will have a bundle before Christmas, sometime in November is my guess. I started being suspicious I was pregnant while we were lambing, but I guess I was scared to hope. I was all set to tell you the night that Laura revealed her secret. After that, I couldn't tell you because I thought you would think I was using the baby to get back to you."

By this time, Ivan had come around the table to Amy. Now he knelt down beside her and said, "Oh, love, you have had such a burden to carry all by yourself. I should have been there for you right from the start. Can you forgive this stupid old man?"

Amy put her arms around him while she gently kissed his lips, then his nose, "I don't see anything to forgive now. You didn't know I was carrying your child. Let's just go on from here and be happy. I never thought I would ever have another child, so this is like a gift from heaven for me. I was worried I would miscarry in the first trimester so I didn't say anything to anyone."

"Does Laura know?"

"She guessed. She said I had a certain glow about me."

"Won't Shane be surprised. He will have a little brother or sister."

"Laura wanted me to tell you a long time ago, but I just couldn't. The last thing I wanted was to use the baby against you. It is entirely too precious."

"You are precious. I don't want anything to happen to either one of you. The baby is okay?"

"It was at my last check-up. I should be feeling movement soon."

"I love you," Ivan pulled Amy to her feet, "Let's go and tell Laura and Shane. I want to see Shane's face when he finds out."

Amy laughed, "Hey, wait a minute. We have to clean up this lunch mess. And I want to check Cuddle Cat's food and water."

"I'll clean up the lunch; you look after the cat."

Making short work of their chores, Ivan and Amy got into Amy's car and headed out.

"Where's your truck?" Amy asked

"Right under your nose. You didn't see it when you left Laura's this morning?"

"No. Where was it?"

"I think Shane put it in the garage, or behind the barn; I'm not sure."

"Boy, you guys are sneaky, but loveable."

"Don't you forget it!"

Shane was working on the garden tractor in front of the garage as they drove into the yard. He stopped what he was doing and wiping his hands on his grease rag, came over to them.

"Well, look who's here. It is nice to see the two of you actually in the same vehicle and smiling."

"Hello to you too, Shane," Amy retorted, "You are just as sneaky as Ivan here. You had a good trainer."

"It doesn't matter how sneaky I was; what matters is you two are back together. You should never have been apart, so don't let it happen again, hear?"

"Yes, boss," Ivan laughed, "Sometimes I think you kids are smarter than old codgers like me."

Shane shook Ivan's hand, then reached out for Amy's, but she reached up and gave him a hug instead.

"Watch for the grease. I don't think it comes out of clothes too well," Shane muttered, but he seemed pleased that Amy hugged him. Amy squeezed his hand and asked about Laura.

"She is very relieved you two made up. She actually ate a bit more lunch. I can see her failing every day. I don't know how I will deal with things later."

"We'll be here to help," Ivan assured him. He then looked to Amy and raised his eyebrows, so Amy spoke up, "Shane, we have some other news for you, too."

"What's that?"

"Ivan and I are going to have a baby."

"A baby?!!? Wow!! That is great news. Mom will be so happy. She loves little babies." Shane paused then added, "but she won't be here to see the baby, will she?"

Amy shook her head, "No Shane, I don't believe she will be. But she knows about the baby. She guessed some time ago."

"A baby! Well, what do you know. You are happy, aren't you, Ivan?"

"Happy isn't the word for it. I have always wanted children. Just think, Shane, you will have a brother or sister."

Shane stared at Ivan, then said, "Say, that is right. I never thought of that."

"Families are forever, Shane. Don't forget it."

Amy left the two men talking in the yard and headed in to see Laura. She found her sitting up in bed, reading. She glanced up as Amy came through the door.

"Oh Amy, I am so happy for you. How did Ivan take the news about the baby?"

"Excited, in shock a bit, I guess, but happy."

"I knew he would be. He loves kids so. You two will make wonderful parents. As long as the two of you are together, everything will be fine."

"I think both Ivan and I have learned our lessons. Nothing is worth not having each other. We made a pact and I plan to stick to it and I'm sure Ivan will too. Family is the most important thing in our lives."

Laura patted the bed beside her, "Come sit down. I have another confession to make to you."

"Oh, no. I'm not sure I want to hear anything else."

Laura signed, "Well, this one is something I felt I had to do and I hope you don't mind. The other day, when my lawyer was out here, I got him to make a new will up for me. I have willed this ranch; the land and the building site to you."

Amy started to object, but Laura hushed her, "Let me finish. I have willed this place to you because you are Abe's daughter. In the will, I have stipulated that when Shane returns from his mission, he is to take over the ranch. So it has been willed to you, in trust for Shane. The sheep can be sold off if necessary for him to go on his mission."

"Does Shane know about this?"

"Yes. I talked it over with him and he agrees. He argued a bit about going on a mission, because he said he needed to be here for me. I think I finally convinced him that is not a problem. I wanted to prepare him for what is coming very soon."

"Oh Laura, I am going to miss you so. I am the one who needs preparation. Ivan and Shane have such a strong faith. What is wrong with me?"

"You were not raised with a strong faith. Lately, I have really regretted that Abe and I did not search more diligently for you when you grew up. That way, you could have known your father and what a difference the church made in his life. He told me he never once regretted joining my church. It put direction in his life and gave him something to hold on to."

"Yes, I do regret not knowing my father. But if what you believe is true, I will have the chance to meet him. Isn't that true?"

"Yes, that is true, but you will have to prepare. Put your trust in Ivan and he will help you to understand more about our church. Someday if you join, you and Ivan and the baby can be sealed together in the temple. I am not sure how it works with Shane, but you could check on it. Maybe Ivan will know."

"My greatest wish is to be with Ivan and my family forever. Do you think there is hope for me?"

"Definitely. You are a good person and have a kind and loving heart. You just need some time to accept things."

"Thank you. You are so special to me. You really are more like a mother to me than my own mother. She would never talk to me about personal things. Maybe she was scared she would reveal some of the things she had hidden away."

"That might be true. Try to forgive her in your heart. God wants us to forgive all that trespass against us. I was wrong when I was angry with you. I was not practicing my church beliefs then, was I?"

"Does God actually want us to let people take advantage of us?"

"No. He wants us to forgive them, but not to make the same mistake of trusting them again. He gave us a brain to figure out things. You have to forgive your Mother, but be wary of further dealings."

"So, if families are together forever, what about my Mother?"

"I don't know. That is another question you should ask someone in authority."

Amy reached over and gave Laura a hug, "Thank you for all the advice. Now I think you had better rest. You look very tired."

"I am tired, but excited too. I can go to my rest now, knowing things are okay on the two ranches. Abe is calling."

"I love you Laura. Sleep well."

Amy tucked the blankets around Laura and handing her the book of Mormon, left and gently shut the door to the bedroom. Ivan and Shane were sitting at the kitchen table. Ivan stood up as Amy came into the room.

"How is she?" he asked as he came over and took Amy's arm.

"Happy. Contented that things are okay. She is ready to go. I don't know how to deal with all this."

"We will support each other," Ivan said as he gave her a squeeze. "Laura would want us to be there for each other and not be sad."

Shane sat staring at the table, then got up and put his cup in the sink. "I am so glad I have a strong faith in God. I don't think I would be dealing with this very well without that. Even so, it is going to be very hard. I was younger when Dad....., Abe passed away, but that was hard too."

"Laura told me about her will. How do you feel about that?"

Shane smiled, "That's my Mom. She is always worried about doing the right thing. I am okay with it. You should be the heir. After all, you are Abe's daughter."

Ivan spoke up right then, "What's all this?"

Amy turned to him and replied, "Laura changed her will and left the ranch to me, in trust for Shane. When he returns from his mission, he will take possession of it."

"I wonder why she didn't discuss this with any of us before she did it?"

"I think she wanted to assure I went on my mission," Shane answered, "It's okay. I trust Amy. After all, she is my biological mother. But what I think I will do, or we should do is sell off all the sheep. When I return, I can decide if I want back into sheep or maybe get into cattle. I am not even sure I will want to ranch. This way, you guys can pasture and crop the land. We can make some kind of deal. We can close up the house until I return."

"You know, Shane, you are entirely too smart for an eighteen year old," Ivan said, as he patted Shane on the shoulder, " Laura has underestimated you. I think you could have handled all this on your own."

"No, I am glad Amy is involved. I need the support."

"You have it," Amy assured him as she reached up and gave him another hug.

"That's good, even if I am the boss, eh?" Shane joked as he hugged her back.

Chapter 53

LAURA PASSED AWAY quietly in her sleep two nights later. Ivan and Amy got the call from Shane at 6:00 AM. Even though they were prepared, or so they thought, it was still a shock. When Amy and Ivan arrived at the ranch, Shane met them in the front yard.

"I have called Bishop Lang and he told me I had to call the police. That is standard procedure when someone passes away at home. I am so upset, I can't even think straight. Did I do right, Ivan?"

"You did just fine. Come, sit down on the porch. I'll stay with you. Amy wants to say her last good-bye, then I will go in."

Amy entered the house and quietly walked to Laura's room. As she gently pushed the door open, she could see Laura laying on the bed. She had a calm, half-smile on her face. Her Book of Mormon had fallen on the floor and Amy bent over and picked it up. She sat down in the chair and stared at Laura. This was the first time she had been in a room with a deceased person and it was a bit unnerving. She reached out and took Laura's lifeless hand and bowed her head. Not used to saying prayers, she didn't know where to start, but finally just blurted out, "Laura, this is Amy. I don't know how to pray for you, but I do hope you were right about everything. I want to believe that you are now with Abe and looking down on us. You have no idea how much I am going to miss you."

Amy started to sob and tears ran down her cheeks. She reached for a Kleenex on the table and wiped her nose. "Good-bye, sweet Laura. I hope we will meet again. I have to go now and let Ivan come in."

The police arrived and then the funeral home. Things had to be signed and people called. Amy tried to keep busy with the arrangements and getting food out for the people that arrived. Women from the church came and brought food. Shane was very gracious and so was Ivan. It was like they were robots, going through the motions. They prayed for the day to end.

Laura's funeral was well attended. She had many friends and church family in the area. Amy had phoned her mother to let her know of Laura's passing and her mother was actually sympathetic and offered her condolences. Amy had told her mother about the baby after she told Ivan. Her mother seemed happy for her, but it was hard to tell with her. She had never made any move to come to visit them, so they didn't push it. Because she had never told her mother about her separation from Ivan for a spell, Amy was glad she didn't decide to come. Now the last link with Abe seemed broken and Amy found herself starting to understand what her mother was feeling. She didn't condone what she did, but she could understand not wanting to lose her daughter. Amy knew she would fight tooth and nail for her baby. She reached down and rubbed her stomach as she sat in the front pew at the church. When the service began, she bowed her head to pray. She prayed for Laura and Abe; she prayed for her mother, and then she prayed for Shane. She knew he needed support and prayers at this time. He was being very strong but Amy knew just how hard it was for him. Last, but not least, she prayed for Ivan and their unborn child.

Chapter 54 - Epilogue

AMY FINISHED LOADING the dishwasher and turned to wipe the counter free of crumbs. As she glanced out the window, she could see Ivan coming out of the barn, leading Belle, his new mare. He was off to check on the cows in the east pasture. Amy smiled to herself as she thought about how dedicated Ivan was to his ranch and to their family. I am so lucky, she thought. This is a dream come true for me.

She turned from the window as the baby started fussing and banging his spoon on the highchair. Baby Abraham was just starting to show an interest in everything and was the joy of his parent's heart, as was his older sister, Laura. Laura had been born a week before Shane left on his mission. There was no question but that her name was going to be Laura, Laura Dawn Johnson. Now at three years old, she was a pretty blond with a pert little nose and an attitude to go with it. She was the apple of her father's eye. From the minute Ivan laid eyes on her in the hospital, he fell in love. Amy thought her heart would burst when she saw them together. Then, to put icing on the cake, along came Abe two and one-half years later. They called him Abraham Ivan. He had Ivan's coloring with curly hair, just as unruly as his Dad's. Now, as Amy gazed at her two children at the table, she could not imagine herself being happier. Ivan was the best thing that could have happened to her. And to think she nearly lost him because of a stupid misunderstanding.

Shortly before Laura was born, Amy had joined the church. She had never regretted it. She had found the balance and support of the church women was what she needed in her life. Just recently, they had journeyed to the temple in Cardston and been sealed together as a family. Ivan had wept with joy as he gathered them all to him. Amy always knew Ivan was a very sensitive guy and his display of emotion was very touching.

Shane had returned home from his mission to Italy over a year ago and had settled in at the Collins' ranch. He decided he did want to ranch and to go into cattle. The sheep had been sold off to finance his mission. Ivan had helped him pick out some nice breeding stock and supplied him with a couple of bulls from his own herd. Shane had taken a job in town for the time being to get a start. He was dating a very nice girl from the church who came from a farm family and was excited about living on the ranch. They were to be married in the temple in Cardston this coming summer. Amy and Ivan were looking forward to that.

Amy lifted Abe out of his chair and carrying him to the bathroom, wiped his face and hands. He had a big smile as she played peek-a-boo with him and the face cloth. "You are all ready for the day, aren't you, you little snookums." She laid him on a blanket on the floor in the living room, "Now you be a good boy, so Mommy can get some work done."

Laura was busy coloring at the table and spoke up, "I can help you, Mommy. I am a big girl now."

"I know, sweetheart, but Mommy has a big job to do. You could keep an eye on Abe for me. That would be a big help."

"Okay, Mommy." With that, Laura slid off her chair and headed into the living room. Cuddle Cat followed her and batted at her little feet as she skipped along.

"She is getting so big," Amy mused. "Soon we are going to have to make some plans. This house is not big enough. We only have two bedrooms."

At the present, Laura had the small bedroom and Abe was in the crib in theirs. But soon he would be outgrowing the crib. They had talked about building on and maybe this coming summer would be the time. Cattle prices had been good and plenty of rain for the crops. While Shane was away, Ivan had seeded most of the Collins' ranch to crops and had used the proceeds to maintain that ranch and improve theirs. Shane's share had been banked for his eventual return, so he had a bit of a nest egg. He had used some of it to purchase his cows, with the rest on payments. Ivan hated to see Shane start out in debt, but he seemed confident and he was very mature for his age. His mission had even matured him more. He knew what he wanted in life and was reaching out for it.

All these thoughts were going through Amy's head as she took the racks out of the oven and put them in the sink. If she hurried, she could get this job finished before Ivan got back. She wanted to have his lunch ready on time, as he was going to help Shane in the afternoon. She could hear the children talking in their own little language and she smiled. Life was wonderful Please God, never let it change.

The End